Other hilarious tales edited by Alf Dotson

from The Jamestown Shakespeare Manuscripts

The True Mystery of Hamlet
"by Watson"

Othello l'Amour
"by Christopher Marlowe"

Romeo, plus Juliet
"by Friar Lorenzo Frier; trans. Richard Barnfield"

TRUE SHAKESPEARE:
The Greatest Stories Ever Told

The Taming of the Pooch

An Actually True Romance

Edited by Alf Dotson

Wicked Good Books

New York

SECOND EDITION

THE TAMING OF THE POOCH

Copyright © 2025 Wicked Good Books, Inc.

First publication: 2015
Font: Baskerville

Cover art: Francesco Hayez, *Il Bacio*, Courtesy of Pinacoteca di Brera, Milan. Cover design by Anastasia Stevens.

Library of Congress Cataloging in Publication Data

DOTSON, Alfred, ed. (1983 -)
    I. Title. *The Taming of the Pooch: an Actually True Romance*
    II. Series title. *True Shakespeare*

ISBN-13: 979-8-9987851-1-5
LCCN: 2014960227

The Taming of the Pooch

Introduction: The Mother of All Codpiece-Rippers

Alf Dotson

> *Hot, faint, and weary with her hard embracing,*
> *Like a wild bird being tamed with too much handling—*
> *Or as the fleet-foot Roe that's tired with chasing—*
> *Or like the froward infant, still'd with dandling—*
> *He now obeys, his stiff resistance, daunted;*
> *While she takes all she can, not all she wanted.* [1]

— William Shakespeare

DISCOVERED among the Jamestown Shakespeare Manuscripts, handwritten upon some forty sheets of fine parchment, is a steamy romance called "The Taminge of the Pooche, by Sig[nora] Isabella [Sforza], the countess Porcigliano." Written in the sixteenth century and published here for the first time (in modern spelling), it purports to be a true story. Lady Porcigliano's narrative is dated July 1555, shortly after the death of her second husband, Hortensio Lando, the well-known Italian comedian.[2] A copy of the Italian original (*l'Addomesticamento del Cucciolo*, not extant) is said to have been brought to London that same year by Sir Thomas Hoby, on his return from Padua; from whence it passed to Anne Cook Bacon (mother to the Elizabethan philosopher, Sir Francis Bacon). Lady Bacon translated Sforza's story into English, and the rest is history.

Hundreds, perhaps thousands, of women's romances were published during the European Renaissance. Countless others were written but not printed. Seen one way, *The Taming of the Pooch is* more of the same — a conventional erotic fantasy by a woman author who has been excluded from the Western literary canon by a mostly male (and dour) professoriate. Seen another

---

[1] *his stiff resistance, daunted ... wanted*] Q3; later eds, in octavo, read *and now no more resisteth, / ... listeth;*

[2] *Hortensio Lando*] b. Milan, 1512. Educated in Milan and Bologna. Became a monk, but resigned. Itinerant wit, scholar, and physician; friend of Pietro Aretino; author of some fifty books (Axon, Grendler); 1. m. 1529 [unk.]; 2. m. 1555, Isabella Sforza, Lady Porcigliano (1503-1561); his books banned by order of the Vatican, May 1555; died in Padua, 1555.

way, *The Taming of the Pooch* — now that it has been recovered from the dustbin of patriarchalist history — could become the most transformative woman's romance since Adam and Eve. By revising the biblical (Shakespearean) model of marriage as a contest that must be won by the husband, ladies Porcigliano and Bacon align themselves with mother Eve, who seduced Adam with fruit from the Tree of Knowledge and thereby revised God's original storyline for all humanity. I would not go so far as to predict that *The Taming of the Pooch* can undo six million years of human evolution or six thousand years of literary sexism. I am not optimistic that close reading will turn a lunkhead husband into a responsive lover. But I don't doubt that when future generations assess the most influential discoveries of the Twenty-First Century, Lady Porcigliano's *Taming of the Pooch*, in Lady Bacon's lively translation, may be right up there with NASA's discovery of water on Mars.

That *The Taming of the Pooch* was written by a woman, and translated by a woman, for the pleasure and erotic satisfaction of women readers, will be viewed by many as a stroke against its cultural importance — as if it were unimportant that English-language romances are fast pushing toward the two-billion-dollar mark in annual sales. Men — in which I include male literature professors — rarely peek between the covers of a paperback romance. Yet many of those same men will examine photographs of naked women and wonder why some guys have all the luck. That is like the knucklehead who drools over automobile commercials, or who covets his neighbor's vintage Buick which is still going strong, but remains clueless about those things that a car needs to keep going (such as gasoline and an ignition key): any ride he gets from her will be a short one.

Recent research in behavioral psychology indicates that the male gaze alone cannot unlock the mysteries of the female heart. The man who desires both a relationship, and pleasure, cannot just look at his love-interest with lust in his eyes and an erection in his trousers; he must look at what she has been reading lately. (Hint to husbands and boyfriends: if your bedpartner loves nothing better, for a headache, than to curl up with a romance novel, try moving a few of those paperback books from her side of the bed to yours, and read them a.s.a.p. You may be quite surprised to learn what your lover was dreaming about, the last time she lay there waiting for you to finish up.)

A randy college boy, or a frustrated husband, or a lonely divorcee, may find himself wondering what women really want. Scientific study has shown (contra Freud) that the correct answer is not: "a penis." The correct answer is "romance" — exemplars of which may be found in bookstores and supermarkets all over the civilized world. With their suggestive titles and eye-candy cover art, these paperback books practically beg to be taken home with you to bed. Yet most men will walk right past the Women's Interest section without noticing. Same way they do at home.

It has often been said, and I believe it, that the man who understands romance can overcome all other liabilities in love, such as a problem with his looks, religion, politics, geography, in-laws, and income. And yet, with so many romances from which to choose, it's often a mistake for a man to glom onto the first one he picks up. Different strokes, same genre, for different folks. Let refined palates (*e.g.*, college professors) savor such flambé classics as Anne Radcliffe's *Mysteries of Udolpho* or Delia Salter Bacon's *Tales from the Puritans* or Emily Brontë's *Wuthering Heights.* The hungry novice may more easily whet his appetite, and PJs, with selections from the Harlequin Blaze and Rakehell Regency Series, all of which are easily digested and smoking hot. For a steady diet of less spicy fare, the leading authorities recommend such masters as Suzanne Brockman, Sandra Brown, Loretta Chase, Julia Quinn, Nora Roberts, and Danielle Steel; all of whom know how to deliver a thrill as you read in bed, and leave you with that familiar rosy glow.

What is it about romance that makes this genre so appealing to exactly one half of the human race? According to the Romance Writers of America, "All romances have a central love story and an emotionally satisfying ending" (RWA Website). "A central love story" that's "emotionally satisfying." That's the key. Let a man learn, from romance, how to make *that* happen, and the secret parts of a woman's being will unfold to his touch like the petals of a blossoming rose.

Romance is not for everyone. Adolescent readers who first learned about the mystery of sex from their parents or youth minister, or from the sex-ed unit in middle school gym class, and whose curiosity was thereby terminated, are advised to skip *The*

Taming of the Pooch and dive instead into *The True Mystery of Hamlet*, which is all mystery and no sex. Those consumers who desire a strictly anatomical model of love may prefer the Internet, which is all sex and no mystery; also, no relationship and not much pleasure. But for those millions of women and dozens of men who savor both historical romance, and their own, Lady Porcigliano's *Pooch* will be a volume of love at first sight.

The publishing industry lately has seen a hugely resurgent interest in books about Christian love — the whole gamut, from the merely devotional, to Christian vampire novels, Christian erotica, and Christian marriage manuals. The sales figures for Christian romance fiction are off the charts. [1] In that respect, *The Taming of the Pooch* packs a double wallop. Isabella Sforza, who wrote the story, and Anne Cook-Bacon, who translated it, were women of faith. Both authors were Protestant reformers who struggled to keep their strong religious opinions in tune with their possibly overpowering and very un-Catholic sex drive. But they were not zealots. When the need for passionate love came on super-strong, these literary ladies did not mind tweaking conventional pieties, thereby to accommodate the heart's desire.

Certain features of Lady Porcigliano's *Pooch* make it of special interest to our own cultural moment. One is that this prose romance is the original history that morphed, through various treatments, into Shakespeare's ever-popular comedy, *The Taming of the Shrew*. Another is that *The Taming of the Pooch* is itself one

---

[1] An Amazon.com book search for "Christian sex" yields nearly ten thousand results. Evangelical romances (published by Barbour House, Bethany, HeartQuest, Summerside, Waterbrook, and Zondervan) edify even as they titillate. Christian vampire fiction includes Tracey Bateman, *Thirsty;* Eric Wilson, *The Jerusalem Undead Trilogy;* John Olson, *Shade*; and the novels of Anne Rice. Erotica by Christians includes such titles as *Seek: the Erotic Lives of Christian Wives,* by Heather Vivant; *Angel's Delight,* by Christian Zillner; *Restless Spirits,* by Christian Black; *The Man I Love,* by Christian Ibegbu; *Licks and Promises,* by M. Christian; *The Honey Lickers Sorority,* by Christian Zanier; *The First Time,* by Rachel White; and *Nasty Night (Spank Me Right),* by Jackie Christian. Best-selling Christian marriage manuals include, *The Thrill of the Chaste,* by Dawn Eden; *What Wives Wish their Husbands Knew about Sex: A Guide for Christian Men,* by Ryan Howes; *Is That All He Thinks About?* by Marla Taviano; *Wired for Sex: What Christian Wives Should Know,* by Barry Franklin; and *Sex for Christian Couples (None),* by Master Larry Bates.

of the four or five greatest stories ever recorded. [1] I cannot promise that high school English teachers, or the mostly student-fandom of *No Fear Shakespeare,* will prefer Lady Bacon's spicy prose translation to Shakespeare's chauvinist stageplay. And yet, Italy in the sixteenth century produced no author more talented than Isabella Sforza, Lady Porcigliano. One mark of her incredible genius is that she lived, and loved, and wrote her bodice-rippers at a time in human history when most wives were still untamed, and when most husbands never ripped anything at all, but farts. If Lodovico Ariosto, Pietro Aretino, and Torquato Tasso should ever get together in Dante's Purgatory, their topic of conversation will be Lady Porcliano (1503-1561). And they'll be saying: "*Porca Madonna*! *Come quella donna fa*?" ("Gosh, how does that woman *do* it?"). Isabella Sforza grasped an eternal secret of true love: she knew it is not enough to rip open a bodice unless the codpiece gets ripped, too.

In Lady Isabella's history, marital hiccups cannot be overcome by shoving a metaphorical sock in the wife's mouth and forcing her to be silent: Petruchio of Verona enters marriage as a shy puppy, considerably less experienced in bed than your conventional Italian rake; and he is a perfect novice when it comes to romance. Having left his home to escape maternal engulfment, he meets his match in Caterina Miniola Ramusio di Baptista, who takes him in hand and grooms him into a manly lover. The Petruchio of Lady Isabella Sforza's history (and of Lady Anne Cook-Bacon's English translation) is a diamond in the rough, a stranger with dreamy looks and rock-hard muscles who requires a woman's touch. True love begins with boot camp. Before the honeymoon is over Petruchio must learn how to talk, think, and act like a romantic hero: to be sweet with praise, steady in trouble, bold in danger, daring in adventure; and to be prepared at a moment's notice for throbbingly good passion in bed, within the confines of Christian monogamy.

---

[1] *Pooch* survived in two separate manuscript chains. One copy ended up in New Haven, Connecticut, where it was read (sometime before 1831) by Delia Salter Bacon, the famous Shakespeare scholar. Another copy was handed down through fifteen generations of the American branch of the Shakespeare family, to Eureka, where it was rediscovered in 2006 by Robert Shakespeare. It is Mr. Shakespeare's copy of *Pooch* (in a modern-spelling text) that is published here. The New Haven copy is no longer extant.

Shakespeare's *The Taming of the Shrew*

> *He that knows better how to tame a shrew,*
> *Now let him speak.*
> — William Shakespeare

IN 1601, Lady Anne Cook-Bacon wrote to her son, Sir Francis, "If I could not write better than this Stratford fellow, [William Shakespeare], I would shoot him." Lady Anne's irritation may have been directed in part at Shakespeare's largely plagiarized and hugely successful romantic comedy, *The Taming of the Shrew.* I include here a synopsis of Shakespeare's plot, for the benefit of those who neither studied *Shrew* in high school nor have seen it performed on stage; and perhaps also as a caveat to henpecked husbands who would look to Shakespeare for self-help advice. *The Taming of the Shrew* is Shakespeare's far-fetched version of Lady Porcliano's *Taming of the Pooch,* as adapted from the Cook-Bacon translation of 1589. Writing for an all-male dramatic troupe and a British audience, Shakespeare had the market sense to remove all of the romance and most of the erotic bits. If there is a moral to *The Taming of the Shrew,* it is that a woman's highest good is to be silent, obedient, and grateful. That is an idea that Shakespeare cannot have picked up from Signora Isabella Sforza; nor from her translator, Lady Cook-Bacon.

Writing just a few years after his own shotgun marriage to Anne Hathaway, Shakespeare begins his romantic farce outside an alehouse in his home county of Warwickshire. Returning home from the hunt, a nobleman (played originally by Shakespeare himself) comes upon Christopher Sly, a poor tinker who lies in the street, dead drunk. For a laugh, the nobleman directs his servants to carry the homeless sot to his manor house and to dress him in silk pajamas and put him to bed.

When he awakes, Sly is told that he is not a poor man, as he believes, but a great and wealthy aristocrat who for the past fifteen years has been suffering from "a strange lunacy" that he is a poor tinker named Christopher Sly. A beautiful lady enters the bedroom, with a curtsy and a smile: it is Bartholomew, the nobleman's page, now cross-dressed as a woman. As the chaste spouse of "Lord" Sly, Bartholomew rejoices in the tinker's alleged recovery from madness but complains of having gone fifteen years without conjugal relations. "What is it my lord will command," asks Bartholomew, "wherein your lady and humble wife may show her duty, and make known her love?" With "kind embracements and tempting kisses," "low tongue and lowly courtesy," the sexy boy gives the tinker an erection under the bedsheets (a favorite Elizabethan stage-gag, accomplished with a long wooden peg on a pull-string). Excited by this unexpected development, "Lord" Sly begs his presumed spouse ("M'dam wife") to strip and climb into bed with him. Bartholomew as the wife coyly begs off until the sun has set, saying that her convalescing lord must first be examined by a physician, both upstairs and down, to ensure that he is healthy enough to have a go. In the meantime, his lordship will be entertained with a comedy, to be enacted straightaway.

The players now enter to perform "The Taming of the Shrew," a drama described as "a kind of history," "a very excellent piece of work," "by Saint Anne" (*Shr.* pr.2, 1.1). But it is only a silly Italianate farce: the story to be acted for "Lord" Sly's entertainment (as also for the real-life theater audience) is not *The Taming of the Pooch*. The actor who plays the drunken tinker instead must sit through Shakespeare's 1594 revision; of Christopher Marlowe's 1591 stage adaptation; of Lady Anne Cook-Bacon's 1589 English translation; of Signora Isabella Porcigliano's 1555 historical romance; which was itself based on three real-life marriages in Padua, Italy, including Isabella's own union with Hortensio Lando. Shakespeare's patriarchalist fantasy of masculine domination stands thus at four removes, and four decades, from reality. [1]

As Shakespeare's play-within-a-play begins, Christopher Sly is not yet fully recovered from his hangover. He promptly falls back to sleep, his head upon the shoulder of cross-dressed Bartholomew, his supposed wife. But the show must go on, if only for the entertainment of the theater audience.

---

[1] Sir Thomas Hoby on his return from Padua in 1555 forwarded Lady Porcigliano's Italian text to Anne Cook Bacon, who translated it into English some years later. Christopher Marlowe's comedy, *The Taming of a* [*sic*] *Shrew* (1591; Q1 pub. 1594) borrows from Lady Anne's unpublished translation and from a play by George Gascoigne, called *Supposes* (1566). Marlowe's *A Shrew* was revised in turn by Shakespeare, and called *The Taming of the* [*sic*] *Shrew* (acted 1594; revised 1601; F1 pub. 1623).

Act One. Shakespeare's play-within-a-play, like its historical antecedent, is set in Padua. Baptista "Minola," a rich merchant, has two daughters. Both are fair-skinned virgins under the age of twenty, which makes them ripe for plucking by an alpha male. The younger daughter, Bianca, is cute, bubbly, and flirtatious. She is waiting for Mr. Right in a city full of over-eager Mister Wrongs. The elder daughter, Katherina ("Kate"), has a strong will, hot temper, keen wit, and sharp tongue. Men do not care for her, nor she for them.

Lucentio, an Italian college student, has come to Padua intending to pursue "a course of learning and ingenious study." As a rich man's son, he is served by two footmen (Tranio and Biondello), who have no interest in books. A minute later, neither does Lucentio. Bianca enters, escorted by her father (Baptista). They are followed by two of Bianca's suitors (middle-aged Hortensio and ancient Gremio). Bianca's fiery elder sister (Katherina) brings up the rear. Falling in love at first sight (with Bianca), Lucentio laments: "I burn, I pine, I perish, Tranio, if I achieve not this young modest girl" (*Shr.* 1.1); *i.e.,* "If I cannot score with that barely legal chaste maiden, I shall fry in my own lust, and die" (which sounds unrealistic, but that is just the way the young men of Italy used to think, in those days).

Katherina disrupts this romantic scene by offering to crack Hortensio's skull with a three-legged stool and to paint his face red with her fingernails. Signore Baptista, eager to be rid of his contentious elder daughter, announces that no suitor shall be allowed access to woo Bianca until bitchy Kate is married off. Hortensio and Gremio (though rivals in love for Bianca) vow to help Baptista foist Katherina upon the first sucker they can find. That man turns out to be Petruchio of Verona, a swaggering chauvinist who has "come to wive it wealthily in Padua; / If wealthily, then happily." Informed by Hortensio of the rich though hot-tempered Katherina Minola, Petruchio promises "to woo curst Katherine, / Yea, and to marry her, if her dowry please." He will "board her though she chide as loud / As thunder" (*Shr.* 1.2).

Act Two. Signore Baptista is thrilled to have a suitor for Kate. He offers Petruchio a huge dowry of twenty thousand crowns (nearly eight thousand ducats, in gold) and gives him some moments alone with the girl, to woo her. The ensuing contest of wits proceeds smoothly enough until Petruchio makes a

cunnilingus joke ("What, with my tongue in your tail?"); whereupon Kate slaps him across the chops and refuses his proposal of
marriage (*Shr.* 2.1). Petruchio tells her not to do that again, or he
will punch her. (The taming has begun.) When the father
returns, he and Petruchio quickly wrap up the nuptial agreement,
over Kate's objection. The wedding shall take place two days
hence, on Sunday.

Act Three. Katherina is obliged to marry the husband whom
her father has chosen for her: Petruchio of Verona is said to be
the man "born to tame" her unruly disposition. She dresses for
the Sunday afternoon wedding, is taken to church, and waits. The
guests are seated, the music is playing, the bride is weeping.
Petruchio, having gone to Venice to "buy apparel," is a no-show.
Just as Kate is about to go home, thinking she has been stood up,
Petruchio arrives at the church, dressed in rags, and riding (we are
told) upon a diseased horse that can barely go.

The wedding, like the horse-ride, takes place offstage. Ancient Gremio comes onstage to tell us what happened during the
ceremony, which we did not get to see: Petruchio, when he stood
at the altar with his bride, cursed the Roman Catholic priest ("by
God's wounds!"), causing the vicar to drop his Catholic Bible;
whereupon Petruchio punched the papist vicar, knocking him to
the floor. Crying, "A health!" ["Cheers!"], the groom quaffed
down the Roman Catholic Eucharist wine before the priest could
stand up. Helping himself to the consecrated wafers, Petruchio
threw the sops into the sexton's face. That done, he grabbed the
bride by the neck and kissed her, thereby to conclude the
wedding service "with such a clamorous smack / That, at the
parting, all the church did echo." (With this report of anti-papist
antics, Shakespeare could count on a big laugh from his
Protestant audience; but in the sixteenth century there were limits
to what you could actually perform on stage without getting
yourself into a Sinead-O'Connor-type situation.)

Refusing to attend the reception, Petruchio commands the
wedding guests to celebrate without him. Seizing his woman
under his arm like a bundle of sticks ("my goods, my chattels"),
Petruchio carries her away, on pretense of rescuing her from a
band of virgin-napping thieves (*Shr.* 3.2). The shrewish bride
kicks and screams, and beats her fists on his buttocks, but
Petruchio doesn't care, he just laughs merrily. He carries Kate

offstage for the trip home to Verona, there to consummate his marriage whether she likes it or not. (The romantic love-formula is basically the same in all of Shakespeare's manly comedies: "I woo'd thee with my sword, / And won thy love, doing thee injuries" [*MND* 1.1]).

Act Four (set in Petruchio's manor house). A cold and muddy Grumio, Petruchio's valet, comes onstage to report more funny-business that took place offstage and out of sight: the bride and groom, he tells us, quarreled all the way home, from Padua to Verona (a trip of 55 miles). As they drew near the house, Petruchio led his bride's palfrey into a filthy swamp, where it stumbled and fell. Kate landed in the mud, with the horse's ass on top of her (*i.e.*, not Petruchio, but the literal ass of the literal horse); whereupon Petruchio cursed Grumio and beat him, blaming the footman for Kate's mishap. Escaping from beneath the horse, Kate waded over to comfort bruised Grumio; Petruchio took that opportunity to make Kate's horse run away. Bedrenched and shivering, the bride and servant had to walk the remaining miles to the house. (Given the limits of theatrical representation in the sixteenth century, this incident could not be shown to the audience, as it might be today on, say, *America's Funniest Home Videos.* But as told by Grumio — played by the clown, Will Kemp — the anecdote was designed to get good laughs from men in the theater audience, who just wished they could have been there to see the bossy bitch fall into the mud, with that horse on top of her, ha ha ha!)

During his first two days and nights of married life, Petruchio deprives Kate of food. He deprives her of sleep. He beats the servants, throws temper tantrums, and harangues his bride with sermons on female continence. He does all this, not just for a laugh, but to train his wife to obey her new master: "To make her come, and know her keeper's call" (*Shr.* 4.1).

Lucentio and Bianca are soon to be married, back in Padua. Before making a return trip to the in-laws, Petruchio orders up a new silk gown and hat for his wife. He allows Kate to see and admire the outfit, tailor-made for her according to the latest fashion. But before she can try it on, Petruchio discards the hat; tears the dress to pieces; and beats the tailor, accusing him of incompetence. Grumio stands by the while, making lewd jokes about taking up Kate's gown and putting his finger in a thimble.

The newlyweds return to Verona dressed as peasants. Along the way, Petruchio forces Kate to swear that the sun is the moon, the moon is the sun, and that an old man whom they meet in transit (Signore Vincentio, Lucentio's father) is actually a "young budding virgin, fair and fresh and sweet." In all things, Kate proves obedient. Hortensio, amazed at Kate's surrender, cheers Petruchio as a victorious military commander. He announces: "The field is won!" (*Shr.* 4.5).

Act Five. Lucentio, needing paternal consent for his marriage to fair Bianca, has commandeered an elderly scholar to pose as his father. Under duress, the pedant signs the nuptial agreement with Signore Baptista. (Lucentio's real father upon reaching Verona is arrested for identity theft.) Hortensio, having lost Bianca to rival Lucentio, proposes marriage to a friendly widow (*i.e.,* the historical Isabella Sforza; unnamed in Shakespeare's plagiarized version). The widow accepts, and marries Hortensio the same day.

The feast for Hortensio's wedding is held at Lucentio's house, Shakespeare having forgotten that Lucentio's house lies in Pisa, two hundred miles away. Lucentio announces that "raging war is done." (This is to be the play's final scene.) Moments later, the wives of Petruchio and Hortensio exchange catty remarks. Their war of words quickly escalates to fisticuffs as the two feisty women assault one another in a knock-down catfight. The men cheer them on.

The onstage brawl between the wives of Petruchio and Hortensio is the play's climactic incident. The two combatants scratch one another, and rip one another's partlets. (Given the limits of theatrical representation in the sixteenth century, neither Kate's nor the widow's partlet could be ripped off entirely, because the women on Shakespeare's stage were played by boy-actors; an exposed chest would have destroyed the illusion of well-endowed women with pleasant cleavage; but neither was there any danger, with boy-actors, of a wardrobe mishap getting the players into a Janet-Jackson-type situation.)

After Kate has put the widow down, it's all denouement. The women exit. The male characters remain onstage, in the dining room, to discuss which of them now has the best-trained, most obedient, wife. The three husbands place bets. Lucentio wagers twenty gold crowns on his beloved Bianca. Petruchio matches, and raises the wager by eighty crowns. Hortensio calls the bet at one hundred crowns apiece.

By turns, each husband sends to his wife, with instructions for her to come at once. Of the three brides, only Kate promptly obeys. From the two losers, Petruchio collects one hundred crowns each.

"Nay," boasts Petruchio, "I will win my wager better yet, / And show more sign of her obedience, / Her new-built virtue, and obedience." Petruchio commands Katherina to fetch forth the other two wives, who sit offstage "conferring by the parlor fire" (*Shr.* 5.1). Kate exits and returns a moment later, hauling the two disobedient women by their hair. To set a good example for them, Petruchio directs Kate to do a few tricks he has trained her to perform, such as take off her new cap on command, and throw it to the floor. She obeys. The other wives are appalled. To tame them, Petruchio orders Kate to lecture Bianca and the Widow on their obligation to serve and obey their husbands. Kate delivers an impromptu sermon, one of the longest speeches in the Shakespeare canon. When she is done, the wives of Lucentio and Hortensio stand before their husbands and the stage audience, silent and shamefaced.

For her final test, Petruchio commands Kate to kiss him, and she of course obeys. (Moral: She has found her bliss in a strong and peremptory male who can dominate her shrewish but ulti-mately dominable spirit.) Signore Baptista is so pleased with the stubborn girl's reclamation that he doubles Kate's dowry to forty thousand crowns. The play ends on a note of congratulations and good cheer. Everyone, even Kate herself, agrees that Petruchio has "tamed a curst shrew."

Shakespeare's *Taming of the Shrew* has been a tour de force of Western culture for more than four centuries. No Shake-speare play has had greater success on stage except his incomparable *Hamlet, Prince of Denmark.* The merry wars of Kate and Petruchio have been performed on screen by such stars as Mary Pickford and Douglas Fairbanks (1929), Lisa Kirk and Charlton Heston (1950), Elizabeth Taylor and Richard Burton (1967), Cybill Shepherd and Bruce Willis (1986), and the Warner Animaniacs (1993). The comedy has been adapted for Broadway and the screen under such titles as *Pygmalion* (1910), *Kiss Me, Kate* (1948, 1953), *My Fair Lady* (1964, 2012), *Taming the Wet Medium* (1987), *Swept Away* (1974, 2002), *Ten Things I Hate about You* (1999), *Deliver Us from Eva* (2003), *Taming the Tushie* (2010), and *Taming of the Screwy* (1993). It has been retold in print under such titles as Alexander Kelly's *The Taming of the Princess Bitch,* and R.S. Tanner's *The Taming of the Brat: M/F Spanking Stories*.[1]   The common theme of these popular shrew-taming tales is that, for a woman, "It is better to love and to lose, than not to be loved at all."

The theme of romance, as pioneered by Lady Porcliano and Lady Cook-Bacon, is that true love is not for losers. But even if Anne Bacon's women readers should happen to have married one, all is not lost. *The Taming of the Pooch*, like every great romance, provides a guiding light for dramatic conflict, a successful rising action, an exciting climax, and a happily-ever-after denouement.

A. D.

---

[1] In the women's tradition of taming-tales, represented by hundreds of *Taming* titles, the heroine is subdued not by a man's cruelty, but by channeling her rebellion into sexual passion.   In hundreds of others, a bestial, or lawless, or promiscuous male hero must be tamed by a strong heroine. Those readers who enjoy *The Taming of the Pooch* may also enjoy such modern imitations as *The Taming;* or *The Taming of the Beast* (five different novels by five different authors and publishers); also, Tamings of: *the Alphas, the Barbarian, the Beastly, the Boss, Chaos, the Cougar, the Dangerous Lord, a Dark Horse, the Duke, the Fire, Him, a Husband, her Irish Warrior, the Lion, the Lone Wolf, her Man, the Notorious Sicilian, the Outlaw, the Pirate, the Playboy, the Prince, my Prince Charming, a Renegade, a Rogue, a Savage, Savage Love, the Scotsman, the Sheik, the Storm, the Tiger, the Texan, Two Fires, the Tycoon, the Texas Tycoon, the Viking's Dragon, the Wicked Wulfe, the Wild, the Wild Man, the Wolf, and a hundred others;* plus a whole sub-genre of less sanguine romances bearing such titles as *Tough to Tame, Too Tough to Tame, Too Wild to Tame,* and *Too Wicked to Tame;* a reminder that while some women may fall hopelessly in love, some men are simply hopeless.

The Taming of the Pooch

By Isabella Sforza del Nero Lando, countess Porcigliano (1555)
Englished by Anne Cook-Bacon (1589)

I. *Collinosa Bianca*

WHEN THE COACHMAN opened her carriage door, Bianca was ready. She took two quick breaths and exhaled slowly. Fans on both sides of the red carpet craned their necks for a glimpse of her. She counted to twelve before making a move. Slowly, she stretched out one hand. Her well-trained chauffeur reached up, took her by the fingertips, and helped her down. Bianca Miniola Ramusio di Baptista descended from the carriage like an angel from heaven, taking care not to snag her yellow silk stockings, nor to let the elevated soles beneath her feet cause her to stumble upon the stone walk.

Head high, elbows back. Shoulder-length blond hair, artfully curled, with a braided up-do by Donna Marie Fischetto. Figure-cinching silk gown by Donilo Donati, powder blue, low-cut with a white partlet front and back, and virago sleeves. Her eyes, lode-stars. Her earrings, diamond chandeliers. Her smile, a rifle-shot to the heart. Joining her now, at her side, was her seventy-year-old father.[1] As she took his arm, the crowd applauded. Someone in the throng called out, "I love you, Bianca! I want you to have my baby!" Another fellow shouted, "No, mine first!"

---

[1] *father*] i.e., Baptista Ramusio (b. Treviso, 1485). Educated at Venice and Padua. Entered public service 1505; cosmographer to the Venetian Republic and secretary of the Council of Ten; m. (1.) 1524, Franceschina Navagero, (d. 1536; his mother's cousin); s., Paolo (1532-1600); m. (2.), 1536, Topa Miniola (d. 1539); dau. Caterina (b. 1537); dau. Bianca (b. 1538). Generous patron of the arts and geographical exploration. Baptista's house in Padua, on Via Patriarcato, was a mansion noted for its collection of paintings, ancient sculpture, and books of geography. Died in Padua 10 July 1557, aged 72; buried in Venice.

Bianca, seventeen, had it all. Looks, style, money, adoring fans. She intended for this to be her night. And what Bianca wanted, Bianca usually got.

Theater people, writers, and celebrities from Venice to Florence had converged on Padua for the city's premier cultural event — the Hercules Awards ceremony, held annually at the Ragione Palace and sponsored by the Accademia degli Infiammati.[1] As a leading patron of the arts, Signore Baptista Ramusio with his wrinkled countenance and mane of shaggy white hair and frivolous beard was a familiar figure at the event, a fixture of the Paduan theater. But tonight all eyes were riveted upon his teenaged daughter. The Academy had nominated Bianca to receive a Hercules for her supporting role as Erotima the courtesan in Hortensio Lando's smash hit, *A Comedy of Erros*.[2]

Hortensio's script — a modern adaptation of *The Menaechmi*, by Plautus — featured a double set of identical twins who were separated when young, one member of each pair having been lost or misplaced in infancy. The two Androphallus brothers were performed by Preslio, the company's biggest star; while the two bondservants, named Dromio, were played by the brothers Colloredo. Hilarity ensues when the long-lost twins of Syracuse disembark in Epidamnus. Supporting roles included five female parts, for boy-actors: Adriana, an elderly abbess; Goody Dromio and Lady Androphallus (wives to Dromio and Androphallus of Epidamnus); Lucrezia, a randy housemaid; and Erotima, a high-rolling courtesan. On a lark, Baptista's younger daughter — who had all the right attributes and did not mind showing them — auditioned for the courtesan's role. Baptista stayed

---

[1] The Accademia degli Infiammati ("Academy of the Flaming Ones") was an influential academy of the arts, founded in 1540 by Leone Orsini. Its emblem featured Hercules on fire on Mount Oite. The Paduan academy was subsequently eclipsed by the Accademia Olimpica, chartered in Vicenza 1555, the year of Signore Baptista Ramusio's retirement.

[2] Not to be confused with *L'Errore* (1556), by Giovan Baptista Gelli, whose comedy of errors coat-tailed on the success of Horatio's *Comedy of Erros* (1555). Gelli's plot is based on a mistaken address; an old dotard, cross-dressed as a girl, is sent to his own wife, and humiliated.

out of it, but he was not displeased when Bianca was chosen for the part — he was, after all, the patron of the company — nor was he surprised when his daughter went on to receive appreciative notice in the popular press.

Having been given a role in Hortensio's comedy, Bianca when playing Erotima did not wish to be mistaken for just another cross-dressed boy, like other ventriloquized "women" on the Italian stage. She dressed for the part like an actual courtesan of Venice, fully exposing her young breasts to the view, without so much as a lace partisan between the eyes of the audience and her lovely bosom. Reviewers agreed that it was not just the two Dromios, or the two Androphalluses, that had made *Erros* a smash hit. Some credit was owing also to Bianca's twin girls, a perfect set of pink plumpers. Moreover, Bianca had spoken her lines as clearly, as seductively, as any boy-actor could have done. Even her father was impressed.

Looking distinguished in his black suit and mop of white hair, Signore Baptista extended an elbow to Bianca for their walk up the red carpet into the Ragione. Hundreds of people had crowded the square, with dozens more looking down from the arched walk of the upper portico. "Merda," said the old man, through smiling teeth. From years of working with playwrights and directors who sought his favors or money, Baptista had perfected the art of saying "Merda" with a warm smile — so that the applicant understood him to mean, "Merda! I love it! I love the concept! Let's do lunch!" — when what he really meant was, "Merda! Your concept sucks. Eat my shorts, and die." Baptista's aesthetic judgment deferred always to good money sense. His personal preference was for tales of bawdry, and tough-guy Senecan fare; or he slept. And yet, he had a soft spot for stories of wise patriarchs with desirable daughters who honored their father above their own buffoonish husbands or suitors. Also, blood. Lots of blood. Nothing brought in the box receipts like a tragedy of blood.

As a producer, Baptista had no time for scripts with obvious literary merit. He always said, and seemed to be correct, that you can never underestimate the lowest common denominator in a theater audience. In the year previous, he had bankrolled two plays — Benedetto Varchi's touching comedy, *Two Very Gentle Men of Verona* and Antonio Molino's *Titus Andronicus: A Musical Extravaganza.* Varchi's play had a smaller gross but enjoyed better net earnings. Molino for the staging of his gory neo-Senecan romp had demanded big-production dance numbers, plus costly props — weapons and butcher knives, wax hands, wax heads, and a hoist — that bit into profits. The laundry bill alone, for weekly cleaning of blood-stained togas, was horrific. And yet no play in memory — not Varchi's *Gentle Men*, not even *Titus* — had packed the house like *A Comedy of Erros.* Baptista had earned enough from *Erros* to refurbish Villa Marsango, his property north of Padua, where he intended to retire.

Like his daughter, Signore Baptista was to receive some personal recognition that night: he been selected for a "Life-time Achievement Award," as they called it. The prize-disposition did not please him. "They're just counting the days till I drop, those people," he said. Nor did the old man care for any event where the rich and famous gathered to stroke one another's ego. He disliked these annual affairs in particular, where theater people glad-handed him from every side. An Academy award for Best Play would write *finis* to his record as a founding patriarch of northern Italy's theatrical Renaissance. But a "Lifetime Achievement Award" felt like a push.

The carriages lining up at the curb pulled forward one at a time to disgorge their celebrities. Bianca made her way inside, on her father's arm. As she walked up the red carpet, grown men and teenagers continued to call out her name. "Bianca!" "Erotima!" "Bianca!" All the men of the Veneto region seemed to want her. The women just wanted to *be* her. "Bianca!" "Over here!" "Bianca!" The teenaged star turned this way and that, smiling to the crowd. She felt the energy. She felt the love.

Inside the Ragione, an usher led Bianca and her father up-stairs into the Great Hall, where tables were set for the banquet that preceded the awards ceremony. The noise of the crowd now gave way to the lilt of familiar theater tunes, scored by Nino Rota and performed by the famed Domenico Venier

Ensemble, over the buzz of cocktail chatter and the clink of crystal wine glasses.

A large table had been reserved for the *Comedy of Erros* party — Signore Baptista (producer), Hortensio Lando (author-director), and the full cast, each with a spouse or guest. Baptista greeted those already seated, but did not yet take his assigned place at the head of the table. He excused himself to go back outside and wait for his elder daughter. When the carriage had come to pick them up, Caterina was not yet dressed and ready to go — a typical stunt from stubborn Kate. But it was not entirely her fault. The delay was partly because Bianca, in a dressing-room mishap, had spilled hot orange candle wax, quite a bit of it, upon her elder sister's new silk dress.

When ushered to her table, Bianca chose a position from which she could see and be seen by everyone who came through the main entrance. To her right sat Luci Speroni, a nervous redhead with heart-shaped lips who dressed as if for Sunday School. To her left sat Lady Gonzaga (Horatio's patroness), a bleached blonde whose swatches of cut-and-slash white leather were artfully arranged to cover the essentials.[1] Competing with *Erros* for "Best Play" were Andrea Calmo's gritty romance, *Pericles, the Errant King of Tyre,* performed by the Lord Cardinal's Men; Cinthio's *Antonio and Cleopatra,* by the Duke of Ferrara's Men; and Leon Sommi's *The Betrothal,* a musical comedy produced and performed by Mantua's Università Israelitica, with innovative stage machinery designed by Sullam and Shalit. Six Mantuan Jews, one of whom was doubtless the playwright, sat on a bench at the back of the hall. They sat without speaking but not without being noticed. Dressed in red pointed hats and red scarves (compulsory garb in the Veneto), the Jewish guests looked conspicuously out of place here in Padua's Ragione Palace, among so many well-dressed Christian celebrities.

---

[1] *Luci*] Lucietta Speroni (1533-1563); daughter of Sperone Speroni, whose play, *Canace* (a tragedy of incestuous love) was performed only once for the Accademia degli Infiammati but fueled bitter academic debates for a century; *Lady Gonzaga*] Lady Lucrezia Gonzaga (1522-1576), one of Horatio Lando's patrons; a famed bluestocking whose letters were published by Horatio Lando in 1552.

"Think we'll win Best Play?" asked Bianca, as a conversation opener.

"Oh, I think you will," said Luci, with her usual perky enthusiasm.

Lady Gonzaga laughed out loud. "Who else is the competition — *Pericles?* Pullease. Pericles is hot to wed Princess Stratonice until he learns the answer to the riddle of King Antiochus: she already belongs to Papa. '*He's father, son, and husband mild. / I'm mother, wife, and yet his child. / 'I sought a man while wearing plaid, / I found that kindness in my Dad...*' Some riddle. Who writes like that? Who even *talks* like that, except Lucrezia Borgia, at age twelve, in her church-school uniform?"

"Andrea Calmo wrote it," said Lucietta. "Who happens to be a very nice guy. So handsome! So debonair! I adore his wavy hair. And oh my god, those dimples! Such a shame, that he's a sodomite."

"Besides which, it's not primarily an incest play," explained Bianca, impatiently. "That twist is for classical verisimilitude. Pericles' own daughter, Marina, a little Miss Goodie Two-Shoes, is to be assassinated by the jealous mother of a girl who is less popular than she. But Barbary pirates come and take her away, so Marina doesn't get killed; but then the Barbarians sell her to a bordello on the island of Lesbos, where she almost gets raped; but she scolds the customers instead of shagging them, which very nearly puts the brothel owner right out of business — she's that good of a preacher against lechery. Very funny stuff. Then Pericles, who's lonely and depressed, goes to the island whorehouse thinking to relieve his sadness with some meaningless sex. But he discovers — in the nick of time, from a mole on her breast, just above the actual nipple — that the teenage puttana they have given him is own his long-lost daughter, Marina; so nothing happens between those two except a paternal kiss and a happy reunion. Then long-lost Queen Thaisa appears, so that the whole happy family is reunited. Meanwhile, the Syrian princess and her wicked incestuous father get blown to pieces by an off-stage petard from the gods. So there's your poetic justice, by the spadeful.

I'll take *Erros* over *Pericles* or *The Pimp,* any day, but I heard Daddy say that the competition this year was awfully stiff."

"Members of the audience were," said Hortensio. "That much I *know* is true."

"Calmo won't win," said Lady Gonzaga, with cool confidence. "*Canace* won the Hercules for Best Play, years ago. *Pericles* is just another *Canace* imitation. That wave already crashed. Like anyone in Italy needs another bad romance? [1] Incest is just so passé ... so *yesterday.*"

"If I go to the theater," said Luci, "I want to see true love. I want to see manly valor. I want to laugh. I want to cry. I want to see cute guys. I want to see the human spirit triumph over adversity. I do not want to see a Syrian king in bed with his daughter."

"In all fairness," said Hortensio, "you didn't actually see her in bed with him. The church censors get their hand into everything, damn them."

Trumpets announced the arrival of Stefano Trevisan, Padua's newly elected Podestà, accompanied by Senator Domenico Venier of Venice, and Helena Artusi, his mistress, half his age. Helena was a sweet girl, with a nice figure, though viewed as a problem by Venier's staff, who called her Hellina Handcart-tushie. (She was unpopular as well with the senator's wife, who called her "your filthy whore.") All rose, applauded politely, and sat down again. Moments later, to everyone's surprise, in waddled Trevisan's petite and stumpy spouse, Wilfredda. She had come to the event dressed (as usual) all in black, from shoulder to foot; with a white partlet over her upper bosom, complemented by a high collar and a head veil of white linen. She wore no makeup, no superfluous bum-roll under her skirt, and no jewelry. Peach-colored shoes.

"Help me out here," said Bianca, "is that midget an English Puritan on holiday, or a nun escaped from the convent?"

---

[1] *bad romance*] Lady Gonzaga's husband, Paolo Manfrone, a cruel and violent man, died in prison ca. 1554; Lady Gonzaga never remarried.

"You haven't seen one of those before?" said Hortensio.[1] "That bird, almost certainly, is a penguin."

Bianca let her eyes range the Great Hall, coolly assessing the hotness factor of every other woman in the hall. She began with Loredana Marcello. "Oh, look," she said. "I just love the pleated drapes that Loredana is wearing tonight. I wonder if her windows — down home at the onion farm — are wearing her dress."

"Beh," said Lady Gonzaga, "I've seen fish at the market who came wrapped better than that."

"Speaking of down home," said Lucietta, "I have some reservations about Laura Bacio Terracina's neckline."

"God, yes," said Bianca. "Someone should remind Laura that a plunging neckline should not literally hit bottom. It makes you wonder: is that just deep cleavage, or is our Laura growing hair on her chest?"

"Yes, and yes," said Gonzaga.

"The cat eye-makeup is interesting, though," said Bianca. "So very medieval. Goes perfectly with her lipstick, from the Fresh Kill collection."

"That cannot be lipstick," said Gonzaga. "It's a nosebleed."

"I wonder where she bought her platform Zoccolis," said Lucietta, trying to be sweet. "They give her height and yet look comfortable enough for walking."

"Well, yes," said Bianca, softening her tone. "That *has* to be a big plus, having comfy shoes that also lift your hem out of the mud, especially if you're someone whose work requires you to walk the street — at night."

"She writes lovely poetry," said Luci.

"Did you hear what happened to Laura at Lavinia's wedding?" said Bianca. "Her braies came untied as she danced a

---

[1] Penguins are first described by Ferdinand Magellan in 1520; in English, by Master Hore in 1536; and are mentioned by Hortensio Lando in *Sette libri* (Venice, 1552). Finding the birds quite comical, the European explorers accorded penguins the usual welcome, killing as many as three thousand adult birds, and collecting as many as 100,000 eggs, in a single day (Hakluyt).

galliard with Senator Badoaro. Pfft! Down they came, to her ankles."[1]

"Well, no great shame," said Lady Gonzaga. "Good way to save the senator a few precious seconds after the dance lets out."

"Yes, except that she tripped on her own undies. The galliard was disrupted. Laura had to walk from the ballroom like a prisoner in leg-irons, or like a duck, before she could find a private place to pull up her bloomers and re-tie the points and return to the dance floor."

"I do wish Elisabetta Buzaccharini, at her age, would wear a partlet over her world-famous jiggly parts," said Gonzaga. "I don't mean this in a bad way, but I always like honeydew melons better in a fruit basket than when I see them popping out of Isabetta's bodice."

"Those are not real melons," said Bianca. "Those are the skulls of her two dead husbands, who remain close to her heart. Her breasts were last seen somewhere below her belt. But I see that Signora Buzaccharini has saved on her wig budget once again, by making her own hairpiece from the flayed hide of a dead sheep-dog. I just wish she would make two more wigs, one for each of her boneheaded husbands."

"What I admire about Elisabetta," said Lady Gonzaga, "is her capacity to find true love after bereavement. Plus, at her age, and with her range of experience, her lovers know she will never get them into a tight spot. She doesn't say, 'Darling, let's fool around,' she says, 'Sonny, let's play a game of Toss the Minnow into the Cistern.'"

Entering the hall now was a rail-thin beauty, large breasts, luxurious hair. On her arm was a Venetian beefcake, mid-twenties, dark curly hair, lots of blingbling jewelry.

"Olympia Malipiera is looking awfully thin," said Luci, changing the subject.

"Yes," said Bianca, "she has an exercise plan: Eat like a horse. Trot outside. Jam fingers down throat. Hurl. Then hurry back inside and dive headfirst into the dessert buffet. Keeps a girl slim."

---

[1] *braies*] linen drawstring underwear.

"She has been known to put other things down her throat, besides fingers," said Androphallus of Syracuse, somewhat dreamily.

" —Which also keeps her slim," said Gonzaga. "I mean, considering the alternatives."

"Were I her tailor," said Bianca, "I'd have recommended some other shade for tonight's gown than pickle-green. That just seems like such a risky wardrobe choice for a skank with olive skin who wears her dresses tighter than a sausage-casing. Olympia could be taken for a spoiled bratwurst, or a zucchini."

"I'm sure it's been done," said Gonzaga.

"Who's the cow on her left?" asked Androphallus.

"Lavinia Titian, the singer," said Bianca. "The famed 'Nightingale of Venice.' Or maybe it was 'The Stuffed Goose,' I forget. She's in a career transition, in the sense that she used to have one, and now she doesn't."

"That's Lavinia *Titian*?"

"Yeah. Got married. To Cornelio Sarcinelli of Serravalle — who toasted his bride, at their March wedding, as 'the next big thing, bigger than Polissena Pecorina.' And that is just so true. Because here she is, two months later, and forty pounds bigger."

"Life imitates art. Her father gave her an extra forty, every time," said Lady Gonzaga.

"Huh?"

"Each time he sketched her. Why, I've seen pictures of Lavinia Titian," said Gonzaga, "where she looks less like the Songbird of the Veneto than like the Great Squid of Bread Dough."

"God bless Tiziano Vecelli," said Lady Porcigliano. "What Caravaggio did for little boys, Titian has done for beefy girls."

"God, yes," said Bianca. "What's the deal with him and Tintoretto and their fetish for white whales?"

"That's the beauty of it," said Hortensio, "Titian's girls have nooks and crannies all over the place. You don't even need to aim, it's all good."

"Those portraits are *not* of Lavinia," said Luci Speroni. "Her papa hires prostitutes to sit for him."

"Where does Titian find them, stranded on a beach holding a sign that says: *Fat, naked, unemployed, will sit for food?*"

"Oh, stop," said Lady Gonzaga. "It's not that hard to find a fat whore today. I mean, just look around the room, at these *nouveau riche* merchants' wives."

"Did you see Titian's latest exhibition?" asked Luci.

"No," said Bianca, "but I'm sure we didn't miss much. Isotta Brembati tells the story that when she sat for Titian, at age sixteen, the old fool whipped out his cazzo and said, 'Do you know what this is, sweetheart?' and she said, 'Maybe. It looks sort of like a cock, only smaller.'"

"From the size of his codpiece," said Gonzaga, "You'd think he was packing heavy artillery."

"Cotton bombast. One dried raisin, packaged in a feather-pillow. What's Titian, eighty years old? Pray god, when he needs to piss, and rummages through all of that extra stuffing, he can find the thing before he has an accident."

Androphallus was gazing now at a slim blonde, entering the hall on the arm of Luigi Lippomano. "What's that candied sweetmeat stuck to the arm of our titular bishop of Methone? She's seems a good deal more titular than the bishop."

"That's the bishop's niece, you pervert," said Bianca cheerfully. "Name's Paola. They're not a couple."

"Nice buns," observed Androphallus.

"Yes," said Peniculus, "and one could say that about his niece, as well. I mean, *I* wouldn't say it, but someone could."

"Paola used to have hot buns," said Lady Gonzaga, "but now she has a cake in the oven, with no wedding in sight. I have that on good authority."

"And yet," said Bianca, "I applaud Paola's fashion choice. The vestal Madonna theme is brilliant. Nothing says 'Assumption of the Virgin' quite like a white silk gown with a vestal blue hat."

"Yes, but the high waistline with a vestal-blue sash tied right underneath her enhanced bubbies very nearly spoils the effect," said Lady Gonzaga.

"Those aren't enhancements you see on her bosom," said Bianca. "Those are callouses. Seriously, she should teach her footmen to use hand lotion. But I do worry about her Uncle Lu. The Vatican is sending his excellency as the Pope's ambassador to Poland."

"Oh, my," said Lady Porcigliano. "My cousin is Bona Sforza, Queen of Poland. I must warn her that the bishop is coming to Cracow. Her majesty has forty Maids of Honor— "

" —most of whom," said Bianca, "already know the Italian tongue, from Gianfrancesco Commendone, the Vatican's last nuncio to Cracow. But I wonder what his excellency Bishop Lippomano will reply when those forty *troie d'honore* ask him why he wears those excellent velvet patches on his face. Does anyone here know a good Polish euphemism for stage-two syphilis?"

Uncomfortable with Bianca's catty remarks about other women, Lucietta tried to change the subject: "I've been read-ing the *Rime* of Gaspara Stampa," she said. (Luci looked heavenward, fetching a deep sigh.) "Edited by her sister, Cassandra. Gaspara's poems of her love affair with Count Collaltino are just the most beautiful I have ever read."[1]

"I hear Cassandra has turned Protestant," said Lady Gon-zaga. "I hear that she practically worships Pietro Carnesecchi."[2]

"Yes, that's true," said Lady Gonzaga. "I think she would do anything for him."

" —in sincerity of Christian love," added Luci, by way of clarification.

"If Carnesecchi told Cassandra to read the entire Protestant Bible from cover to cover, would she do it?" asked Bianca.

"Absolutely," said Lady Gonzaga.

"If Carnesecchi told Cassandra to steal from the offering plate for the Protestant cause, would she do it?"

"Yes," said Lady Gonzaga, "I'm certain she would."

"If Carnesecchi told Cassandra to poison the Pope, would she do it?"

---

[1] Gaspara Stampa (1523-1554), a musical performer at men's homes, was one of Italy's greatest love poets; also, a courtesan. *Rime* (edited by her sister Cassandra) appeared posthumously in October 1554.

[2] Pietro Carnesecchi, leader of the Reform movement in Venice; beheaded and burned as a heretic in 1567.

"I have no doubt."

"Oh, my," said Bianca. "Pray God Carnesecchi does not ask Cassandra to give him a blow job."

"Nay, that's past hoping for," said Gonzaga. "The best we can do is pray that she does so with less gusto. The poor man has lost weight."

The food was coming round. As servers brought the antipasti, the guests brought out their clean flatware from purse or pocket.

(Here in civilized Italy, socialites never share one another's silverware. Spoons and knives and toothpicks are considered personal items, no less than bath-towels and underwear. The ladies at this moment glanced around the table, to ensure that no man was without a table fork. This pronged utensil, not yet known to the troglodytes of Northern Europe, and seen only rarely in France, allows socialites to eat without using their fingers. Men at first scorned the food-fork as a feminine hygiene utensil, and Holy Church has condemned it as a fastidious nicety, invented by pagans. Undaunted, the women of southern Europe have inched civilization forward with a crusade against greasy fingers at the dinner table. It is fair to say that, in Italy, the table fork has gained social acceptance as the only fashionable means whereby to deliver solid food to the mouth. In the Veneto region, gentlemen today were better to go about with their hair unwashed, their breath foul, and their codpiece untied, than to use their fingers at the dinner table like a common ape or a rude peasant or an Englishman.)

As the food came, the talk shifted inevitably to table etiquette. Everyone had a story to tell of his first fork, or tips to share on how to eat such difficult foods as spaghetti without simply grabbing a handful and shoving it in.

"I have a little story about dinner forks in America," said Hortensio. "Just last year, three explorers to the New World, a Frenchman, an Englishman, and an Italian, were captured by savages in the West Indies, and taken to the chief, who pronounced their execution.

"The Frenchman was the first to be slain. The Indian chief said to him, '*From your bones, we shall make tools; and from your skin, a canoe. How do you wish to die?*'

"The Frenchman said, '*Like Denis, patron saint of Paris, I shall be beheaded. Vive le France!*' Taking up the Frenchman's own sword, the chief took a mighty swing at the man's neck and with one blow toppled his head to the ground. Four of the savages who were standing by quietly picked up the man's body where it fell, and carried him off, to be flayed, to make a canoe.

"The West Indian chief said next to the Englishman, '*From your bones, we shall make tools; and from your skin, a canoe. How do you wish to die?*'

"The Englishman said, '*Like valiant Henry Percy, Hotspur of the North, let me be shot in the head. God save the Queen!*'

So the Indian chief put the Englishman's own gun to his forehead, and pulled the trigger, and shot him dead. The savages carried away his body, to be flayed, to make a canoe.

"The chief said next to the Italian, '*From your bones, we shall make tools; and from your skin, a canoe. How do you wish to die?*'

"'*I shall fall like a hero of Rome,*' said the Italian, '*on mine own weapon.*' He reached into his pocket and withdrew a silver dinner utensil. '*I shall die upon my table fork,*' he said, bravely. '*Fratelli* d'Italia!' The Italian then suddenly stabbed himself with the fork — all over his chest and belly and thighs — then laughed, maniacally, saying, '*So much for your* fucking canoe!'" [1]

"Oh, my god, oh my god," said Bianca, clutching her bosom.

---

[1] *canoe* | MS Italian *canoa*. Christopher Columbus introduced the *canoa* to Europe from the islands of the West Indies, where *canoas* were made from silk-cotton trees. The first recorded use of the form, *canoe,* is supplied by the French explorer and fur-huckster, Jean Nicolet (whose writings are cited today, by linguists, in their studies of 17th-century dyslexia [Hofstadter]). In a journal entry of 1640, narrating his foray south from Ontario into what is now Wisconsin, Nicolet writes: "I may be flayed (I am down with the Sioux). / Wrote to say, 'Need punts & canoe'; / Reply came today, / Said, 'Girls on the way / — But what on earth's a *panoe?*'" (Nicolet, 1640, trans. Dotson [2014]).

Hortensio pouted. Because of this sudden outburst from Bianca, no one had laughed at his joke.

"What's the matter?" asked Lady Porcigliano, startled.

"Look what just fell from Heaven!" said Bianca. She pointed to the entrance, where stood a young gentleman and his valet, seeming unsure where to sit; yet both were grinning. The servant, mid-thirties, bit of a paunch, was nothing special. But his aristocratic master was a knockout: well-built, with a shock of curly blond hair, grey eyes, and rosy cheeks, age twenty, tops. He was elegantly dressed in the style of a Florentine nobleman.

"That guy is so cute I could get pregnant just looking at him," said Bianca. "Name, please, someone?"

"Never saw him before," said Lady Gonzaga.

"Me, neither," said Luci, "but he's scrumptious."

"Nor I," said Lady Porcigliano.

"He's mine," said Bianca. "I'm in love."

At the very moment when Bianca's gaze met the eyes of the mysterious young lord, the ocular flirtation was interrupted by the return of old Signore Baptista. At his side was Caterina, looking beautiful but bored. Kate hated getting herself "tarted up." She disliked having to play nice to celebrities and theater people who could talk of nothing but their next show, or their last one, or about getting laid, or about *haute couture*. Kate had come dressed as a boy in a white silk shirt, black tunic and French slops — supplemented with diamond-stud earrings, and several ropes of pearls carelessly slung about her neck for a touch of blingbling esclavage. Her open shirt and tunic, partly unlaced, revealed just enough topography to excite interest. Her man's tights showed off a shapely set of calves. Utterly feminine in her boy's garb, Caterina Miniola Ramusio di Baptista as she entered the hall turned the heads of men and women alike, including the head of that aristocratic stranger on whom Bianca had just called first dibs.

"Well, good evening, Kat," said Bianca, when she reached the table. "I'm thrilled you could make it. Sister, you look as lovely in that outfit as you did at your seventeenth birthday party, in the same outfit."

"Why, thank you Bianca," said Caterina. "I'm comfortable. And you looked quite stunning last year, when you were still able to squeeze into your Little Princess outfit without a corset. Personally, I'd rather save a new dress for some unusual occasion, such as going to church, don't you think? But come, Bianca, can you introduce me to your friends?"

"I really don't see why that should be necessary," said Bianca. "Hey, everybody, this is Caterina, my big sister."

"And which of these handsome men," inquired Kate, "will be bringing you home tonight? or should I say, tomorrow morning?"

Bianca deflected the jibe with a tolerant smile. "Let's just say I like to keep my options open," she coyly replied.

"Oh, really?" said Kate. "That's what you call them — *options*? Most people call them *legs*."

"Go screw yourself," said Bianca, suddenly irritable.

"Oh, I wasn't finding fault," said Kate, sweetly. "I read somewhere that sleeping around is a great way to meet people."

"Girls, *stop* it," said Baptista, wearily. "Not here, not tonight."

"Oh, yeah, now I remember where I read it," said Kate. "It was in her journal."

"Vaffanculo," said Bianca.

"Vaffanculo? I have a little story about that," interjected Hortensio, as a welcome distraction. "Just last year, three explorers to the New World, a Frenchman, an Englishman, and an Italian, were captured by savages in the West Indies, and taken to the chief."

Bianca interrupted. "You already told us this one," she said. (Bianca had no patience with repetitive old men, such as her father.)

"No, different incident. Young lady, when an old man feels pressured to tell a tale or to let a fart, you were better to lend ear to his tale, than your nose to his tail." Hortensio chuckled, as usual, at his own joke. "Hear me out." Bianca rolled her eyes. Hortensio resumed his anecdote: "Three explorers to the New World, a Frenchman, an Englishman, and an Italian, were captured by savages in the West Indies, and taken to the chief.

"The Englishman was the first to stand before that savage tribunal.

"'*Buzo-buzo, or death?*' asked the chief.

"The Englishman did not know what buzo-buzo could be, and the chief refused to explain. But it could not be worse than death. '*I choose buzo-buzo,*' said the Englishman. '*Long live the Queen!*'

"Some half-dozen godless savages promptly ripped off the Englishman's hunting-breeches, and buggered him, by turns, and sent him on his way.

"Many savage warriors yet stood in queue, waiting quietly for their chance with a white man. The chief commanded the Frenchman to stand forth. '*Buzo-buzo, or death?*' asked the chief.

"Having witnessed the lamentable fate of the Englishman, the Frenchman answered, '*Mon dieu! I'll take buzo. I'll take buzo-buzo any day of the week, and twice on Sundays. Vive le France!*' A second band of eager savages fell upon the French-man, and buggered him, and sent him on his way. The Frenchman was not displeased.

"The Italian was the last to stand forth. '*Buzo-buzo, or death?*' asked the chief.

"'*Death,*' said the disgusted and courageous Italian. '*I choose death.*' So the chief — "

Baptista interrupted Hortensio's story. "Come again? An Italian said that?"

"Yes, sir," said Hortensio, impatiently. "Just hear me out, will you? This really happened, I'm not making it up. The Italian gentleman chose death. Like you, the West Indian chief was surprised at the answer. '*Seriously?*' said the chief, in amazement. '*You choose* death *over* buzo-buzo?'

"'*I have spoken,*' said the Italian. '*I choose death.*'

"'*Come, my warriors,*' said the chief. '*This fellow has cho-sen death. But first — a little buzo-buzo!*'"

After dessert was served, Master of Ceremonies Pietro Are-tino led off the disposition of awards with a number of stories,

which are best left unrepeated here,
because they were indecent.

The first Hercules to be awarded
that night, for Lifetime Achievement,
went to Signore Baptista. The old man
hobbled to the stage and delivered a
number of thank-yous, which I shall not
repeat, because they were tedious.

Next up was Best Supporting Role.
Of four actors nominated, Bianca was
named by book-makers as the hands-
down favorite. But politics, personal
rivalries, and back-room financial deals

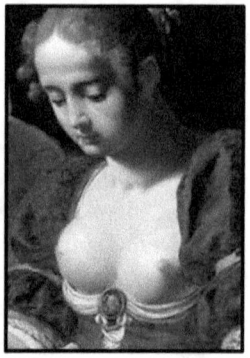

Bianca di Baptista

always influence the vote. You can never be sure until the
winner is announced. To heighten suspense, Signore Aretino
launched into another one of his naughty monologues.

"Merda!" said Kate.

"Shhh!" said Bianca.

"Sorry," said Caterina, "but I seem to have dropped my
diamond-stud ear-ring." She pushed back her chair.

"Forget it!" hissed Bianca. "Let it go!"

"I can't," said Kate, with furrowed brow. "That diamond
once belonged to our mother."

Signore Baptista gave his elder daughter a look that would
have stopped a lion in its tracks. But it did not stop Caterina.
Before anyone could intervene, she was under the table, on
her hands and knees, hunting for her lost diamond earring.

Bianca was visibly furious. So was Baptista. "Caterina!" he
snapped, while leaning back and trying to peer between his
own knees. "Get up! Get back to your seat!"

To diffuse the tension, Hortensio suddenly placed both
hands on the table, palms down, and began rocking back and
forth, first gently, then wildly, as if Caterina was fooling around
with him down there. He opened wide his eyes and whispered,
"Oh, Kate, oh yes, oh, YES!"

This buffoonery fetched raucous laughter from the cast,
easing tensions, for a moment. Androphallus flagged down a
young waiter. "Garçon!" he said.

"How may I help you, sir?" inquired the youth.

Androphallus pointed to Hortensio, who was just now reaching the height of his pantomime. Adapting a line from another comedy, Androphallus said, "Garçon, whatever Hortensio is having, I'd like some of *that.*"

Another burst of disruptive laughter.   Signore Baptista frowned. Bianca pursed her lips, and fumed.

By now, guests at nearby tables had noted the commotion: a young woman in boy's garments was crawling around beneath the banquet table, bumping into shins, while the cast of *Erros* was laughing aloud, and ignoring the comic routine by Aretino, master of ceremonies.

"I'll kill her," muttered Bianca, under her breath. "I'm gonna kill her."

The moment of crisis had arrived.

There was a drum roll as Aretino broke open the wax seal. He began to read the announcement: "The WINNER of this year's Hercules Award for Best Supporting role...."

At that exact moment, the head of Caterina popped up again from beneath the table, looking jubilant.

"Sit!" snarled her father.

Caterina climbed back into her chair, held aloft her diamond earring, and whispered in triumph, "Found it!" She then twisted her chair to face the stage, with the rest of the table guests, as if nothing had happened.

"...goes to BIANCA di BAPTISTA, for her role as Erotima in *A Comedy of Erros!*"

The Hall erupted into applause.

Bianca stood. She then sat down again — quite suddenly — and frowned. The guests, expecting her to make her way to the stage, continued with their applause. But Bianca sat wriggling about in her chair, and grimacing as if she had got ants in her pants, or was suffering from hemorrhoidal burning and itching.

"Good sister," said Bianca, "this is not funny. Wrong me not. Nor wrong yourself. Undo it — immediately — or I will fucking kill you!"

"I beg your pardon?" said Kate. "I'm here to enjoy the show. Go collect your Hercules. Hurry, sis. Everyone's waiting!"

Sensing trouble, Aretino improvised: "Ladies and Gentlemen! may I introduce .... Signorina **BIANCA DI BAPTISTA!** .... awarded Best Supporting Role ... for her performance as Erotima, in Hortensio Lando's *A Comedy of Erros!*" The applause continued, but it was losing steam. "A high-five," said Aretino, "for the part Bianca made famous.   And another high-five for the other one.   And now, let's all give her a real big hand." But the young star remained at her seat, grimacing. "Bianca, please come forward.... You know, friends, Bianca is a local girl, the daughter of Signore Baptista, the play's producer....   Only that, of course, is not why she won the Hercules..."

"Someone tell Aretino to shut up," muttered Bianca. "I'm coming. Just give me a sec."

The guests glanced about with furrowed brow and worried eyes, puzzled by Bianca's odd behavior. "Are you feeling all right, sis?" asked Kate.

"Papa!" said Bianca, on the verge of tears. "Sister has tied my feet to the chair!"

Bianca now was in a deep panic, desperate to free herself either by breaking the ties or by pulling her feet from her shoes. Pausing in that struggle, she looked Caterina straight in the eye and silently mouthed her opinion (two words, it didn't take a master lip-reader). Pretending not to notice, Kate lazily scratched at her chin with one finger.

"Caterina!" said Baptista, sharply.

"Yes, Papa?" said Kate.

Baptista stood. With arm outstretched to silence the applause, he bellowed: "I beg your pardon, friends! We have had a little mishap. It's nothing. Bianca my daughter wishes to thank— "

Bianca strained so violently that the laces of one shoe gave way. Ka-CHUNK! The plates bounced and glasses shook as Bianca's knee slammed into the underside of the banquet table. She then let words slip out that one does not ordinarily hear in a lady's dinner conversation. Still grimacing, she reached down to her other foot. In a frenzy of fast finger-work, Bianca removed her second shoe. She had escaped.

Bianca stood and smiled (though looking somewhat purple in the face). She waved to Aretino, and hallooed, "I'm coming, I'm coming!"

Without her Zoccolis, Bianca was suddenly six inches shorter than when she arrived; and her evening gown was now four inches too long. As she made her way to the front in her stocking feet, she had to hold up her skirt and petticoat and silky camica with both hands. Reaching the stage, standing beside Pietro Aretino in a dress that dragged upon the stage floor, Bianca looked to be wearing an outfit that was far too big for her petite frame. Aretino stepped back and laughed. A joke was coming. Bianca, whose feminine instincts are always spot-on, did not let him get it out. She also ignored the bronze Hercules that Aretino extended to her. "Friends," she said — speaking loud enough for all to hear — "I thank each one of you for your support. I love you all. But I never expected to win this honor. So as I sat at dinner, silly me, *I took off my shoes!*" With that remark, Bianca hoisted her skirt all the way to her thighs, revealing her unshod feet, her stockinged calves, her garters, and the lacy hem of her bloomers. The Domenico Venier Ensemble quickly struck up a few bars of "Io, io, scrollarsi di dosso," a popular galliard. Bianca, responding to that musical cue, gave her petticoats a good shake left and right, and launched into a high-kicking cinquepace that drove the crowd wild with admiration.

The music ended. Bianca smiled and curtsied.

Guests from one end to the other of the Great Hall — all of the men, plus many of the women — leapt to their feet and applauded, and stomped their boots on the floor and pounded their fists and the table, and hollered for more. The thunderstorm of applause that ensued very nearly brought down the roof of the Ragione Palace. I believe the ovation she received was the most deafening roar the Italian theater has seen or heard since the fall of the Roman Empire. "Thank you!" said Bianca, shouting into the din, as she accepted the bronze Hercules from the hand of Aretino. "Thank you, my friends!

thank you!" — and thus, all the way back to her seat — "thank you, my friends, thank you!" She returned to the *Erros* table with her golden Hercules tucked under her arm, and with her skirts hoisted so that her adoring fans could gaze upon her liberated ankles and feet.

"That's my girl!" said Baptista, beaming with pride.

Taking her place at the table, the award-winner flashed her elder sister a look of meaningful disdain. She then summoned a waiter to assist her with her abandoned footwear. The lucky lad with trembling hands took the next several minutes to put the goddess's feet back into her shoes and to mend her shoe-laces, a service that he would doubtless remember, forever after, as the most thrilling moment of his human existence.

After Bianca's triumph, all else was anticlimactic. Best Actor was awarded to Andrea Calmo for playing the lead in his own *Pericles.* And by some mistake no one could explain, the Best Play was given to Leone de'Sommi's Jewish musical, *The Comedy of Betrothal.* Bianca's eyes meanwhile had found and reconnected with the gaze of the mysterious young stranger, three tables distant. When the awards ceremony had ended, on her way out the door, Bianca slipped a note into his hand: "Bianca di B., Palazzo del Ramusiao, Via Patriarcato, Padua."

II. *Petruchio il Bambolotto*

ON THE DAY he arrived in Padua, the temperature of the air was feverish. The city was steaming, a limestone brach in heat. But Master Petruchio di Antonio, gentleman, age twenty, minded neither the scorching sky nor the sprawling, paved wasteland called Prato della Valle. Padua was the best city in Italy for live theatre, and therefore the most thrilling.

Petruchio's mother had warned him that Padua was dirty — and hot and crowded. She was right about that. But intermin-gled with the squalor, litter, noise, carriage-traffic, stray dogs, humidity, and strangeness, Petruchio felt a thrill, a heightened sense of life. The cracked and narrow, horse-dungy streets of Padua made the trees and open boulevards and clear air of Verona seem tedious. In Padua, homicidal scholars and greedy merchants and sly pickpurses bumped shoulders on the sidewalks with a careless abandon and *gioia di vita*. Soldiers and priests swaggered through the central market with a convulsive excitement. Here in Padua, it was as if everyone had just been born, with no family heritage to acknowledge, nor actions to regret, nor skeletons to hide under one-hundred-fifty pounds of too much female flesh and a peach-fuzz moustache.

Petruchio had no immediate plans to return home. He hadn't just left Verona — he had escaped. Escaped from his mother and his aunt, and from marriage to Rosaline Capulet, a solid Verona girl, from a solid family, who would have subjected him to the solid, respectable life of a henpecked husband. The same respectable life his father had lived. And his father's father. In the same respectable house. A house that a good Veronese family had owned for generations, its male inhabitants engulfed in respectable maternal affection, their manliness stifled within that creaky iron maiden called "a woman's love."

Petruchio's nicknames, at home, were "Pet" and "Poochi": "A gentleman never laughs out loud, Pet." "Cover your mouth when you sneeze, Poochi." "Pet, a gentleman *never* sheds tears in public."

("But the kitchen isn't public! I'm crying to *you*, Mama, because Josephine just died. I loved that little poodle.")

"Well, a gentleman never sheds tears in private, either. You're not a little boy, Pet! you're eighteen, and Auntie Bettina is here in the kitchen, too. Now go to your room, you little pussy." [1]

Petruchio was still attending Saint Zeno's Academy when he made the decision to leave Verona for good. He announced it to his mother and Aunt Bettina during his Easter vacation.

---

[1] *pussy*] This word, when recorded by Lady Cook-Bacon in 1561, may possibly have lacked pejorative connotations, as in a popular 1560 drinking-song: "Adew, my pretty pussy, Yow pynche me very nere" (=Adieu, my pretty sweetheart, [I like how] you squeeze me so tightly!), *Mod. Lang. Notes* 34 (1919): 347. Cf. also the Puritan polemicist, Philip Stubbes, who writes: "You shall have every sawcy boy...to catch up a woman & marie her... So he have his pretie pussie to huggle withal" (*Anatomy of Abuses* [1583], vol. 1, sig. H1ʳ).

"Mama, Aunt Betty, when I finish at Zeno's, I'm going to Padua."

"No, you're not. That's a horrid place for a vacation," announced his mother.

"I want to live there."

"Have you discussed this with Rosaline?"

"Why should I?"

"Well, you've been friends since you both were seven. Everyone naturally assumes..."

"Exactly. In Verona, *everything* is assumed. I hate that."

"Don't you raise your voice at me," said his mother, calmly. "Rosaline Capulet is a darling girl. Your father went to school with her father."

"But I don't think she's sexy," said Petruchio.

"Girls are not supposed to be *sexy.*" This, from his Aunt Bettina.

"That makes no sense, to me. Did you never really want my father, Mama?"

"Of course I wanted him." Her voice bristled. "I wanted him to behave as a gentleman. I wanted him to bring home a satisfactory income. I wanted him to keep his foot out of brothels and his hand out of petticoats. Your father was a difficult man, peremptory, irascible, and he liked to drink."

"I never saw him drink anything but milk," said Petruchio.

"That's just it. I broke him of wine-bibbing before it could ruin him. Had he not been married, he'd have come to a bad end, almost certainly."

"But he *did* come to a bad end."

"There was nothing wrong with that steamed risotto," said Aunt Betty, sharply.

"Oh, Pet, your Papa had wild ways, at first. His grandfather was English, you know."

"The English are always a little loco," Aunt Betty agreed. "They think they could rule the world, if given the chance."

"You must understand, Poochi, that while there was nothing abnormal about your papa, he was, after all, a man; and one man in an Italian family is quite enough."

Petruchio wished he had not been such a mama's boy, while growing up. "There was nothing wrong with my Papa!" he blurted.

(It now seemed so long ago, the day his father toppled forward, right here at the kitchen table. It was Petruchio's twelfth birthday. The man never even finished saying "Happy Buh—" He just slumped quietly forward, face-down, into a bowlful of warm risotto and died. The holy friar came, arriving too late to administer last rites. Petruchio wondered, sometimes, if it would have made any difference, had he been quick to leap from his chair and grab his unconscious Papa by the hair and pull his face out of the bowl and maybe even unclog his nostrils. That thought haunted Petruchio — that his father might still have still have been alive while face-down in Aunt Bettina's mushroom risotto.)

"But Mama, I mean, wasn't it ever wonderful with Papa?"

"Wasn't what wonderful?"

"You know...knowing...wonderful to know one another... in the biblical sex. Uh, sense. You know, was it never like, *Wow, that was really good?*"

"Poochi, hush, for shame!" snarled Auntie Bettina.

Petruchio cringed, expecting to be slapped, but his aunt checked herself, for once. It was like that time when he happened to break wind during Holy Mass, not just once, but a thundering sequence of echo-producing farts, owing to an upset stomach. He held it in as long as he could, squeezing his buttocks muscles, his stomach growling uncomfortably, but he finally couldn't hold back. The offense caused three famous Veronese artists — Orlando Flacco, Bernardino India, and Michele Sanmicheli, who were sitting in the pew just behind — to leave church before the service had ended: the men could not contain their laughter at the sequence of stentorian farts, coming from such a pipsqueak. His mama and aunt waited till they got home, then hollered at Petruchio, and sent him to his bedroom. "Gentlemen do not fart in church," his mother had said. But Pet felt it was seriously not his fault. His aunt was the one who had fed him the fagioli cannellini for dinner the night before, plus a forced second helping. "Poochi, a gentleman appreciates what his mother and aunt have cooked for him," she had said. "Gentlemen do not leave fagioli, uneaten, on their dinner plate."

(But then, evidently, a gentleman must not suffer gas afterwards — not unless you were a grandfather; in which case you didn't suffer, you were allowed to rip them off, one after another, all day long, and the whole family just had to pretend they did not even *hear* anything.)

Another thing that eighteen-year-old gentlemen were not supposed to do was to wonder if God actually created such a thing as sexual intercourse. "Sorry. Just curious," said Petruchio.

"Unfortunately," said his mother stiffly, "after marriage, a man is not satisfied with *kissing.*" Then, cautiously, "Has Rosaline ever kissed you, son?"

Petruchio grimaced. "Yes, of course. A few times."

His mother frowned. "And did you enjoy it?" It wasn't a question. It was an accusation. His mama, Lady Maria di Antonio of Verona, was a strict Catholic.

Petruchio paused in his reply. Rosaline had soft lips, which felt nice; and she had been growing a bosom, which also felt kind of interesting. But her breath defied all comers, smelling of garlic and onions. Besides, by age sixteen Rosaline Capulet was overweight and sported a peach-fuzz moustache. Petruchio had no desire to spend the rest of his life with her. "I *hated* her kisses!" he said. And he meant it.

"Have other girls kissed you?"

Petruchio shrugged. "At Rosaline's fourteenth birthday party, we played *Winkem*, and *Going to Jerusalem.* I guess most of the Capulet girls got around to kissing me, and their friends, and their mothers. Not one of them really did it for me."

"*Did* it?" His Mama looked at him in horror.

"You know, *did* it, made it exciting. I think there has been only one decent kisser in this entire town, and she's dead. Along with her crazy Montague boyfriend. A lot of good it did *him* to kiss."

A beatific smile returned to Lady Maria's countenance. "You're a gentleman, Pet. That's why you don't like to kiss. No real gentleman does."

"O Mama, I don't know if I'm a real gentleman, or who I am, or what I want. That's why I need to go east, to Padua. And then, who knows? Maybe onward to Venice."

His mother scowled. "Pet, you have ten thousand ducats. Your Papa left that for you to sow your wild oats. When I'm dead — when you have broken my heart and have driven me to the grave — there will be a good deal more. I shall leave everything to you, Pet, and I won't expect you to bring flowers to my grave, I know you're busy. In the meantime we're comfortable enough, not rich, not like the Capulets, but our name stands for something in Verona— "

"Well, mine doesn't stand for Rosaline, or for any other Verona girl, I can tell you that."

"And I can I tell you that you cannot run around and forsake your adult responsibilities. When you are done roaming, you must marry and settle down. In this house. Your father and grandfather were born here. Of course, Rosaline may wish to make some capital improvements, but this is our house, after all."

"Whose — yours and Aunt Betty's?"

"Also, yours and Rosaline's."

"But Mama, I don't *desire* Rosaline Capulet!"

"Let me tell you something, son: If and when desire comes, it dies very quickly after marriage. Go to your Padua. I won't stand in your way. I'm sure Rosaline will wait, too. But mark my words, Pet. After a few weeks you'll come running back home. To your mama, who loves you. You'll be happy to leave that dirty city, and the dirty women who live there."

Petruchio looked his mother straight in the eye and said: "I know what I want."

"What's that?" asked Lady Maria di Antonio.

"I *do* want to live in that dirty city. And when I get there, I want to do one of their dirty women."

Petruchio grinned when he said it, but he should have ducked. Aunt Bettina clocked him on the jaw with the back of her hand, then boxed his ear on the return swing. The flesh under her arm was still jiggling, back and forth, when his mother joined in. "Time out!" she yelled, taking his aunt's side, as usual. "To your room! And you're grounded."

As he made his way up the stairs, Petruchio heard his Aunt Bettina mutter, "Piccolo perverte! Maria, you are headed for trouble with that boy. He has not yet got a full beard on his chin and already he thinks only of sex. Ché ragazzo! Ché italiano!"

Petruchio took strange comfort in Aunt Betty's vexation. Upon reaching his room, instead of crying on his bed, he took up a charcoal pencil, and opened his sketchbook, and turned to a half-finished drawing of his favorite subject: the Flagellation of Saint Catharine of Siena.

• • •

AT TWENTY, Petruchio was no longer interested in saints or in mortification of the flesh. Nor did he really want a "dirty" woman. He had said that only to horrify his mother and aunt. He had done some growing up. As a gentleman and the son of a gentleman, what he desired now, somewhere in the bottom of his confused heart, was to find his soulmate; or at least, a girlfriend with a pretty face and nice curve; ideally (someday) a wife; at best, a woman with a sweet disposition and lots of money and a firm abhorrence of adultery. But he had no idea where to look or what he would do next if he should happen to find her. He remained a virgin. It's not that he was opposed in principle to sexual intercourse — he was not that good a Catholic. But girls made him nervous. To speak with a maiden his own age, or with a married one who found him attractive, afflicted Petruchio for hours afterward with stomach upset and flatulence. Opportunities to dance with the fair sex made him so weak with anxiety that his knees buckled. And he feared he could never be a success at making love to a woman of flesh and blood. Just to imagine himself naked in bed with a girl (which is something he actually did, quite often) gave him cold feet and caused him to sweat like a horse.

The one great question Petruchio had not been able to answer, despite his years of research into the feminine soul, was: "What does a woman want?" His other great question: "If making love is what a woman wants, what then?" He had read all of the most popular manuals, from Ovid to Aretino, but he still felt as if he wouldn't know what to say or do or think, if he were left alone with a woman who wanted him. During adolescence, his father was unavailable for counsel, being dead. With his mother and aunt, sexual intercourse was a taboo subject. For a long time, Petruchio had toyed with the idea of visiting a brothel — not to have sex with a prostitute, but to be tutored by one. It had occurred to him that he could enter a bordello somewhere far from Verona, and for a reasonable price inquire of the girls there what he needed to know — such as, how does a guy please a woman in bed without making a fool of himself?

Arriving in Padua, Petruchio booked a room at the university, checked his bags, and made a few discreet inquiries. Of all the brothels on the Piazetta della Bambola, a house called La Sorellanza was said to have the most talented women. Petruchio made that his first tourist stop. But the dumb buck at the door, who had been lazily cleaning his teeth with a silver toothpick, would not let him in. "Business has been slow," the fellow said. "So many men, off fighting the Turks. But you're a doll. You don't want to enter here, to purchase your diseases. You can do better. Honest, honey, if I had your looks I'd head straight for the palace of Signore Baptista. You could be grabbing a frisky one."

"A frisky what?"

"Baptista is father to the hottest girl in town."

"I'd like a girl with money," said Petruchio. "But you can put a hold on 'frisky.' I have a friend back home in Verona who married frisky. It didn't work out."

"Baptista is one of Padua's wealthiest men. Powerful, too. He's secretary to the Council of Ten. And he has put his two daughters on the marriage market. Trust me, you could be just what he's looking for."

"Right now," said Petruchio, "What I'm looking for is an opportunity to perform as a player with one of the licensed theatrical troupes."

"Looks like you just hit the trifecta, kid. Baptista is also the patron of Padua's leading dramatic company. Where you from?"

"Verona. But if I wanted a wife, I'd have stayed at home. 'Soon married, soon marred,' my father used to say."

"That can happen anywhere, kid. Here's Thurio, a local merchant, who grounded his bride for getting a leg up on Sir Eglamore. So when the major part of her dowry came due for payment, his wife ran away from home, taking with her all of Thurio's bonds, bills, jewels, his gold watch and rings, under the pretense of his having the pox — and then sued him for maintenance. Here's Lord Bellario, a learned doctor, one of the city's most celebrated peacocks, who had his wings clipped by a shrew with a pretty face. As a married man, they say, Bellario cannot go to the jakes to relieve himself without first asking permission of his wife. If the maids of Verona have so curst a disposition, you have left home in good time."

"In my experience, your typical Veronese virgin is only too willing to please — "

"Send one to my arms, dear Lord!"

" —in exchange for a testicle."

"Well, in that case, maybe not."

"Would you have any good-looking virgin who wants you?" Petruchio was curious. He was thinking of Rosaline Capulet, a girl who, since turning fourteen, must have gained thirty pounds, and who wanted him.

"My dream," said the doorman, "is to find a virgin who can supply me with money, a coat of arms, a part-time chambermaid, and let me sleep to noon. If that's not true love, it's close enough. But I'm a poor man's son. All of the women I know earn more money than I do. I can't compete."

Petruchio grimaced. Rosaline, the girl back home, never missed morning mass. She was not the sort of Italian woman who would let you sleep till noon, with or without a chambermaid.

"So are you coming in, or aren't you," said the doorman. "It will cost you a thousand crowns for an aglet baby — "

" —an aglet baby?"

"A virgin. But I can get you fairly fresh wares, about your own age, for as little as two hundred crowns."

"I need some advice. Just for the sake of conversation, how many minutes could I have for, say, ten or twenty ducats?"

"For ten ducats, I can give you five minutes with Gummy Bear."

"Gummy Bear? What's she?"

"Gummy is a wornout trot with as many diseases as two-and-fifty horses, and not a tooth in her head. But the old gal can do some pretty amazing things with those gums."

"You don't understand. I just want to talk. I have some questions ... about technique."

"If you don't want the whole package, the *négotiation entière*, as we call it, we do have a lovely conversation-only package, priced accordingly. Striptease, extra."

Petruchio's eyes grew suddenly wide. Not ten feet inside the door was a heavy-set woman, about the age of his own mother, in a silky negligee, with her breasts exposed. Spotting him, the beefy prostitute broke into a smile. She hurried to door and said, "Hey, big guy, I love you. I want you."

"Sorry, I just remembered that I have to be somewhere," said Petruchio. "I'll come back later." Clutching his stomach, he turned to go. The woman ducked back inside.

"Ciao," said the bouncer, returning his toothpick to his mouth.

Petruchio stopped. "Just one thing?"

"Shoot."

"As long as I'm out and about, where might I find this Signore Baptista?"

"Palazzo del Ramusio, on Via Patriarcato."

• • •

III. *Micia Caterina*

ON THE MORNING after the awards, Caterina remained in her room, reading by candlelight behind a locked door, pulled blinds, and closed shutters. The earlybirds — those first few annoying Bianca-worshipers, noisy as alleycats — had appeared on the curb before dawn. By mid-morning, a great throng had gathered — dozens of fans, plus some ten or fifteen wealthy suitors, all seeking access to Caterina's lovely little sister, or at least a glimpse. Children and adults stood on the walk with playbills, goose-quills and ink, looking for an autograph. As the crowd swelled, a band from the university appeared, comprised of two lute players, a trombettista, a flautist, and singers. Parking themselves on Baptista's front steps (before an open lute-case, to receive donations), the students serenaded the neighborhood with love ballads, hoping thereby to earn a few extra scudi by drawing Bianca out of the house. Street vendors arrived with beer and fast food. There was chanting, there was laughter. Some idiot set off fireworks. It was like Carnevale. And for what? For Bianca!

Caught up in a novel of summer love, Caterina ignored the din on the street until shortly before noon, when a noisy quarrel erupted between two of Bianca's suitors. Pietro di Paragonadi, a handsome young football player with shoulder-length hair, became suddenly abusive toward Guglielmo di Menarelancio, a wealthy but overweight gentleman-poet. Kate got up from her bed, walked to the casement and cracked open the shutters, to watch. Pietro snarled, "I am he, sir, that must marry this woman. Therefore, abandon the society of this female, you clown, or I will kill thee a hundred and fifty ways. Tremble, and depart." A defiant Guglielmo stood his ground; whereupon Pietro delivered a series of kicks to the man's fat posterior, first with one pointed boot, then the other. Pietro drove his adversary down Via Patriarcato. Guglielmo howled curses and mooed like a dairy cow until the two men disappeared around a corner, where Kate could no longer see what became of them.

Her father must have heard the quarrel, too, because he came to the front door. Calling out to the crowd, Signore Baptista asked them to disperse. "Friends! neighbors!" The crowd paid no attention. "Countrymen!" he shouted. "Lend me your ears."

"You come a minute too late," joked Hortensio. "Our friend Guglielmo, just moments ago, lent his rear to Pietro di Paragonadi, only not for the usual."

"Lend me your *ear*," growled Baptista. "I said, 'your *ear*.' I said it very plainly. And now, please go! Bianca shall not be seen today!"

A hush fell over the crowd. "What did the old man say?" asked one.

"He said she's not coming out," said another.

"That's not fair," said a third.

"Leave!" shouted Baptista, his voice hoarse. "Hence! Disperse! Abandon! Avaunt!"

Baptista's announcement prompted much grumbling, but most of the crowd honored the old man's wishes, and left. Only the diehard suitors remained, each fearing that a rival would be first to get his foot in the door.

"Gentlemen!" said Kate's father, with impatience. "Pester me no more. Under no circumstance will I bestow my younger daughter before I have a husband for the elder. If any of you loves Caterina, you have my permission to court her at your pleasure. Otherwise, go!"

"To *cart* her rather," said one, directly below Kate's window. "Your Caterina is too sour for me. She needs a sugar-daddy. Wed her to Gremio."

Caterina recognized the voice: it was Hortensio Lando, the famous scholar and comedian. He had come to the house to discuss geography with Signior Baptista, and stayed over. That was two weeks ago. Finding good food and excellent accommodation, Hortensio had yet not found occasion to depart. Kate did not find his jokes all that funny.

"No match for me," said Gremio, in his wheezy treble.

Caterina opened wide the shutters and leaned out.

"I have a match for you," she said. The men looked up. "Signore Gremio! Signore Lando! Stand cheek-to-cheek, you'd make the picture of a billygoat's arse, and no telling which buttock is the better half until some shepherd comes between you." Kate pulled her head back inside and closed the shutters without waiting for a rejoinder.

Gremio, stroking his white beard, shouted after: "Until you are of a milder mold, no 'better halves' for *you*," he said. This quip received a buzz of approval from the other men.

Signore Baptista without looking up hollered his paternal displeasure at his daughter's outburst. "Caterina!" he shouted. "Get thee in!"

Caterina, who was already in, opened the shutters and poked her head back out. "Signore Pantaloon! Baldpate! No, not you, papà! Gremio, yes, you! It is not halfway to my heart, to be your 'better half.' But if it were, be sure I would take wifely care to comb your moldy scalp with a garden rake, and scratch your face with my nails, and use you like an ape in Hell."

Kate disappeared back into her room, and slammed the shutters. She felt contemptuous of Bianca's suitors. (*So many men, in Italy! So few wealthy ones, who are not lechers! So few charming ones, who are not paupers! So few young ones, who are not blinking idiots!*); and yet, she remained a little jealous of Bianca's mysterious sex appeal. (*How does that minx do it?*)

"Good Lord," said Hortensio, "spare me from the tongue of a shrew."

"And me, too, good Lord," said Gremio.

"That depends on what else she can do with it, besides talk," said Lucentio.

Caterina left her bookmarked romance on the nightstand and headed downstairs for a bite of lunch. From the corridor, she heard Bianca scolding Tabatha, her chambermaid, for laziness. Kate caught only a bit of it: "Shape up, or you're fired. I do *not* understand why you find it so difficult to match up the shoes in my wardrobe closet. And you *know* I don't like to have my stockings put into the drawer, unfolded.

Worse and worse, it has been four days since you last emptied out my chamberpot — "

"Three," said Tabatha, in self-defense.

" — one more night, and the room will begin to smell like a pissoir."

Caterina knocked on the door.

"Yes?"

"It's Kat. May I come in?"

"No."

Caterina entered. Bianca was stretched out on her bed in a white robe, her face coated with a facial mask. Covering each eye was a cucumber slice to reduce puffiness from the previous night's alcohol. Her hair was in rollers. And as she lay there scolding Tabatha, she was receiving a foot massage.

"Sister," said Caterina. "I regret our quarrel, last night. In all humility, I would like to make it up to you. I was going downstairs anyway. I will take your chamberpot."

"Surely, you jest, sister," said Bianca, talking to the ceiling, but with a note of amused scorn.

With bowed head, Caterina walked quietly over to Bianca's bedside, and stooped, and picked up the porcelain pot, keeping the lid firmly in place.

"Tabatha, perhaps you can close the door behind me?" said Kate. "My hands are full."

Bianca was so gobsmacked, she lifted the cucumbers from her eyes and sat up. "Be sure you bring it back," she said.

"I will," said Caterina. Bianca's chamberpot was a pricey affair of hand-painted porcelain from the Danae's Revenge collection, by Capodimonte. It probably cost as much as the whole outdoor latrine in a less wealthy neighborhood.

Moments later, Caterina Miniola Ramusio di Baptista thrust open the shutters of her bedchamber and called out to the men below. "Good sirs!" she said.

"Yes, milady Amazon?" said one.

"I have a private message for you, which comes from my sister Bianca."

"Oh, yeah?" said one. "What's that?"

Without further ado, Caterina emptied the chamberpot on their heads and quickly drew back inside. To muffle the ensuing thunderstorm of unpleasant curse-words, she closed both the shutters and the casement window. She left her room, and closed the door, glowing with happiness. Knocking once at Bianca's bedchamber, she announced: "Delivery"; deposited the empty pot at the door; and proceeded downstairs, to forage for breakfast.

In the kitchen, Kate washed her hands and helped herself to a repast of carrots, celery, and bread. Returning to her room, she peeked out the window. The street was empty now in both directions. The boys had evidently taken the hint. Caterina knew there might yet be hell to pay for her behavior. In the meantime, that large wet spot on the stone patio, where the shower had hit, painted upon her mouth the barest hint of an enigmatic smile. When she returned to her romance, it was with a feeling of personal accomplishment and deep satisfaction.

Not long afterward, less than an hour, a knock came on her door. "Caterina? It's your father."

Kate bookmarked her page and sat up. "Come in, Papa." She braced herself for a lecture. It was not unthinkable that one of Bianca's would-be husbands had already threatened legal action for having had his spirits dampened, unexpectedly, from on high.

Baptista upon entering her room said, "Tell me, daughter Caterina, how stands your disposition to be married to an honorable gentleman?"

"'Tis an onager that I dream not of," said Kate.

"You have a visitor. A gentleman caller. Downstairs, in the parlor."

"Say what?" Kate understood that her father wished to dispose of her but she had not expected him to find a potential customer so quickly. Her father was beaming. For the wrong reason, no doubt.

"I say, there is a young gentleman downstairs who seeks your hand, to be his lawfully wedded spouse.

"Let him seek his own awfully wetted hand," said Kate, returning to her book. "I'm busy."

"It would please me if you would at least come downstairs to meet him. Shall I tell the gentleman to return at another time, or to wait?"

"No need to make the man return," said Kate. "Let him wait."

Her father left, shaking his head with annoyance, and closed the door behind him.

It was now mid-afternoon. Caterina had not yet gotten dressed. She was wearing only her silk camica, and a robe.

What to wear?

A gentleman caller seemed an opportunity for good sport. As much to befuddle and disappoint her father's suitor as to amuse herself, Kate decided to meet him dressed as a peasant. Pulling several rustic outfits from her walk-in closet, she chose a front-fastening gown with linen sleeves, a hoopless under-skirt, and a green apron. Her hair she left uncovered, and tousled.

When fully dressed, she inspected herself in the mirror. The camica, with its ruffled collar, was somewhat too modest for a market wench. She loosened the ribbon, to expose her neck and show some cleavage. Incantavole! All she lacked now, to look the part of a street hawker from the Padua farm market, was a basket of fruit.

Caterina sat back down on the bed, fluffed the pillows, and returned to her romance, expecting to be called. No one did. So she kept reading. She read straight through to the end, to the climactic union of true hearts, which gave her a nice little buzz and left her with a familiar warm afterglow. Setting the book aside without further thought of her gentleman caller, she rolled over and fell asleep.

A knock came on her door. Her father, again. "Caterina," he said through the door, "if you don't come down at once, I shall tell the young man to leave. He has been waiting for hours."

Kate got off the bed and walked to the door without opening it. "What young man?"

"The young man I told you about."

"You didn't say he was *young*."

"He's young."

"*Young*, meaning, under sixty? or *young*, under forty?" (Her father, at age seventy, had a skewed notion of youth.)

"Young, meaning, more like a child. I think his mother's milk is scarcely out of him. Will you open your door, please?"

"No. I'm not decent. What's he look like?"

"Like Phoebus Apollo."

"Or a chubby putto. And he has waited all this time?"

"Yes."

"Doing what?"

"Sitting in the parlor, with his hands folded in his lap."

"I'll be down in a minute."

"Please."

Caterina heard the wooden treads creak as her father retreated to his library by the back staircase. She returned to her closet for sandals or slippers or suede pumps, something suitably rustic. All of her shoes were too upscale. Fine. She sat back down on the bed, undid her garters, and pulled off her stockings. She would hear this man's lovesuit, barefoot.

Tiptoeing downstairs, Kate stopped in the kitchen, where she cobbled together a fruit basket (apples, oranges, peaches) to complete her ensemble; then poured herself a drink, a glass of tomato juice.

It now occurred to Caterina that she did not know whom she was to meet. She had not thought to interrogate her father on that point. At the time, it had seemed unimportant: she already knew all that she needed to know of the strange youth in the parlor, which is that she would not like him. A man of flesh-and-blood, on the best day of his life, could not hold a candle to those that inhabited the world of sixteenth-century romance. In the sheets of a paperback novel, a girl could find love with a shirtless but ultimately tender beefcake, any day of the week.

And yet, it would be inaccurate to say that Caterina was unmoved when she entered the parlor and set eyes upon her suitor for the first time. In fact, her heart very nearly jumped into her throat. He was young and pretty — tall, slim, muscular.

He had dark curly hair, a puppy's earnest eyebrows, deep-set eyes, rosy cheeks, dimples — and he was sleeping like a baby.

"Ahem!" (He stirred awake.) "I understand a gentleman suitor, and a circus buffoon, and a broom-maker's apprentice, have been waiting to see me. Which one are you?"

Petruchio opened his eyes, seeming unsure where he was, or who had spoken. Setting eyes on Caterina, he sucked in his breath and sat up.

"Buon giorno, ragazza dolce!" (Good morning, sweet wench).

"The buffoon, then. A suitor would say, 'Buon pomeriggio, caro dea.'" (Good afternoon, dear goddess).

"What is your name, signorina?"

"Caterina di Baptista," came her reply.

At the sound of her name, Petruchio stood bolt upright, and blushed, and pulled his hat over his face.

Caterina curtsied. "I am sorry, good sir, if I have offended you."

He lowered his hat. "No. No, not at all. I— it's just that— I beg your pardon. I mistook you for, never mind."

"What? You took me for a fruit-wench?"

"Yes. I mean, No. No comparison."

When coming up Via Patriarcato, Petruchio had stopped two sullen gentlemen and a surly footman coming the other way. He asked them for directions to Signore Baptista's house; whereupon they became quite animated. Gremio, an elderly gentleman, introduced himself to Petruchio as the future husband of Baptista's younger daughter, named Bianca. The other introduced himself Bianca's true love, Lucentio. But the rivals were allied in this, that they both wished to find a suitor for the elder daughter, Caterina. ("Bitch," "bag," 'ball-breaker," "bluestocking," "crone," "hag," "harpy," "harridan," "hoyden," "vamp," "vixen," "Kate the Curst." These were a few of the epithets they had applied to the young woman; from which Petruchio inferred that they did not like her very much. Even the footman joined in, with a few unprintable epithets.) Gremio, an old man, and Lucentio, not above twenty, professed to be quite wealthy, and therefore hopeful of their

ultimate success with Bianca, were it not for the shrew, her
sister. Finding Petruchio to be a handsome, well-spoken youth
from out-of-town, they offered him a deal he could not refuse:
if he would woo, seduce, marry, or otherwise occupy saucy
Caterina, then Gremio and Lucentio would underwrite
Petruchio's expenses (a promise that neither self-interested
signore intended to keep).

On the received information concerning Caterina, Petruchio
had set his expectations low: he resolved that anything above
three on a scale of ten would be worth the wager. A five would
be welcome. Six, a blessing. Above that, he dared not venture
to hope. He was just happy to get his foot in the door with her
father. This overture to Caterina, he surmised, could lead to a
role with Padua's leading dramatic company. And then, who
knows? He might never return to Verona.

But the young woman who stood before him now was as
perfect an angel as Petruchio had ever hoped to love. All
thought of a stage career passed from his mind. She was more
than just pretty. A finer daughter of Eve, if any walked upon
the earth, would have given him catastrophic heart failure.
Caterina di Baptista looked as if she had stepped out of a
romance novel — a heroine with dark silky hair, flawless skin,
eyes of liquid sapphire, rosy cheeks, sweet smile, and a curve
to die for. Petruchio half feared that, during his nap, he had
died and gone to heaven. The other half of him feared that he
hadn't. He was starting to sweat. His stomach growled. He
took a few deep breaths, to settle his nerves.

Petruchio realized now what a fool he had been to believe
those scoundrels on the street, with their vile remarks about
Caterina di Baptista. For one thing, they were in love with
Bianca, the younger sister. For another, Petruchio could not
help but observe (from the lingering air, after they had gone
their way) that the gentlemen smelled very much like horse-
piss. He should not have trusted them.

"How long have you been waiting?" inquired Caterina.

"Not long."

"Oh, because my father said you have been waiting for
hours."

"Maybe. I'm not sure."

"So are you irritable?"

"N-no. Why would I be?"

"You're a man. You're waiting for a woman. One plus one."

"No, I was happy to wait, gentle signorina."

"Well, now, isn't *that* romantic!" said Caterina, quite suddenly, as if taken aback by something beyond him.

Petruchio turned and looked over his shoulder. He saw nothing of interest but for a few framed oil paintings: one of five dogs smoking tobacco and playing at cards; another of Adam and Eve, starkers naked, their faces and bodies composed entirely of fruits and vegetables; and a third showing a kitten in the arms of a ragged street urchin, a waif with wide, sad eyes as big as the cat's entire head, who also had big, sad eyes.

"Yes, that *is* a nice picture," said Petruchio, unsure which one was intended.

"Not that. Your patience. Romantic. The paintings are trash. My father, who has the biggest art collection in Padua and no taste, exhibits only such pieces as will be certain to amuse his guests and embarrass his daughters. But you're a man, what would you know? Italian men are so damned disagreeable."

"I wish to agree with you, gentle lady."

"Oh, I doubt that," said Caterina, showing her teeth. "The last man I ate did not agree with me at all. But it was good of you, to be patient. I was in the midst of a heart-wrenching romance, about this incredible girl whose boyfriend catches some kind of terrible cancer in his, you know, down there, and he breaks up with her, so she very nearly marries his employer instead. I could not wait to see how it turns out. Happily, of course. Do you mind if I sit down?"

"No, of course not. May I sit down, too?"

"Please do."

Petruchio hardly knew what to say next. "Well, here we are," he said at last, "sitting down."

"Yes," said she, unhelpfully.

"Your book. I don't think I know that one. What's it called?"

"*Only True Love Waits.* Which is so true, don't you think?"

"I do now."

"Only it should be called, *Only True Love Waits without Complaining.* Make a man wait for anything, for more than a minute, and he gets grumpy, I don't care if it's his coachman, his dog, his dinner, an oxcart at an intersection, or sex with his fat wife. It's a rare ability, in men, to wait."

"Oh. Well, I was just, I was just, um, you know, waiting. It was no trouble. I had nothing special on my plate, today."

"That was not a very romantic thing to say," said Kate, annoyed. Recovering: "But I suppose that's what a libertine says to all of his lady friends: 'I'll wait for you if I've got nothing important to do.' There's a man for you."

Petruchio blushed. "No, not at all, I never even really had a, a, a, no, that's not how I meant it."

Caterina found herself intrigued by this shy boy. Perhaps it was just the elation of having come down from the high of Orora Abrahama's latest romance; but she actually felt goosebumps on her legs. Kate wished now that she had not removed her stockings. "What's your name again?" she asked. "My father must have told me but I forget, silly me!"

"Petruchio di Antonio, of Verona."

"And mine's *Caterina.* You may call me *Kat.* Or *m'lady.* Or *madame.*"

"Yes, Madam. Thank you, Madam."

"Not *Mad*-um. M*'damm.* Here in Padua, a *mad*-um is a businesswoman who gives a lecher his just desserts, such as the French Pox. So let's try that again, from the top: Bonjour, Monsieur Petruchio. Bonne journée."

"Est-ce que vous allez, oui, oui, m'dame Kat?"

"Well, it seems your French is not of the best. To you, plain Caterina will do."

"To me," said Petruchio, "you're *beautiful*, not p-plain at all."

The crimson flush, when Petruchio uttered this compliment, did not escape her notice. Caterina wondered if this gorgeous boy from Verona could really be so innocent, or if it was just an act. She felt suddenly playful. "If you like, sir, you can call me Wild Kat. Grrrr!" (Here, she curled her fingernails, and took little swipes at the air.) "Or Sweet Kat — purrrrrr" (trilling her tongue). "But I do have claws, and a reputation," she added, with a dimpled smile. "Call me *Domestic, Fat, Feral, Tom, Bob,* or *Hell* Kat, and Sonny, there will be nothing left of you for burial but a coughed-up hairball."

"No *Kitty* Kat either, I suppose?" Petruchio was feeling flirty, for once, without a panic attack. He felt strangely at ease with Caterina Miniola Ramusio di Baptista.

"I'll save *Kitty Kat,*" said Kate, with a sigh, "for my special someone, someday."

"I suppose no *Pussy,* either."

Kate's jaw dropped open. She frowned. "I beg your pardon, sir?"

Realizing his mistake, Petruchio buried his face in both hands. His stomach growled, and he broke into a sweat. "Oh, God," he said, "I am such an idiot. I beg *your* pardon! Excuse me, I need to go now." He stood to leave, beet-red, fearing nothing worse than the onset of a gastric disturbance when alone in the same room with a pretty girl who had seemed, quite possibly, to have been interested in him, for those glorious first two minutes.

"Not so quick, buster. We're not done talking. Sit down." Petruchio sat. "So do you have a nickname, back home?"

"Oh no, not really. My mother calls me *Poochi,* short for Petruchio, which I hate; or *Pooch,* which I also hate, or *Pet.* But why do you let people call you *Kat?*"

"Because I'm special. When spelled K-A-T-E but pronounced Kat, the name sounds almost *primitive,* don't you think? — less Renaissance Italian, more Elizabethan English."

"Do you say *tomahto?* Because I say *tomato.*"

"I say *tomato,* also. And *vase,* not *vahse.*"

"Me, too. I think *vahse* sounds pretentious."

"Pretentious? No, *vahse* sounds unpleasant, like something you would find in a man's testicle."

"Oh."

"Your father, I suppose, is a wealthy Veronese merchant."

"No, not really," said Petruchio.

"Good. A great nobleman, perhaps. Or a humble country vicar."

"Papa's dead," said Petruchio. "Has been."

"Come again?"

"As in: he has been dead for a long time."

"I'm sorry," said Caterina, sounding pleased. "I imagine your father as a cold and distant man."

"No, not so much," said Petruchio. Caterina raised one eyebrow at this information. "I mean, yes, sort of," said Petruchio, correcting himself. "Buried in Verona."

"My advice? Don't over-idealize the man. Children never really know the score with their parents. Law of averages. Your so-called 'papa' was probably a rakehell, a devil-may-care libertine, rich and wild and reckless until poisoned by an illicit lover or killed in a duel."

"More like, poisoned by Aunt Betty's risotto and died in the gruel."

"What's that?"

"Joke. Sorry. Not funny. He died of a heart attack."

"At what age were you, when he passed?"

"It was my twelfth-birthday party."

"Oh, that is so *sad!*" Caterina remained quiet for a moment, as if savoring the sadness of it. "So as a fatherless orphan, did you grow up in a slum, or in a sweet little cottage, or in a country estate?"

"Yes."

"Which?"

"Country estate. Manor house, just outside Verona. On the banks of the Adige."

"With whom?"

"My mother, and my aunt."

"Oh. With a cruel uncle, I suppose, as your guardian. God shield the villain has not robbed you of your inheritance!"

"No, my legal guardian was my mother. And my inheritance is quite adequate."

"Very nice. But in your father's absence, did this guardian control your every move?"

"Yes, absolutely."

"So you were an only child, then. No brothers or sisters?"

"They all died as newborn infants. Except Sophia, who got run over by an oxcart. And Eddie, who died of typhus."

"Oh, well," said Caterina, deftly concealing her pity. "But why does your aunt live with you? Is she an invalid? or quite possibly insane?"

"Is this for the record, confidentiality assured, not to be quoted?"

"I promise."

"Quite possibly insane. Not possibly. Definitely. My mother, also."

"And does one of these madwomen live upstairs in the attic, in your country manor house on the banks of the Adige?"

"Huh?"

"I'll take that as a No. How about you. Are you incredibly intelligent?"

"Intelligent? Yes, I would say so. Maybe not incredibly so. Credibly smart."

"Your mother and crazy aunt say that? Or do other people?"

"My teachers, mostly. My mother was never impressed with me, all that much."

"Have you suffered?"

"Yes, of course. Hasn't everyone? I'm almost twenty years old. I have suffered horribly."

"Do you see yourself as a loving and attentive hero? Or are you the sort of man who will choose to live in town, where you can drink and gamble and squander your wife's dowry on harlots, while your long-suffering spouse manages your lonely country estate and at last falls in love with a migrant worker who was hired to muck out the stables?"

"No, that would be beastly. I want my wife, my future wife, to be happy."

"Do you desire children?"

"No! Of course not."

"I don't mean like a priest. I mean, can you see yourself as a father to my children?"

"Children? No one said. I mean, wow. Could I possibly meet them, first? How many do you have?"

"None, yet. We're speaking hypothetically."

"Phew."

"Do you, Petruchio of Verona, wish to father children by your future wife, whoever that woman may be?"

"Oh, sure. I mean, I guess so. Probably."

"Yes or no?"

"Sí. Definitely. Um, I just never really thought about babies as something a person *wants* — you know, it's not like people say, "Hey, bro, I really want new boots," and "a faster horse," and "a baby." It's just what people do. They get married, they have bambini. I thought. But I'm totally okay with it."

"And will you be a real father to your children after they have been born? Will you be there for them, as they grow up?"

"Oh, yes, absolutely," said Petruchio.

"You won't just die and leave them, as your father did?"

"No, I would hate that."

Caterina's manner changed. She leaned forward, and spoke in a whisper. "Petruchio, do you have a dark secret, from your past?"

"I would say, no."

"Nothing? Have you never seduced your best friend's bride, or your best friend, or maybe fathered a bastard, or run like a coward from the battlefield?"

"No, nothing like that. Once, I stole a cinnamon bun from the Verona bakery. Also, I— but never mind."

"Please — with me, your secret will be utterly safe."

"Well, I— ." Petruchio stared at the marble floor. "I — I carry a load of emotional guilt about my father's death, like I'm to blame for it. I feel as if his death was my fault."

"Get over it. No big secrets, then? No ancestral curses?"

"You mean, like red hair, or short stature, or weak kidneys?"

"No. Red hair is lovely. But you seem to fit the profile of the earnest young man whose family, in some past generation, was cursed with a prohibition, the violation of which can lead to an unforeseen catastrophe. Like, maybe you have opened a room, or a cedar chest, or a grave that ought not to have been disturbed. Next thing you know, you're up to your neck in vampires and twists of fate."

"No, nothing like that, not in my family. We're upper middle class Republican Italian Roman Catholic."

"No secret transgressions, even on a small scale? — such as exploring your mother's underwear drawer?"

Petruchio flushed crimson. "Okay, once, maybe twice. But I was only fourteen years old then, and curious."

"If you should happen to meet a young virgin with a romantic disposition on a Highland moor, or on a dusty cattle ranch, how would you describe yourself to her?"

"How do you mean?"

"How would you measure yourself, against other men?"

"Oh, I would never do that," said Petruchio.

"Put it this way. What do people not understand about the true *you*?"

"I dunno," said Petruchio.

"Okay. Hypothetical. Imagine yourself on the ramparts of a ruined medieval castle. You have just saved, from drowning in the moat, a young woman. She's dripping wet, but pretty. She has a lively intellect. Her heart is powered by ardent and enthusiastic feelings. Her love for Nature has been nourished by lonely rambles in a haunted wood. Her romantic imagination has received further encouragement from her reading, from her association with the best authors. But the damsel has also a certain pure and fearless independence of soul, a character some men cannot love, and which only the select few, with spirits like her own, can even appreciate. She seems to inhabit a world inaccessible to the common masses of men, who prefer her younger sister. Let us grant that she has also a kind of unconscious superiority in the curl of her coral-red lip. Though not haughty or capricious, such horrid epithets as 'shrew' or 'bitch' attach themselves to her name — though she has asked nothing more than the indulgence of her innocent tastes and feelings, without opposition or restraint. What ordinary workaday man could ever love such a woman?"

"Gosh," said Petruchio. "I think I could."

"Well," said Kate, looking a bit dreamy. "Well, then. Maybe you're not as ordinary as I supposed." They sat quietly for a moment. "But who is the real you," said Kate, finally, " — that is, the private you, the one whom no one knows?"

"I dunno," said Petruchio.

And yet, he was definitely not keeping up his end of the conversation.

"Okay, look. You're outgoing and debonair. You never take anything seriously, so the people back home don't realize you have a passionate nature. You keep a mistress, and you have a reputation throughout Verona, as a rake. When you meet your soulmate, rather than despoil her innocence, you desperately fight your attraction to her — until you realize that you can do without a mistress but you cannot live without your truelove, and so you arrange a marriage for your doxy back home, and seek— ."

"No!" said Petruchio. "No! You have me all wrong. I'm not like that!"

"So you're not a rake, then?"

"No, I am not a rake. And I don't hang out with hoes. Heh. Sorry, dumb joke."

"Don't apologize, it was cute. I may be able to use that pun myself, someday. Seriously. Because I have a little sister who's a hoe. But you're not a rakehell, then?"

"No. I'm sorry if that disappoints you. I wish I were, I wish I could be one. I have tried on occasion, but I'm not convincing."

"Brooding and passionate?"

"My mother says I brood. I've never been passionate, but that is something that I would definitely like to try."

"You're used to giving orders and having people obey them."

"I'm used to *taking* orders. From women. The same two women."

"Unorthodox. Unconventional. Here in Italy, almost bizarre." Kate took a first sip of her glass of tomato juice. She set down the cup, and smacked her lips. "But not entirely displeasing. You are a young man of strong moral character?"

"Most definitely."

"Also, a young man of strong muscular definition?"

Petruchio blushed, again. He had not blushed so much in a single hour since that morning in church, years ago, during the ecclesiastical aftermath of his mother's fagioli cannellini. "I do work out," he said. "I get lots of exercise."

"Well, anyway." Caterina stood up from her overstuffed parlor chair. She seemed to be ending the interview. Petruchio's face expressed sudden disappointment, followed by resignation, the look of a forsaken puppy. As he gazed on her, with his smitten heart, he surmised that his first-ever wooing scene had gone poorly. Perhaps he had given offense — or seemed too afraid of offending. He was unsure, now, whether to stand or sit, or to speak, or to remain silent. He was not experienced enough to sweep Caterina off her feet, nor brave enough to try it. At that moment, a familiar feeling of black despair welled up in his heart.

And yet, Petruchio's inexperience in matters of love was offset by good instincts. Rising from his chair, he took a long step forward on his right foot and dropped (clumsily) to his left knee. He swept his arms outward, and bowed his head low and said, "Your duteous servant, m'lady."

Next thing he knew, the back of his shirt was drenched.

"Oh, no! oh, my, I'm so embarrassed!" cried Kate. She had spilled her tomato juice all over his back. "I'm terribly sorry," she said. "I'm such a clumsy ox."

"No, you're not," said Petruchio. "It's nothing. I took a room at the university. I have clean shirts there."

As Petruchio stood, he could feel the juice running down his back and into his breeches, and into his crotch area, which felt uncomfortable.

"You're drenched to the skin, poor thing. Here, let me help you out of that."

"Huh?"

"Take off your shirt. We'll get you fixed up with a fresh one for today, and we'll launder yours. Oh, I'm such a foolish girl! How could I be so clumsy?"

"No prob— " But Caterina was already tugging the shirt out of his waistband, quite vigorously.

"Come on, cooperate. I'm doing my best here. Raise your arms and bend forward."

Startled by her impatient tone of voice, Petruchio obediently leaned over so that Caterina could slip the soaked linen over his shoulders and down his arms. To keep juice from dripping onto the floor, she wadded the shirt into a bundle and used it like a bath-sponge to dry off his back. "Fiametta!" she called. "Or Tabatha! Come quickly!" And to Petruchio, softly: "Not that it matters, Pet, but I'm glad to see that your shoulders and back are not all hairy, like on some Italian men. Back- and shoulder-fur is just such a *totally* unoriginal way for a man to be primitive."

One of the domestic maids appeared, chewing casually upon a stick of beef jerky. "Fiametta," said Kate, "this poor gentleman has spilled tomato juice all down his shirt. Please put this wet thing in the laundry, and fetch him a clean one. Any shirt about his size will do — from the servants' livery, if necessary. Thank you, darling. Quick! Be about it!"

"Jesus God, you're a pretty thing," said Fiametta, giving the stranger a once-over, from head to foot.

"Go!" hissed Caterina. The maid took the wet shirt and shambled off.

An outside observer at that moment would have been unsure which of the two young people seemed more self-conscious — Caterina, having spilled the juice, or Petruchio, for standing in Signore Baptista's parlor, before the man's unmarried daughter, with his shirt off. But he had the presence of mind to suck his stomach in, and to flex his arms, and to curl his shoulders inward slightly so as to enhance his pectorals, while seeming to appear relaxed; a trick he had practiced in the mirror, many times.

Kate walked a circuit around him once or twice. If she was impressed by the bronzed sheen of his wedge-shaped torso, sculpted as if from golden oak, or by his powerful arms and tight abs, she gave no indication. Nor did she touch his skin. Petruchio felt unequal to her close scrutiny. He wished he could have his shirt back.

Finally, Caterina spoke. "I can't believe it," she said. "I just can't believe it."

"What?" said Petruchio, in a misery of suspense.

"You look like my *first husband*," she said.

A look of alarm swept over the young man's countenance. "How many have you had?"

"None," said Kate.

• • •

IV. *Ballo di Nozze*

NEVER WAS A MATCH clapped up more quickly. Petruchio and Baptista came to terms and signed the prenuptials that same afternoon. A novice at marriage negotiations, Petruchio accepted Baptista's initial dowry offer of twenty thousand crowns, half embarrassed to be taking the old man for a ride. Baptista quietly rejoiced. Eager to divest himself of both daughters, he expected to go as high as sixty thousand crowns for the elder daughter; and twenty thousand for Bianca, who was an easier sell.

The wedding ceremony — held Sunday afternoon in the Basilica di Sant'Antonio on short notice — was a conventional affair, with candles and flowers and church music. Four musicoes from the Priory of Santi Fermo & Rustico sang a lovely madrigal that brought tears to the eyes of many. The bride was beautiful; the groom, handsome; and the priest, adequate. (Father Giovanni's sermon in the vernacular, like his premarital counseling, provided Petruchio with no fresh or useful information of a practical fleshly nature.)   The cathedral was half full.   Caterina had thought it best not to delay the ceremony; which meant that Petruchio's mother and aunt and Veronese friends were unable to attend.   There was no time even to send them invitations.   As a result, the pews to the right side of the aisle were empty.   Petruchio was okay with that.

Immediately after the service, the guests lined up along the main walk of the Orto Botanico.   They were armed with bags of rice (to ensure fertility), and garlic (to ward off evil spirits); or else, with pen and paper (to seek Bianca's autograph).   When Kate and Petruchio appeared at the head of the gardens, the happy couple kissed once; waved to the crowd; then ran the gauntlet, from the church to the street, through a shower of rice and garlic.

Reaching the curb, Kate and Petruchio drew up short.   The carriage was gone.

No, not gone: it was parked on the far side of the square. The carman lay asleep in the driver's seat, trusting the horses to stay where they were.   To reach the carriage, the bride and groom would need to cross the cobblestone pavement, which from here to there was wet and dirty, and strewn with trampled horse manure.   On the church side, near the curb where the bridal coach should have been parked, was a fresh wet pile.   It looked golden-brown and steaming ripe in the morning sun. "This is Bianca's doing," muttered Kate.

"Not possible, my dear," said Petruchio.   "That's from a carriage horse."

"I mean, someone has told the coachman to park over there so that my wedding dress and petticoat will be ruined."

"I'll tell him to come around."

"No, don't."   Caterina threw her arms around Petruchio's neck and pulled him close in a lover's embrace.   She whispered in his ear: "Quick, remove your cloak."

"Why?"

"Romance does not start in bed," she whispered.   "It starts right here, right now.   Quickly.   After you spread your cloak over the mess, just leave it there.   Keep smiling, the while."

The priest during premarital counseling had impressed upon Petruchio that he must embrace his new responsibility as the husband, lord, and master to Caterina his wife. He must command, she must obey. This, now, was Petruchio's first opportunity to assert his conjugal authority. He gave it his best shot. "Surely, you jest," he said. "This is a new cloak, not a throw rug. First time I've ever worn it."

"My papa's tailor will make you another."

"What, would you destroy a cloak of ruched velvet that cost me nearly two hundred crowns?"

"What, would you destroy the hem of a lovely wedding gown of white silk that cost my father more than one thousand crowns?"

By now, Signore Baptista had come forward and seen the problem. The old man called out to the coachman, "Holla! Foolish knave! Come around!" But the fellow seemed not to hear over the din of traffic and the clip-clop of passing horses.

"Petruchio," sighed Caterina, "You are a dreamy man and you promise to be a wonderful husband." (She stood on tip-toe, and pecked him once on the nose, her fingers still locked behind his neck.) "But you *do* need tweaking."

The impatient crowd began to clap hands in unison, chanting, "Kiss! kiss! kiss! kiss!" Petruchio gently lifted the chin of his bride. He pressed his lips to her lips. The audience whistled and cheered.

Petruchio, while kissing, opened his eyes and looked up to see what was happening with the carriage situation. The coach remained where it was. But in that moment of distraction, the groom did not see what he should have seen coming: Kate's knee.

Reader, she kicked him. A straight shot to the groin, like a fist through a window-pane. A cudgel. Petruchio doubled over. If it were not for layers of silk and the hoops of her underskirt, the kick might easily have dropped him to the sidewalk like a shot duck.

Petruchio's hat fell off. Kate caught it before it hit the street. "Oops, sorry, Pet," she said, demurely. "I thought I felt a wasp or something sting my leg, and I jumped. Mi scusi!

Stand up straight now, darling. You'll be fine. Just give it a moment."

The suffering groom remained bent over, feet apart, his hands resting on his knees. He was gasping, as if short of breath, unable to speak.

"It's okay, honey," said Kate, sweetly. "No need to feel bad. I've got your hat."

As Petruchio stood hunched-over, Caterina took a step into the street, holding the groom's hat in one hand and hoisting her skirts with the other.

Before Petruchio could say, "NO!" she dropped his slightly worn, perfectly comfortable, broad-brimmed capitano hat, ostrich feather and all, directly over that mound of horse poop. Then she stepped on it and twisted, as if she were killing a cockroach on the ballroom floor. Twirling about on that same foot, she turned to face the wedding guests, further grinding his hat into the pavement.

Smiling gracefully, Caterina called to the crowd, "Thank you, thank you! Love you all! Pet and I will see you at the Gran Guardia, for the reception!" She then snagged Petruchio by the elbow and hurried across the square to the coach. Limping Petruchio muttered something under his breath, to which Kate paid no attention.

The bride snapped next at the carman, who had climbed down from his perch to offer his belated assistance. "Get moving, Tony," she said. "And when we arrive at the loggia, don't drive away. I intend to have a little chat with you about your parking manners."

Extending her hand to the bridegroom rather than to the coachman, Caterina stepped gaily into the carriage and pulled Petruchio in after her. When seated, she waved to the crowd, all smiles, glowing like a beauty queen on parade.

The carriage pulled away. When it had rounded the corner and was headed north toward the Piazza dei Signori, Kate removed her white gloves and set them in her lap, beaming with happiness. "Well, that was lovely," she said. "Don't you think?" Petruchio made no answer. She noticed he was not smiling. "What's the matter now, honey?"

"You call that *tweaking*?" he said, strangely grumpy. "Tweak me a little harder, you'd have killed me. And now you can just forget about making babies. You flattened my balls into ducats."

"Oh, hush."

"Our children will be born freaks. Flat, two-dimensional."

"You don't need to be so melodramatic. The street was all poopy. Trust me, you would not have wanted your bride to step in it. We had to do think fast. We did our best with a complicated situation. You'll be fine."

Petruchio was not satisfied. "God damn it, Caterina," he said. "That was my favorite hat. I wear it to all the games, when my academy plays other schools. It was my good-luck hat. I loved that hat."

"And now you love *me*," said Kate, cheerfully. "Anyway, honey, that bauble did not really become you. Those hats went out of style two years ago, and ten minutes ago yours went out of commission. We'll find you something better, more dashing, more debonair. You'll get over it soon, I'm sure. Men always recover from millinery disappointments *so* much more quickly than we girls do."

Resting her hand on his knee, and then a little higher, Kate gently massaged the inside of his thigh, as if to console him. She looked so beautiful, as they rode through the streets under the Italian sun, that Petruchio soon forgave her. By the time they reached the Gran Guardia, he had forgotten the loss of his hat; and he had recovered also from the blow to his groin. Stepping down from the carriage, he still walked a little funny, but for another reason.

Inside the reception hall, Petruchio was left to his own devices as the bride barked orders to the kitchen staff, the caterers, the musicians. The napkins had been folded in flat rectangles. Kate very nearly called off the celebration, when she saw that. This was not as she had directed. They were to be done up in the shape of white swans, as in Nicola Scintille's *The Wedding*, a best-seller. The exasperated bride had to instruct the maids how to do the fold, wasting precious minutes with the guests already on their way from St.

Anthony's. The floral centerpieces of roses and green hydrangea looked gorgeous, just as the bride had imagined from their appearance in *The Wedding Machine*; but they had to be cut shorter; and the white magnolia limbs in the fireplace invited rearrangement. The musicians had to be resituated, farther from the door; their musical selections had to approved for romantic content; and their instruments, re-tuned.

While bustling about to ensure that everything was just so, Kate stayed looking remarkably cool and utterly happy. Not so, Petruchio. The groom had begun sweating like a horse over the thought of going to bed with her, fearing he would disappoint his bride's expectations for an accomplished performance. He also wondered what his mother would say when he returned to Verona as a married man. He wondered if his bride and his mother would like one another, or kill one another, or join forces. To take his mind off all of that, and to keep his bowels from rumbling, Petruchio during the aperitivo stood by the door and greeted the arriving guests, most of whom walked right past him without a word of congratulation, a few of whom mistook him for the concierge. Everyone at this gathering of Padua's rich and beautiful seemed to know everyone else — except the groom, who felt invisible and small.

The main courses were spread out on sideboards at either end of the hall, the food being served buffet-style, by waiters. The bride took a bunch of grapes, raw carrots, buttered broccoli, quiche Lorraine, and a cup of turnip soup. While in line chatting with friends, she failed to notice that her husband, following behind, took a bunch of grapes, raw carrots, buttered broccoli, quiche Lorraine, and a cup of turnip soup. His reason was not that he wished to imitate Caterina's low-calorie diet; rather, he worried that the heavier foods would give him stomach trouble.

It was not until they sat down at the head table that Kate said, "Oh, no!" and giggled so hard she had to put her hand over her mouth and very nearly fell off her chair.

"What's the matter, love?" asked the groom, sensing he had committed a faux pas of some sort. "What amuses you?"

"That's not your dinner, is it?" said Kate, tickled.

"Well, sure," said Petruchio, his confidence shaken. "It all looks quite healthy and medium delicious."

"Keep us trim, huh? — my thighs, your tummy? Petruchio! Get real! Those menu choices were *for the ladies*! For the men, we've got braised loin of beef with mustard, we've got the pork sausage, we've got the fried eels. If you need a veggie, try the buttered asparagus-spears in bitter orange juice, or the fried green tomatoes. Besides which, this is our wedding night. You should be having a few sliced peaches, plus a first and second helping of the *pie de testículos de toro* in béchamel sauce, which is absolutely *divine*, I sneaked some myself, before the food was served."

"What do you want me to do?" asked Petruchio.

"*This!*" said Kate. She picked up Petruchio's plate, slid it underneath the table cloth, and quietly dumped the food onto the floor, sparing only the cup of turnip soup, which she passed to her left.

One lone grape rolled out from under the white table cloth and stopped forlornly at the edge of the dance floor, directly in front of Petruchio's place at the head table. The bride laughed gaily as she handed her groom a clean platter. "Don't worry," she said. "Good thing about lady-food is that it doesn't leave a mess. Here's your trencher, honey. Now go find yourself a manly dinner, and be quick about it, I want to give you a big kiss on the cheek."

Petruchio started to say that he was actually quite keen on meat and gravy, smoked ham, salami, heavy tomato sauce, and all of that; but he just thought—

"Hurry!" said the bride.

Petruchio went to the buffet and heaped his plate full of meat-and-sauce dishes, which he brought back to the wedding table and then neglected to eat. The bride hardly touched her food, either. She was too busy talking with friends, relatives, and other socialites who came by the head table to meet the groom and to offer congratulations to Caterina. No big deal. He was not that hungry. And yet, the incident left Petruchio feeling ... not unhappy, just a bit uneasy.

Kate throughout the dinner felt ebullient and looked radiant. Midway through the meal, she reached over and squeezed the groom's hand and said, "Oh, Petruchio, don't you just love it? Here we are, you and me, in this romantic loggia, with sweet chamber music, a splashy fountain, lovely flowers, gently swaying lanterns, and the subtle, intoxicating scent of the sea..."

"You can smell the sea?" asked Petruchio. "But we're twenty miles from the Adriatic."

"Oh, I forgot," said Kate, cheerfully.

"The intoxicating scent of the river, perhaps."

"Whatever."

Hortensio Lando as master of ceremonies told jokes that put the crowd in stitches. Petruchio, lost in thought and anxiety concerning his wedding-night, paid scant attention and missed the punchlines. He was still sunk in that reverie when Kate began to speak of the dance. It did not immediately occur to him that this was a subject that involved him in any way. "We will start off easy," she was saying, "with a pavan, to get other couples off their bums and onto their feet. Then you and I will take the floor with our galliard. I'll step back and let you cut a caper, solo. When the allemande begins, you and I will lead, and the other couples will fall in line behind us. That will give us a chance to catch our breath, before the canary."

Petruchio's eyes grew suddenly wide. "Oh, let's not do that," he said. The groom now wore on his face the concerned expression of a chaste nun who has just been commanded to ride naked through an army camp. "Let's just eat, and chat," he said.

"Let's not do what?" said Caterina.

"Dance."

"Ha ha. Oh, dear Petruchio, for a moment I thought you were serious."

"Sweet love," said Petruchio, as cheerfully as he could, "I cannot dance. I never learned. If you should ask me to dance, I would embarrass us both and do an injury to your toes. I lack the training, and the natural grace."

The bride's panic now rivaled the groom's. "You cannot *what?*"

It was if he said he could not change his own diapers. She gave him a look. He winced. She gave him another look. He felt small. She gave him a third look. He felt like that lonely grape, at the edge of the dance floor, which had since been stepped on.

Never had Caterina Miniola Ramusio di Baptista met an adult male in her own social circle who was unable to dance. Never had she read of a romantic heroine who fell in love with a man who could not dance. It had therefore never occurred to her to interrogate Petruchio on this point in his curriculum vitae. To have asked her fiancé, whom she had only just met, if he knew how to dance would have seemed rude, like asking him if he knew how to tie his own shoes, or how to ride a horse, or how to use a dinner fork.

"If you're just teasing me, Petruchio," she said, clutching at her bosom. She was unable to complete the sentence. Kate's eyes darted about the hall, in search of a man who might sub for the bridegroom, just for the afternoon. Her eyes settled desperately on Francesco Portinaro, the madrigalist, an old love-interest.

Caterina did not understand how such a thing was possible, in the modern world. Cannot *dance?* Dancing seemed to her, though evidently not to him, a social skill as necessary as dental hygiene. It was said by Fabritia Caroso, one of the best instructors, that "a man who cannot dance has the heart of a pig, the head of an ass, and deserves to be fed like a Puritan, upon goat's meat cooked in a pie without bacon." That was her *husband,* then, oh god, oh god. She had married a social freak. "Oh, dear Jesus!" she said aloud, "What shall I do?" Her prayer came out in a thin and raspy whisper. Caterina's dream of a perfect wedding and romantic marriage was collapsing like a house of cards in a high wind. She had fallen for a man who cannot dance. Entire tragedies had been written of men with lesser flaws.

Something had to be done, and quick, before the musicians began the pavane. Excusing herself, Kate left the head table.

Moving gracefully about the hall, she spoke briefly and privately with the musicians. She spoke with Portinaro (and excused herself moments later, with a frown, whatever that was about). She spoke with her father, leaning over to whisper in his ear. Petruchio with worried eyes followed her movements about the room. Suffering deep humiliation, he cursed his mother and aunt for having neglected his education in the subjects that mattered most to all other ladies of the world, such as wooing and dancing and making love. He had been able to fake his way through the wooing. But he was about to fail, and fail miserably, in the other two departments. In fact, he was already miserable and he hadn't even failed yet.

Caterina returned to the table with a plan. She gave Petruchio's hand a squeeze and said, "Honey, what do you suppose if I were dancing the pavane with my father, and the heat and excitement got to me, and I fainted— "

"Heat and excitement? From dancing with your father? I suppose that would be pretty creepy."

"Hush. And I fainted in a dead swoon. What would you do?"

"I would call for a medical doctor, of course."

"No, you would *not* call for a doctor. You would scoop me up in your arms, and hold me close without letting too much leg show. You would announce to the wedding guests that I'm all right — that I just need a little fresh air. In a strong, commanding voice, you would instruct the guests, if they love our family, to stay, and dance a round or two, and drink, and have a good time. Then you would carry me out. As we reached the doorway, you would take me through it feet first, without banging my head on the doorframe. Our carriage is parked out front. Just get me into the coach, and we'll figure out what to do from there. Do you think you can manage that?"

Petruchio thought he could manage it. But he was puzzled. "All this, is because I don't know how to *dance*?"

"Do you have a better plan to stave off disaster?" asked Caterina.

"No."

"Well, then."

"Question. Do I take off my shirt first, before I carry you out?"

"Heavens, no!" said Kate. "Why would you do that, in front of all these other women?"

"Sorry," said Petruchio. "Bad idea. It was just something I got from the romance you gave me to read, *Beloved Enemy.* When Gian swooned, shirtless Alessandro scooped her up in his powerful arms and pushed his way through the stunned crowd and carried her to safety. I was pretty impressed, with that."

"Oh. I mean, *maybe.* Could be romantic. Ya think?"

"Gian thought so," said Petruchio.

"I've never seen it done at a wedding," said Kate. "But I suppose there's no reason you should not expose your chest to the whole world. I mean, my little sister has done it, and look at her." Kate corrected herself. "I mean, *don't* look at her. But look at the fact that she won an award for it."

Signore Baptista approached the head table, as instructed, to ask Caterina for the first dance. The musicians struck up a pavane by Dalza, slow and easy, to accommodate the old man. Father and daughter glided onto the dance floor, holding hands. Signore Baptista looked proud and happy. The old man's movements were surprisingly graceful: he danced better than he walked. But the couple had not completed the second counter-clockwise turn, when Caterina stopped. That focused everyone's attention. With the fingertips of her left hand, the bride gently stretched out a handkerchief at arm's length. Placing the back of her right hand to her forehead, she looked toward the ceiling, and said, "Oh, my, it's awfully warm in here" — and swooned dead away, dissolving into a puddle of white silk and lace.

The crowd gave a collective gasp. Someone cried, "Look to the lady!" But in that one split second, the groom had already jumped up, knocking over his chair. Placing both palms on the tablecloth, he vaulted the banquet table with a nimble leap, landing on both feet on the far side. "Caterina! My darling!" he cried. Fully clothed, he dashed to the fallen maiden, to check her forehead, her pulse, her breath.

One thousand one, one thousand two, one thousand three ...
The guests were buzzing like a swarm of locusts. Many rose to
their feet.

"She's all right!" cried the jubilant bridegroom, at last. Baptista looked confused but relieved, all of this having happened
too quickly for his elderly brain to absorb.

With a dexterity more easily observed than imitated, Petruchio peeled off his slashed leather jerkin. "Everyone! Please
be seated!" he barked. Kneeling now over his fallen spouse, he
addressed the guests. "She is coming to!" (left doublet sleeve).
"She needs only fresh air!" (right doublet sleeve). He placed
the padded sleeves beneath the bride's head, for a pillow. "If
you love the family, please stay, and dance, and drink, and have
a good time!" As he spoke the words, his fingers were dancing
down a line of buttons from his neck to his waist. Off came
the body of his doublet. Off came the linen shirt.

Scooping up Caterina in his arms as easily as if she were a
sleeping child, Petruchio stood to address the wedding guests.
His bronze torso, his broad shoulders, his powerful arms,
sheened with perspiration. "Feast, and revel, and celebrate!"
he said. "Carouse full measure to the bride's maidenhead! Be
merry! But for my bonny Caterina, she must with me!"

The reviving bride reached up and placed her hands
around his neck, to be carried out. Cuddled in against his
strength, she now felt thrilled, from head to heel, with
immeasurable happiness. Her face was just inches from his,
and flushed with desire. She pressed her ear against his left
pectoral. She could feel the slow, powerful, *lub-dub, lub-dub,*
of his heart. She could feel, with her earlobe, the topography
of a male nipple, one of God's most extraordinary creations.
She could feel, deep inside, ... but never mind what she could
feel deep inside, we'll come to that.

"Father," said Petruchio, "Kat and I will head on back. No
hurry, but when you come, grab my clothes, will you? My
cloak, too, please. Here's the coat-check. Thanks. Ciao."
With a few long graceful strides, he carried his bride to the
door. He turned once, to extend a last farewell to the guests —
"Grazie! Buon umore!"

The bride, much recovered now, reached up and gave him a kiss, which he bent over to receive.

The guests applauded, when they saw that kiss. Some whispered: "Phew, she's okay." Others said: "That is the most gorgeous man I have ever seen"; or: "How come the wrong women have all the luck?"

Petruchio twisted slightly as he passed through the door with his bride, and was gone.

Out came the ladies' fans. Women who just a week ago were gossiping about Baptista's spinster daughter felt obliged, now, to cool themselves; lest they, too, should faint from heat and excitement on the dance floor and have no man like Petruchio to carry them out.

• • •

"OH, PETRUCHIO! You were magnificent, on the dance floor! You are so! damn! strong! I was peeking, you know. Just wait! When you have learned the galliard, you are certain to be the highest-leaping, most graceful triple-meter gentleman in all Padua."

Caterina was now back on her feet and feeling refreshed, full of energy, a dynamo.

The newlyweds found the bridal carriage exactly where it ought to be. Kate was glad to see that Tony had dutifully tacked to the boot a large sign that read, "SPOSI NOVELLI," as instructed. They found him napping in the passenger seat. "Maybe we should let him sleep," suggested Petruchio.

"Why?" said Caterina. "We've got a two-hour carriage ride ahead of us, before we can do *anything*. Tony! Wake up! Villa Marsango!"

Tony obediently jumped down from the coach and prepared for departure. He glanced the while at Caterina in her bridal gown, chatting gaily with a shirtless groom, a stranger from Verona. The puzzled coachman did not ask, nor did Kate offer to explain, why the bridegroom was delivered to the reception fully clothed but had returned to the carriage an hour later, half naked. As chauffeur to Italian aristocrats, nothing shocked him any more.

Signore Baptista's country house, a newly refurbished villa ten miles north of the city, was situated on a vast parcel of land between the River Brenta and the Canal Marsango. Caterina and Petruchio were to spend their first night there.

When Kate first mentioned Villa Marsango as a possibility for their wedding night, Petruchio had said, "Oh, I thought we would just go to my place, in Verona, for that."

Caterina seemed to disagree. She rolled her eyes and said: "*He* thought we would just go to *his* place in Verona, for that; where, if we're lucky, we can take a room with two beds, one for him and me, the other for his mother and his aunt; or maybe even one big bed for all four of us."

"Okay, bad idea. Where, then, shall we have our wedding night?"

"Villa Marsango," said Kate. "I've spoken with Papa, and made the arrangements."

The truth is that she was not given much choice. Signore Baptista was old school: he required that his daughter consummate her marriage either at his city mansion or country villa; and he required further that the wedding sheets be saved, and signed in ink by the groom, for surety against a fraudulent claim that the bride was not a virgin.

Kate's eyes lit up when she spoke of Villa Marsango. "We can stay on for a day or two if you like," she told Petruchio. "We'll have the entire place to ourselves, except for the steward and his wife, and they've got their own cottage. We can go for walks, ride horses to the Cittadella, gather flowers, go punting on the canal, swim naked, make love in front of the fireplace."

Petruchio felt that he could be at a disadvantage on the bride's home turf. But he was grateful for a refuge where he would not face his mother and aunt over breakfast the next morning, and be required to answer their demanding questions about how well he did on his wedding night, and for how long, and how many times, and be criticized.

Tony knew the way to Villa Marsango well enough. But first they had to get out of Padua traffic; and the sooner, the better. It appeared to bystanders on the sidewalk as if the passing carriage contained a driver, a newly married bride, and a naked man. This was something that many pedestrians on the street found risible. Even children pointed and laughed. While waiting at intersections or just driving along, Kate and Petruchio were pestered with wolf whistles and lewd remarks shouted from streetcorners and sidewalk cafes. Slouching down, Petruchio expressed his willingness to hide on the floor between the seats until they were beyond the city limits. But Caterina made him sit up. "It's about time the people of Padua learned what a real man looks like with his shirt off," she said, proudly.

The bride felt quite contented with the day's events; the groom, somewhat less so. And yet, for Petruchio, his partial undress on the streets of Padua was a modest embarrassment relative to his still-rising anxiety about Caterina's expectations for their first night. He had never prepared himself for these conflicted emotions about married life. He felt hopeful, anxious, happy, sentimental; but mostly, he felt unsure which was worse, being stiff with desire or petrified with performance-anxiety.

As the carriage bumped along the rutted dirt road toward Limena, Kate chatted merrily of the wedding, the reception, their future plans. Petruchio sat quietly and fidgeted. Finally, Kate asked, "Is something bothering you, honey? You seem quiet."

Petruchio could hold it in no longer. "Darling," he said, "I have not told you the whole story, about me."

Caterina cringed. "You don't have perfect curbside manners, you don't eat well, you don't know how to dance. All of that is easily remedied, and we have plenty of time now to work on it. What else? If you have a dark secret — a naughty past with other girls, gambling debts, a love-child, whatever — I forgive you. I'm quite sure it won't happen again."

With sad and beseeching eyes, as if appealing for mercy before a state executioner, Petruchio blurted his confession (but whispered it in her ear, so that Tony could not hear). His face flushed crimson. "I don't really know how to hump," he said.

"Oh my god," said Caterina, out loud. She rode on in silence, the fingers of her right hand toying nervously with the wedding ring on her left while Petruchio squirmed. This was shaping up to be a very long marriage. Or else, a very short one. Kate wondered vaguely if it was too late to seek an annulment. "I do not wish to be *humped*," she explained at last, grievously disappointed in the groom's diction. "Not by you, not by anybody."

"Phew," said Petruchio. "I mean, when we're *ready,* of course. I just don't want to disappoint you. This whole marriage thing just happened so *fast.* Give me a day or two. I feel I need to speak with some married guys, to get a few pointers, that's all. In the meantime, let's just hold hands, shall we?"

"My married girlfriends," said Kate, "will tell you that Italian husbands are not a reliable source of information. Married men know less about how to satisfy a woman than they think. And most don't think. But what I'm hearing from you is that you're twenty years old and still a virgin. Is *that* what you are trying to tell me?"

"No!" He blushed. "I mean, no, I wasn't trying to tell you that. But in answer to your question, I guess you could say that I am still *technically* a virgin, yes, you could say that."

"Oh, Pet, that is *so* sweet," said Kate, reassuringly, "and so romantic. Also, so unexpected, these days, in a man! So then you *did* have a secret, that you saved for sharing just with me! Plus, I don't have to worry about catching syphilis from you, and that's just very important, too."

"I don't want you to be disappointed," he mumbled.

The carriage passed through the tiny hamlet of Santa Maria di Non, a pastoral resort made famous by Pietro Bembo. It was now less than a mile to Baptista's villa. "Well, don't worry so much," she said. "We'll figure things out." Kate rested her head on Petruchio's bare shoulder and smiled contentedly. "I actually know my way around the block pretty well," she said. "I'm quite the reader."

At that moment, Petruchio felt deeply grateful to his bride. He felt totally loved, totally accepted. Also, greatly relieved, from the technical point of view, in terms of like, what do you do first, and what do you do second, when you're all alone, and naked.

A few moments later, with her head still on his shoulder, Kate said, "But surely, you must have made out with girls your own age?"

"Yes, of course," said Petruchio, exaggerating.

"Done some petting?"

"Oh, yeah."

Caterina seemed reconciled to his past as a matter that required no further investigation.

After a bit she sat up. Cupping her hand to his ear, she whispered: "So have you done ... *cunnilingus?*"

"Never!" The thought occurred to Petruchio that Caterina may have a secret past, more dark and disturbing than his own. "Gosh," he whispered, "you have done *cunnilingus?*"

"O mio dio, no," said Kate. She looked indignant, at the insinuation. Petruchio cringed and shut up. The couple bumped along in embarrassed silence, looking straight ahead.

Finally, Kate spoke. "But I do *know* about it," she said, shyly, and gave his hand a familiar squeeze.

"I beg your pardon," he said, "I didn't mean to take you the wrong way."

"Because it might be quite nice, to be taken the wrong way. Not every time, of course."

Petruchio felt his eyebrows twitch. He blinked, several times. "What, with my tongue in your tail?"

"That, I'll try," she said.

"Come again, good Kat. I am a gentleman."

"O Petruchio, in true romance, there can be nothing more lovely than your own très gentle man with whom to come and come again. And there are so many wonderful ways. It's every heroine's dream — one man, infinite variety, happily ever after. If there be cuckolds in Italy, let those men blame themselves."

Petruchio was again silent; his face, beet-red. He fell to chewing his lip.

"What's the matter, darling? Cat got your tongue?"

He winced.

She gently elbowed him in the ribs, and winked. "That was a joke," she said. "Relax. You know me, I'll try almost anything if it strikes me as romantic."

"Cuffs?"

"No cuffs. You see a lot of that, these days, in romance, but when the cuffs come out, I skip to the next chapter."

"Good. Because I may not want to be tied down."

"You and I are so much alike!" sighed Caterina. "So *simpatico.*"

They had reached their honeymoon destination. Baptista Ramusio's house on the Marsango was a two-story villa, peach-colored stucco walls under a red-tiled roof. Beneath the front gable stood a pillared portico, with balconies on the upper floor. Along the drive out front, just past the small gatehouse, was the steward's cottage. All of the buildings — the stone carriage house and stables, the feed barn — had been newly tuckpointed without and painted within.

While Tony tended to the coach and horses, Kate gave Petruchio a tour of the estate. The terrace garden, embellished with cartloads of flowers, offered a panoramic view of the Brenta. "As the sun goes down, the whole valley turns golden," said Kate. "I can hardly wait."

Petruchio felt he could wait. The prospect of a splendid sunset, though attractive, seemed at this moment less breathtaking than sexual intercourse, the thought of which, though attractive, suffocated him. What began as an intestinal growl had developed into full-blown stomach cramps. His heart was racing. His palms sweated. Before the night was through, he would be expected to make love to Caterina, and he quite literally did not know how he was going to do that; though he certainly wanted to. The whole activity seemed scary and complicated. Kate seemed to him so much more knowledgeable than he, about romance.

The front foyer was quite grand for a country villa, with marble tile, frescoed walls, and a curving staircase. Baptista's library and bedchamber were on the ground floor. What was to be the honeymoon suite was on the upper floor, overlooking the river. Tony brought in the bags and carried them upstairs.

The parlor was neatly stacked with wedding presents, which Baptista's servants had transported from the church, following the ceremony. The family would be gathering here after the reception, to join the fun as Kate and Petruchio opened their gifts. "I cannot wait to look underneath all of that wrapping," she said.

"Same here," said Petruchio, unconvincingly.

Allowing some time for the reception to wind down back in Verona, the newlyweds had perhaps an hour, maybe more, before the family arrived. Caterina had a busy afternoon ahead of her. She had written a one-act romantic comedy of "Antonio and Cleopatra," to be performed later that evening for Petruchio and the family, by two actors from her father's dramatic company, just before she and the bridegroom retired to their wedding bed. At this very moment, Guillaume and Bertramo were rehearsing out back, in the carriage house, where Petruchio would not see them. The performance was to be a surprise.

"Tell you what," said Kate. "Here is the key to my bookcase. Take time for romance. I have Old Century Regency. Highland. New World. Harlequin. Tragical. Comical. Historical. Pastoral. Gothic. Christian. Vampire, even. Every novel contains practical information about love, from that first fatal glance, to the warm afterglow. Go upstairs. Do some reading. Take notes. I've got some chores, but I'll be up, in a little. Our first time is important. It's a night we shall always remember. So we *do* want you to know what you're doing, darling."

• • •

V. *l'Inizio di Sempre*

A carriage came up the drive alongside the house, then another. There was laughter, there was animated chatter. The wedding reception had ended. Time to face the in-laws.

Petruchio remained seated at Caterina's library table, under an open casement window, in a robe that Kate had lent him. His thumb and fingertips were stained with ink.   It was now well past eight o'clock and getting dark. He put down his book and rubbed his eyes. Before him, on the blotter, lay a sheaf of conscientious notes and a few worn-out goose quills. To his right were dozens of paperback romances, loosely heaped, all of which he had started, none of which he had finished. To his left, there waited another, neater, stack, of books not yet consulted.   In Kate's bookcase were at least one hundred romances, and god knows how many more in the family's main residence, in Padua. The printing press and movable type had come to Italy only a few decades before. Petruchio had no idea that so many novels had been published, by so many different woman authors; and Caterina seemed to own them all. Which was worrisome. Plus, the poetry. Kate had in her collection at least twenty volumes of love verse by women poets that he had not even bothered to look at, yet. Lucrezia de Medici. Antonia Pulci. Camilla Scarampa. Barbara Torelli. Veronica Gàmbara. Leonora Falletti. So many others. "Who reads this stuff?" Petruchio wanted to know. Back home in Verona, there were not more than a dozen books in the entire house. Most were old schoolbooks. Not one woman's romance. And it was a big house.

While reading and taking notes, the time had gotten away from him. With a stretch and a yawn, he wondered what had become of Caterina, his wife.

His "wife"! He did not feel yet like a married man. The whirlwind courtship, the ceremony, the reception, the fainting incident, the long carriage ride, seemed now like a dream. Here in Caterina's study, he felt alone in dangerous territory. While lost in Kate's books, the thought had occurred to him, with the force of a revelation, that he was unwise to have gotten married so suddenly, and so young, with so little experience —

and with so little flexibility, under Italian marriage law, to correct a mistake. Plus, the mistake of not telling his mother, who would be apoplectic when she found out.

Would he have gone through with marriage at all, he wondered, if it were not for the promised dowry of twenty thousand crowns?

Maybe, yes. Petruchio therefore forced himself to keep reading, to keep learning, keep taking notes. Having known his bride for just three days, Caterina remained a virtual stranger to him, but Petruchio felt attracted to her as to a great enigma. There was something about her that he sensed was terribly thrilling and mysterious, though he had not yet put his finger on it.

Speaking of whom: Kate at that moment came storming into the room. She closed the door gently — she felt like slamming it — and paced.

"What's the matter?" asked Petruchio.

"Oh, that I were a man! I'd eat her heart out in the marketplace. I'd stifle her in her bed, with her own pillow. I'd feed her hot coals. I'd feed her to the crows. I'd put an Egyptian asp down her slutty dress. I'd poison her beer. I'd have her carted through town naked, and hanged from her lace garters, and dunked on a cucking stool."

"What's the matter?" asked Petruchio.

"What's the matter? My sister, of course."

"What could she have done, to put you in such high rage?"

"Married. Guy she met at the Academy awards."

"Is it a crime now to get married?"

"Her engagement is not why someone ought to kill her. Today, after you carried me out, Hortensio Lando returned to the podium, cracked a few jokes, proposed a toast. He signaled for the musicians to play, and invited everyone to dance a pavane in our honor. So the music resumes, our guests take a quick turn a two on the dance floor and go home; end of a beautiful wedding and a lovely reception, right? *Wrong.* During the dance, my sister, my father, a priest, and this stranger from Pisa are off in a corner, in a huddle. Papa walks to the front, beaming. He clinks on a champagne glass with a spoon until he has everyone's attention. The musicians stop playing. Everyone stops talking. A hush falls over the hall.

"'Friends and loved ones,' says my father, 'I am pleased to announce the engagement of my younger daughter, Bianca, to Signore Lucentio, son and heir to Signore Vincentio of Pisa.'"

"Don't ask me when *that* happened," said Kate. "I don't even know this man. I don't think *Bianca* knows him. I never even met him until a half hour ago, downstairs."

"Nice guy?"

"Who knows. I would have thought my sister would fall for someone younger, and more handsome. But his father is fabulously rich. Owns a fleet of two dozen merchant ships. Four manor houses within Pisa's walls. Plus others, in Florence and Rome. My sister is receiving two thousand ducats per annum — that's just her *allowance* — plus her own personal coach and horses, with attendants. So, yes, she seems very keen on him."

"Has he any gifts he did not inherit?"

"Good taste in clothes. Well manicured. Perfumed like a milliner. Smells of April and May. Bit of a dandy. He gets his hair, and nails, and beard, done by a professional beautician. And they say he's a wonderful dancer— ."

"Zounds, he dies! Where is my sword? Or shall we poison him?"

"Quiet, just listen. 'A wedding is planned,' my father said, 'to which all of you are invited... *and it shall take place right here, five minutes from now!*' Everyone applauds. Well, probably not everyone. I suppose there were a few of Bianca's disappointed, teary-eyed suitors who did not clap and who have *no* idea just how lucky they are, to do without. Anyway, so now, suddenly, it's Bianca's wedding day. Father Giovanni joins my father up front. Lucentio makes his entrance. The musicians strike up Constanzo Festa's "Wedding Music." Then here comes the bride, sweet little Bianca. Everyone rises. My father gives her away, Lucentio takes her, the priest marries her. Five minutes later, my sister is married and sitting in my chair at the head table, and Lucentio on yours — can you believe that? — as if our wedding was just a prologue to the main feature."

"But you and I had already left, of course."

"What's that got to do with it? Lucentio and my sister danced, and took a break, and danced some more. Show-offs, both of them. And between dances, they went from table to table, charming the guests. Bianca signed autographs, basking in adulation, that's just like her. The reception dragged on for hours, and they're saying it was wonderful, wonderful, a good time was had by all. By all except by you and me, of course. Because I was downstairs getting ready for our honeymoon, and you were up here, reading. And do you want to know what my father says to me, just now?"

"Mazel tov?"

"No, he puts his arm around Bianca and he says, 'Daughter Caterina, you owe a big thanks to your precious little sister. When you left early, Bianca stepped forward, and saved the day.' Right. That little tart would not have saved my day on her *calendar*, if it was up to her. And now it's not even *my* day, she stole it. The whole town, tomorrow, will be buzzing with talk of Bianca di Baptista's wedding. Well, what do I care. Bianca's wedding was not high on my list of essential life experiences. But I can already see the headlines on the broadside news sheets: 'SHOW-STEALER BIANCA DOES IT AGAIN.' Which, come to think of it, would be an *excellent* motto for that girl's wedding night. Which, come to think of it, should be any minute now, in the room right next to ours. *You* may call this a wedding-day. *I* call it a fucking disaster." Kate sat down on the bed, and pouted.

"I'll do my best," said Petruchio.

"Huh? Oh. No. I wasn't referring to you, you're fine. I said 'a fucking *disaster*,' not 'a *fucking* disaster,' there's a difference." She looked up. "I'm sorry, Pet. That was unfair. You didn't deserve that."

"Well, now that your family is here, I guess we should go down and open the presents."

"No. We can open the gifts again tomorrow, after my family leaves."

"Again?"

"I peeked."

"So when do we open your big surprise for me?"

"It wasn't something you *open*. Something else — God, I could just kill Bianca. The surprise can wait. What do men see in her, will somebody please explain that to me? — Two of my fathers' players were to perform a little play I wrote."

"Your father's players? Wow. I'd like to meet them."

"You will. Is that all you have to say?"

"And get to know them, of course. Become friends."

"I *thought* I just said, to my soulmate, that I have written an original play, to be performed by professional players, to celebrate our love. But maybe I forgot to mention it."

"Super! Wow, that's great, Kat. So let's see your play, then. I would rather watch your play than read another of these books."

"What's wrong with my books?"

"Nothing. They're great. Lots of good stories."

"What's wrong with my books?"

"Maybe I have some concerns, is all."

"Concerns? Like what?"

"I'm sorry I mentioned it."

"Like what?"

"Like for starters, how come the hero always has to receive a leg-wound before she loves him?"

"That's not true," said Kate.

"Well, I mean, in all of the ones I've read so far." Petruchio picked up a sheaf of papers from Kate's writing table. "I've been taking notes," he said, "as you suggested."

"I didn't mean literally, take notes," said Caterina. She looked over his shoulder. "Alphabetized, even. You're a well-organized man, darling, when it comes to taking notes on other people's romances. I don't think I've ever seen that done before."

With the papers shaking in his hand, not from aggression, but nervousness, Petruchio read off some titles: "*Angel Seeker. Born of the Night. Burning Wild. Celia. Colter's Wife. Desired. Ecstasy. Ever After. Fever Dreams. High-*

land Warrior. His Lordship's Dilemma. A Hunger Like No Other. In the Kitchen. The Last Prince. The Lion's Lady. A Love So Deep. The Marriage Spell. An Old Maid's Love. Our Lady of Pain. Our Little Secret. The Princess and her Pirate. Rebel Heat. The Reluctant Suitor. Splendor. The Temptress. Three Times a Bride. Under Cover with the Enemy. What a Rogue Desires. Wildfire. Winter Fire. With This Ring. So many others. Something terrible always happens to the man, before she loves him; and it always happens to him somewhere between his navel and his kneecaps."

"Not really. I'd like to see *one* example of that," said Caterina.

"Not me, I hope." Petruchio riffled his notes. "Case in point. *The L*** Word.* The heroine has 'a perfect leg' while the male hero has an 'injured one.' And his 'injured leg was contorted at a strange angle.' Speaking of which, I don't understand the book's title. What is the unmentionable L word? I'm thinking it may be *limp.*"

"*Love.*"

"*Love?*" said Petruchio. "The boys in *The L*** Word* are not up for *love*, they even say so. *Lust,* maybe, they're teenagers. But what is a 'strange angle' supposed to mean?"

"Not up, certainly."

"I rest my case."

"Not on the first date," said Kate. "Where's the suspense in that?"

"Suspended, dangled, and strangely mangled. *Promises to Keep*, page 76: 'she saw him sitting on the edge of his bed, his injured leg sticking out stiffly.' *The Temptress*, page 193: 'she tore off a long strip of her petticoat and began to bind his leg, his wounded leg stiff in front of him.'"

"See?" said Kate. "You can't keep a good man down. Not after he meets the heroine and falls in love."

"Maybe you can't, but these romances can. With a knife. *One Good Man*, page 10: 'Cut off my leg?' said Signore Legno — that's his name, *Legno*, which is not funny — 'Most of the time,' said Christina, 'we didn't have a whole lot of choice but to amputate.' He's hurting, and she amputates? My god,

Kat, this is creepy stuff. Do you mind if I sit? I'm getting weak in the legs, just reviewing my notes."

"Be my guest," said Kate.

"*The Fire Within*, page 30: 'Caleb lifted the quilt and looked down. He was naked under the covers and there were bandages on his right thigh. She didn't seem to mind that he was showing more skin than was decent.' Page 74: 'They amputate?' he inquires, coming to. No — not *yet*. *Velvet Song*, page 86: 'It doesn't matter if they do, said Alyx callously, moving to the far side of the cot, to Signore Pioggia's wounded leg.' *Heartless, Helpless*, page 477: 'He felt Isidore's soft fingers examining the bandages on his right thigh.' 'Penis?' he asks, coming to. 'You still have one,' says Isidore, 'though it's circumcised now, and stitched where it was nearly severed. I'm fairly sure it will still function, but I don't recommend touching it for a while.' She's like, ooh, yuck, maybe *you* can touch that mangled thing, but I'm not going to do it. *Flash of Splendour*, page 7: 'They say it will go rotten in three days and kill me if you *don't* cut it off,' says Hugh the hero."

"Life is hard," said Caterina. "A man needs to be strong."

"Fine, but for aught that I have read so far, one thing is *not* hard for the hero. Ever."

"Then you have not read far enough, obviously," said Caterina.

"*Saving Doctor Gregorio*, page 10: 'she changed sides so that his injured leg was next to her.' She gives it a massage. Nothing happens. *Perchance to Dream*, page 31: 'Dragging himself to the edge of the bed, he swung his injured leg gingerly over the side.' It just dangles there."

"You can stop citing page numbers," said Kate, with a pout. "I know the stories. And a person's *legs* are not something that *I* need to look up."

"Okay, fine, then. *Just Another Pretty Face*: 'The groan turned to a strangled sound of pain and frustration as his injured leg protested.' Time for love, but the bodily member is still hurting, still dangling. *The Diamond Slipper*: 'Simon walked toward her, ... trying to hide the slight drag of his wounded leg.' It embarrasses him, the way his wounded leg just dangles along behind. *Outlaws and Lovers*: 'He staggered ... on the injured leg. He started toward her.' But he cannot come. *Guarded Moments*: 'on his injured leg, he winced ... Yesterday, inside the vault, the size seemed large.' But that was yesterday, before he got clipped. Worse and worse. *Married to the Man:* 'she would have to cut off his legs at the knees, to get him to fit.' My god, Kat! Would you want to read a horror novel, by a male author, in which a moral monster shaves a lady's legs, in her own bed, with a carpenter's saw, for a better fit?"

"Maybe," said Kate. "Depends on whether true love conquers, in the end. If it doesn't, then it is no true romance."

"*Destined to Love*: '*I could've easily left you, and that injured leg of yours, a long time ago*, she said. *Then go*, he said.'"

"But see? that's the beauty of it," said Kate. "Giuseppina won't ever leave Signore Coitisio. She loves him. Though wounded, he is her destiny. Omnia vincit amor. Love conquers all."

"Unless it's cut off at the pass. *Beloved Rebel:* 'They say Signore Carmaccio got a *leg injury* in the fracas at the *gap*.' Nan Etter is concerned. 'I hope his leg will soon heal,' she sighs. 'He just couldn't *stand*, being a cripple.' On the same page, this author gives her hero an 'honorable discharge.' Well, that's just dandy! So long as Carmaccio can have no heated encounter up there in Nan's gap, he's safe, he can have a pleasant discharge at his convenience. Besides which, 'Nan Etter' totally looks like an uncorrected misprint for Man Eater."

"You're reading too much into it," said Kate, in a huff. "If I had known you would be like this, I would not have let you into my books."

"Oh, here's a kinky one: *Daddy of the House*: 'Leonardo was hobbling at Jay's side, his injured leg still encased in a cast matching that of his now-beloved rescuer.' Jay is the hero. Leonardo is the injured hero's dog. In romance, even the boy *dogs* get whacked. *Daughter of the Forest?* Even kinkier: 'Rosso sat down by his mother, stretching out his injured leg.

Her face was soft and round under the delicate lawn of her veil...' His *mother?* Oh. My. God."

"Stop!" said Kate. "You're totally missing the point."

"No, but Signore Holdeno may be missing the whole point and then some, when he awakes to find a 'bloody, filthy bandage wrapped around his thigh,' in a romance aptly titled, *Missing.*"

"The hero's wound is merely the outward sign of a tortured soul, a mark of his vulnerability, his need to be cared for by his lover."

"Plus, it makes him limp. And stay limp."

"Until he receives the heroine's healing touch."

"Or his own healing touch. *Conquer the Night:* Draegan Youngblood has an 'injured leg' (page 5); he suffers a 'persistent ache in his thigh' (page 62); 'his limp was evident,' but wait, here comes the rising action: 'distracted, he kneaded the flesh of his left thigh' (page 177). If Lady Fallon Deane loves her Draegan-boy so much, then why doesn't *she* knead the flesh of his aching member?   'I was wounded at university,' explains the sad-eyed Draegan, matter-of-factly. 'The injury is something I've tried since to forget' — as if there were *ever* a university student, or a giant lizard for that matter, named Draegan Young-blood."

"Well, there you go," said Kate. "The hero is typically wounded down there by another man — in battle, or in a duel, or at university."

"Or by his wife, or by an old girlfriend, or by his mother."

"Just don't blame the heroine. She wants just the opposite. She wants her man to be big and strong, and to stand tall, and to feel good, and to desperately need her."

"*Tame the Wild Wind:* Christian Faith — that's the heroine's name — takes a pitchfork and 'jabbed at him as hard as she could, sticking him in the left thigh.' Now, there's a feel-good, stand-tall affair! 'But then Clete himself slumped to the floor, a bloody hole in his lower— '"

"One, Clete is not the hero, and two, you're making a big deal out of nothing," said Kate.

"No, no, no," said Petruchio. "A big deal is what Clete *used* to have, before his encounter with the pitchfork of Christian Faith. What he has now, on page 172, is 'a bloody hole.' And besides, where does this writer come up with her names. What man was ever named 'Clete Torres'?"

"You're misremembering. It's Clete Marrone."

"These novels are a horror show," said Petruchio. "I'm gonna have nightmares for a month. *Rocky Road:* Matteo has 'a bullet in his groin and a sickness in his soul.' 'Ask him how he got a gunshot wound in the groin,' said Gina. '*What?*' Carena shrieked. So she asks Mattie about the you-know-what, 'in his leg.' 'She could feel the tension radiate. It's in my groin, he corrected. Yes, it's a gunshot wound.' Thereafter, every time he was aroused, 'the nightmare would start again — he'd be staring *at the bloody hole in his groin.*' Verbatim quote. But when lucky Matteo discovers true love, it registers as an 'ache in his groin that had nothing to do with the four-month-old bullet wound.' Yeah, right!"

"You need to read on, to the happy ending. Trust me, there's no connection."

"If there's no connection, it's because Matteo has got nothing left to connect with, after the author for maximum entertainment-value has shot him between the legs, or tied a bomb to his penis and lit the fuse."

"There are lots of romances in which the hero is perfectly healthy," said Kate.

"Like which ones?"

"Like lots of them," said Kate, irritably. "No amputations, no wounds, no nothing."

"Name one."

"Okay, let me just think .... *Knight in Shining Armor.* Sir Jamie."

"I haven't seen that one yet. I've only skimmed the novels on your top shelf. I've still got at least a dozen shelves to go."

"*An Unpredictable Bride. La Pazza Nella Soffitta.* Almost anything by Carlotta Brontolone. Guilla Catheri's *Mio Fuoco di Sant'Antonia....*"

"Petruchio browsed his notes. *An Unpredictable Bride*: Sir Simon is down. 'Where is he wounded, Captain Digby?' 'His leg — his left thigh, that is.' 'Then would you mind uncovering it?' Another man, mangled. A few pages later, Captain Digby also gets whacked. Predictable."

"*Deception*, then."

"Give me a minute," said Petruchio. He seemed not to notice that Kate was feeling cross, and losing her patience with him. "*Deception, Deception*. Ah, here we go, no, oops, you're right. *Deception*, page 101: 'The knife sliced his thumb. Kate' (that's the heroine's name), 'Kate looked up. 'You okay?' He turned back to cutting the stir-fry vegetables, ignoring the pain in his thumb and his shorts.' End quote. Well, I guess I'd rather have my thumb sliced than to have my testicles and penis shot off and stir-fried, or knifed, and replaced with a bloody slit."

"Don't be disgusting."

"Don't blame me, I didn't write it. *Luci Gets Married, Beyond All Reason, Hunger Like No Other, Make Believe, River Wife,* same thing. Bend, staple, mutilate. There is no injury too cruel to be inflicted on a man's appendages. *Miranda:* 'He held up his hand. In the shadowy candle glow, she studied the last finger, cut off at the first joint....Giovanni: with his blunt workman's hands and the missing finger that he loathed to show the world."

"You're making me angry," said Kate. "These men are walking wounded until they meet their soul-mate. The hero-ine is the *answer* to their pain, not the cause."

"And if the man is not already wounded when they meet, then it's her job to deliver a world of hurt: *Outlaws and Lovers:* 'Daddy was teaching Kat and me how to knee an unwanted admirer in the groin, she said.' *To Catch a Thief:* 'He smiled ... she had to bite back the urge to knee him in the groin.' *Paradise Island:* 'If he spread his legs just a little farther apart, she might be able to kick him in the groin.' *Surrender to a Stranger:* 'she struggled and tried to lift her knee to strike him in the groin.' *Bearskin Rug:* 'She kneed him in the groin. He went down, retching. *Don't hurt me, my dear*" he cried. Shall I go on?"

"No. I get it. I get it, that you have a very one-track mind," said Caterina. "I get it, that you do not understand the first thing about romance. Or the second thing. Or third. True love is a blessing."

"Well, at least I understand now where your notions of romantic *tweaking* come from. Here's a romance with *Blessing* for its title: 'She kneed him in the groin, ... this time pummeling it with her fists.' Or was it from *Birdie:* 'Using her head as a battering ram, she struck him a brutal blow between the legs. *Ow!* He doubled over to grasp his wounded crotch with both hands.'"

"You are being disgusting. And I should not have to listen to this." Caterina hissed the words at him.

He hissed right back. "*Treasures:* 'He saw the shoe, felt a hard kick in the groin and curled into a ball. Bile sprayed up the back of his throat...' 'Only a little piece of the dirty flesh caught between her teeth, but Tommy let out a howl and she moved quickly, bringing up her knee.' What? 'Bile sprayed up the back of his throat'? 'Dirty flesh' caught in her teeth? You don't think that's scary? Creeps me out. The hero in these books would be better off humping a hungry tigress, it would be safer for everyone."

"Don't call it *humping*. I don't like that."

"Making love to a hungry tigress."

"Thank you."

"*Million-Dollar Bride*: 'He felt aroused, and erect, and ashamed of himself. That can't be normal, he said. The last syllable came out in a shriek as Eliza Ricardo jerked her knee up, hitting him in the groin and clobbering every amorous thought he had ever entertained. Every muscle in his body clenched in protest against the pain....'"

When Petruchio looked up, he saw that Caterina was staring at him, scowling, with her fingers in her ears. He stopped reading. She stopped holding her ears.

"I feel for these men," said Petruchio. "I feel their pain. You have no idea. These women should wear kneepads, at least."

"Maybe some do," said Kate. "Only not for that. You've got to stay with the story until you reach the happy parts."

"All the happy parts are cut," said Petruchio. "Or shot off. Or stabbed with the pitchfork of Christian Faith. I take no pleasure from a story in which cruel women aim for the hero's groin, just so they can say, "The hero was kneed in his private parts! He was shot in the groin! He was knifed! He was forked! Hoo-hah! And then we made love, it was soooooooooo romantic.""

"Don't raise your voice at me, Poochi. Your male sarcasm is neither attractive nor pleasant."

"Mi scusi, Kitten, but your feminine entertainments are neither attractive or pleasant."

"Don't call me Kitten."

"Don't call me Poochi."

"Like male pornography is sexy? Pietro Aretino: *The ladies of Italy*, he writes, *will sit with their legs spread over the sides of a chair with their petticoats and smocks in their mouths, and their bloomers around their ankles, whilst their male comrades, with their lances out, run a-tilt at their touch-holes in that posture, paying twelve pence a time for holing.* That may not be verbatim, but it's close. Aretino writes about sex, sex, sex, and he is the most unsexy writer in Italy. Where, in his *Secret Life of Wives*, is the mystery? Where is the tender feeling? Where is the love?"

"You have *The Secret Life of Wives*?"

"I threw it away."

"Anyway, that's satire," said Petruchio, "where no one gets hurt. We're discussing romance. *Gift-Wrapped*: 'Tell him if I see him before he has bought many presents, expensive presents, presents for both of us, I will cut off his ... you know!' Okay, big mystery, let me guess: she'll cut off his allowance? *Dark Victory*: 'You're attempting to neuter me, he cried. I didn't succeed?' says Chesca, her mission incomplete. 'Then remind me,' she says, with a 'razor smile,' 'to bring my castration kit.' Where is the mystery in *that*? or the *love*? I'll grant you, it is not hard to find, in romance, the *tender feeling*. It's located right between the hero's legs, after being kicked. And by the way, I'm still a little tender myself, down there, thank you."

"That is *so* not fair, to drag that up again. You said you were over it."

"*The Devil's Own:* 'I threatened Joe with castration by machete,' she gloats, 'if he left the cellar before I came. He argued with me, of course.' C'mon, Kat, what kind of woman castrates a man just for leaving the cellar?"

"Me," said Kate.

"Well, I don't want you reading this stuff."

"That was a joke. Relax. And I'll not be told what I may or may not read." She put her fingers back in her ears. Petruchio raised his voice.

"*A Greek God at the Ladies' Club:* Cytus realizes 'she was gonna take my balls off.' 'Maybe she *should* cut it off,' Claudia said.' 'She aimed for his groin.'"

"*A Greek God at the Ladies' Club* is one of my favorites," said Kate.

"Hell, I can see where *that* story is going, just from the title. Same place as *Rides a Hero* — straight into a massacre: 'I can castrate at least six of you,' Shannon promised. At least six of the men took a step back.' *Father Found:* 'Castration might be good, for *starters*, she said. His hands dropped from her and he took a step backward.' For *starters*? What else might be good, for the main course — spaghetti and meatballs? *No Strings Attached:* 'She goes straight for their balls and doesn't let go until they've been castrated.' Verbatim quote. Still dangling by a string? Snip! Nope! Got it!"

"Tap my knee when you're done," said Caterina, "because I'm not listening."

"*An Officer and a Hero:* 'She could think of nothing short of castration that would give her satisfaction.' Enter the hero. 'She tried not to stare at the shape of his muscled calves, or the curly blond hair on his legs, or the intriguing scar on his thigh.' Meanwhile, *His Brother's Bride* has 'castrated the male calves, tossing the testicles into a bucket to be cooked up later as

prairie oysters for the adventurous.' *The Night Orchid:* 'If
Roberto Halio were a bull, they wouldn't cut his balls off.' No,
they'd save whatever squirted from his father's male member
'to form such a tall, good-looking man, and try to spread it
around.' Quinn doesn't care, she'll do it to him anyway. 'I'll
shoot your balls off, she said — if you have any, that is.' Exit
Roberto. Enter, by time-travel, a half-naked warrior from the
third century, named Alek, who is not smart but at least he's
muscular and shirtless. Marissa: 'How could anyone castrate
this man? She couldn't bear to think about it.' Well, I say,
God bless Marissa, for sparing the poor savage. *An Obsolete
Man:* 'Even bulls were becoming obsolete. The losers were
castrated.' Signora Witherspoon warns Clint, if given the
chance, 'I'd probably castrate you. She said that quite calmly,
as she examined the cards.'"

Kate shook her head. "She was just joking with him."

"Big Ha. Ha. *Escape Not My Love*: 'He wondered if she
had ordered them to castrate him, for the seven men began to
laugh. Soon it was no laughing matter, when Jay found himself
trussed like a goat at a barbecue.'"

"Yes, but only as a playful threat, a fantasy," said Caterina.

"God save all Christian men from a playful romance heroine. *Something Borrowed, Something Blue:* 'With a hiss, Eva
lashed out maniacally, stabbing toward his groin. He sagged
backward, clutching at the letter-opener she jammed into his
bloody crotch.' O Lord, I have just married a woman who
likes to read about heroines who stab letter-openers into a
man's bloody crotch."

"Only in self-defense."

"You call this self-defense? *Fortunato*, a best-seller, page
87: 'Alice had cut off his balls and used them for earrings. He
died six months after.' Page 100, the new guy: 'If she hadn't
resorted to slamming him in the balls with her elbow she
would probably still be there.' Page 169: 'it was like cutting off
his balls, although Carlo took it calm as a priest.' Page 266: a
granddaughter shoots Enzio 'in the balls, three times.' Page
278: 'she just walked in and blew his balls off. He deserved it,
said Carrie.'" Petruchio's voice had become shaky. "Deserved

it?" he said. "In a romance called *Fortunato,* 'Lucky,' the man *deserves* to have his private parts blown off?"

"Maybe you're taking the phrase, 'blew his balls off,' too literally," said Kate. "I seem to remember in that same book, certain men who were only too happy to be blown."

"Do you not understand, Caterina, why a man might find such fantasies as these a little frightening ... horrific, even?"

"No."

"Mio Dio, if the husbands of Italy were paying attention to what's going on in the sixteenth-century book trade, they'd be sleeping in battle armor, for fear of being mangled in the night by their own bedpartners."

"Anyway," said Kate, "the castration of villains and oxen has got nothing to do with the literary convention of the gentle hero with a wounded leg, which is perfectly romantic and is nothing to be so worried about."

"Sure, why worry? *Raging Hearts:* 'Kitty stepped forward and placed her hand on his brow. *'God, don't let them do this to me, lady,* he shrieked, seeing her through fevered eyes. She had heard the same plea so many times in the past four years that she knew, by heart, every word that would come from his trembling lips. Her eyes went to the exposed flesh' (with a gleam in her eye, no doubt). *'I've got to have my leg!'* he cries. *'God almighty, what good is a man with just one leg?'*"

"Well, for starters," said Kate, "he won't participate in any more ass-kicking contests."

"Oh, funny. You think that's funny? Trust me, it's not funny. Here's another, *Abelard and Heloise,* by Isabella Sforza, Lady Porcigliano. "Abelard falls in love with — "

"Stop it! Just *stop* it!" said Kate, stomping her foot. In a fury, she slapped Petruchio's papers from his hand, scattering them over the bedroom floor. "You are so ... *clueless!* If the man is her soulmate, and wounded, then the heroine restores him, and they find true love. If the man is a jerk, or a rapist, or a buffoon, she knees him in the groin, or puts his balls in a vise, to teach him a lesson. Sometimes, okay, she knees him, or stabs the wrong man, by mistake. But he forgives her, and together they create a union of true hearts. What's not to understand, about that? You are making me so ... angry! Yes, angry! And you are such... such a disappointment, Petruchio!"

The word, *disappointment*, hit Petruchio like battering ram, or like a letter opener. He did not stoop to pick up his notes. He collapsed in the chair by the writing desk, looking dejected. Worse than dejected. "This is not what I wanted, on my wedding night," he said. "Here we are, quarreling."

"Look," said Caterina. "I don't know if this marriage is going to work. You have way too many hangups. So much ... *negativity.*"

"I'm sorry."

"You *should* be. You don't dance. You hate romance. What's left, after that? You're cute. Well, cute guys are a ducat a dozen. I could have 'cute' any night of the week. I thought you would be different. I thought you *were* different. You *fooled* me, pal."

"Okay, okay. What do you want me to get, from romance, that I'm not getting? Besides, of course, castrated? Because maybe I *would* like to be different."

"For starters, buck up, and wipe that sad-dog look from your face. *Sweet talk* me. There are only two kinds of men in the world, those who know how to make a woman happy, and those who don't. Pay me some compliments. Tell me what you think of me. Praise my parts."

Petruchio pondered this assignment. "Well, I do still think you're pretty hot," he said at last.

"No, Petruchio. I am not '*hot.*' I am nowhere close to '*hot.*' I am not halfway to *warm.* If you want to see *hot*, do better. C'mon, sweet-talk me."

"You're beautiful."

"Okay, we'll run with that. Who says I'm beautiful, darling?"

"Lots of people. Guys."

"And what do you say?"

"Same thing."

"Dealbreaker. If you can do no better in conversation, or on the dance floor, or in bed, than everyone else, then someone's unnecessary, and it may be you. Okay, I'm ready for romance. Show me what you've got."

Petruchio — obediently, he thought, though bashful — began to untie his codpiece.

"Leave it!" barked Kate. "Not yet. You need to woo me. What else am I? Try again."

"Um.....um, um, you can be pretty funny."

"Funny, ridiculous? or funny, witty?"

"Witty. Biting sense of humor."

"All right. I am beautiful and witty. What else?"

"Nice hair. Great figure. Nice personality, mostly."

"Continue."

Petruchio paused, cautiously racking his brains. "Rich?"

"Unromantic." Kate frowned. "'Beautiful' was a given. 'Witty' counts for something. But if you pursue a woman for her money, that's not love, that's greed."

"And if a woman pursues a man for his money?"

"That's different. Women have no earning power. Hurry up, you've got *beautiful*, and you've got *witty*. What else?"

Petruchio was starting to panic. He looked around the bedchamber. "You have a nice book collection," he said.

"Insincere. Your Fakeness Rating just shot through the ceiling, Bud."

Petruchio sighed, with frustration. "I don't know what you want, Kat."

"If you cannot sweet-talk me, you're not my guy."

"But I don't know what to say that will please you. I don't know *how*."

"Humility, so rare in a man, is welcome. Here's a suggestion, mister. Any reasonably intelligent man who wishes to satisfy his beautiful and witty lover can acquire, from romance, what he failed to learn at university. Next time, when you dip into my book collection, read more attentively, and think about something besides your own castration anxiety."

"Anxiety, these days, is not unwarranted," said Petruchio. "Case in point: those choirboys who sang the madrigal this afternoon, at our wedding."

"Well, at least now they have nothing left to worry about. And they have beautiful voices.

"Let me tell you a secret, about men..."

"Oh, goody! I *love* secrets."

"This is just for an example. I'm perfectly normal, Kate, so don't go thinking I'm weird. When I was five or six, I had a nightmare. In my dream, my uncle came after me with a sheep shears and tried to cut off my thumb, to punish me, just like in one of your romance novels."

"Punish you for what?"

"For nothing. For a head cold. I was looking through my mother's purse for a handkerchief to blow my runny nose when my uncle accused me of trying to steal her money. Which I wasn't."

"Cruel."

"Yeah. You could say that. And in another dream, one I'll never forget, I was paddling a little punt across the ocean, to meet a mermaid. Progress was slow, because my oar was too little to fight the current. But just when I caught a glimpse of the mermaid, that's when I saw the fin of the great white shark. He circled around me, and then he smashed my little boat with his snout."

"Did he bite you?"

"No, but he ate my paddle. I was terrified."

"And so you woke up and said, Hmmm, I must have been dreaming; because in Verona, *we don't have any sharks.*"

"I don't have any uncles, either. My point is that when I told my dream to other boys, I found out they had the same nightmare."

"Power of suggestion," said Kate.

Petruchio sighed. He felt as if his bride did not understand his concerns, and that she did not even wish to try.

Caterina sighed, too. Petruchio needed feminine mentoring, or he was a lost cause. He was seeming more and more, with each passing minute of their marriage, like a typical man. "Compare me to something," she said. "What am I like?"

"You're like ... pretty difficult," said Petruchio.

"And you may be impossible," said Kate. "My eyes. What do my eyes remind you of?"

"Stars?"

"Ooh-ooh, 'stars.' Haven't heard that one, before. Eyes, like stars. For un-original, Pet, that's ten twinkling points on a scale of ten. Twelve on a scale of twelve, if I were Jewish."

"Okay, orbs. Your eyes are like grey *orbs*. Gosh, I don't know! How would *you* describe them?"

"My eyes are not grey. Stones are grey. My eyes are the color of moonlit clouds on a stormy April night, with soft flashes of lightning. We'll come back to my eyes. How's my nose?"

"Cute as a buh — as a bunny rabbit's. No fur, of course, I wasn't saying that."

"My hair is like — ?"

"Golden silk."

"Except that it's black. Hello?"

"Your hair is like sable silk ... whose mourning curls turn all my griefs to joy."

"You're improving. My teeth are like — ?"

"Fangs! No, just a joke! Seriously, Kat, your teeth are like, they're like pearls, okay, no clichés, I get that, but....Caterina, your smile is my, my *sunlight*....and when you frown, all the world turns to blackest night!"

Kate smiled. "You're a quick study," she said. "We might get somewhere tonight, after all."

"And your voice is like the song of larks, after a bleak and hungry winter."

"Very nice, Pet. Do you like my breasts?"

"And your breasts are like..." Petruchio's face flushed. "Well, I haven't actually seen them," he said. "But I imagine that they're quite nice, like ripened peaches, only sweeter."

"Would you like to see them?"

Petruchio swallowed hard, and nodded in nervous silence.

"Would you like to touch them?"

"Y-yes," he said. "I would like that. Very much."

"Maybe you would like to lean over my shoulder, and slide one palm inside by bodice and caress my breast until your fingertip finds the nipple? and maybe then brush the pink nub lightly with your thumb, making it pert and stiff at your touch?

And as your left hand gently fondles me, the other hand begins to unlace my bodice?"

"Yes," said Petruchio. "That sounds really great."

"Later," said Kate. "First, we need to think about our words. What do you call your male organ?"

"Cazzo."

"Absolutely not.

"A penis?"

"I don't like *penis*. Too urological-sounding. *Pee. Niss.* Call it a *penis* in the doctor's office, if you like, but not in the bedroom."

"Cock?"

"Please, no. When I hear *cock*, I think, male chicken. I think cockfights. I picture a stuffed capon, roasting on the spit. Save your cock for the barbecue grill. My grandmother, God rest her Christian soul, had a proverb: 'What good is your craven cock, but for getting up at the crack of dawn and going doodle-oo?' Of course, Grandma's name was Dawn, but still. I'll have something nicer than a rooster stuffed inside my warm wet nest of desire. Ditto for *sausage* and *salami*. Ditto for *bone* and *boner*. Not romantic."

"*Gun?*"

"Not a *pistol*, for reasons already noted. Nor *breech-loader*, for another reason. A *handgun?* Not when I'm around. If it's gun-play you want, I'll be in the next room with a good book. Have fun, and just don't shoot your eye out."

"Sword?"

"Makes me wince just thinking about it. A *rapier?* Not on your life. Not an *epee*, for reasons twice noted. *Love-stick?* Maybe. Parry, thrust. That's a maybe."

"It's Petruchio."

"Yes?"

"Not 'Perry.'"

"Oh. I get it. Petruchio, thrust!' Not yet, darling. Your romance-training has only just begun."

"I've read enough," he said.

"Rule number one. Take your time, but finish what you've started. That's the great thing about romance. It starts out painful, but it leads to bliss. Tragedy is just the opposite of love."

"Right, like Romeo and Juliet."

"I don't know *Romeo and Juliet.*"

"Friends of mine, back in Verona. They got married, but it didn't work out."

"Romance," said Caterina, "leads inexorably to a happy ending. Joy cannot be avoided. In the final chapter, the hero and heroine find their bliss. It's their destiny."

"Oh, yeah?" Thinking to prove his point that the romance hero's suffering is relentless and undeserved, Petruchio grabbed a random novel from the stack, flipped to the last pages, and started reading.

And then kept reading.

He turned a page and continued reading. His eyes grew wide.

He sat down on the bed and kept reading.

"Petruchio?" He was too absorbed in the action to hear. "Pet!"

"Sorry?"

"We were searching for a romantic term for your sex."

"How's this: 'The fiery serpent pushed deep, deep into the moist warmth of her.'"

"Meh," said Kate. "I am so totally *not* into Highland Romance meets Gothic. A Scottish Pee Ness Monster in holy wedlock, I'll none of that, thank you. The raging beast of lust probes the lady's dank dungeon of love while he sucks blood from her neck. Forget it. I hate that. Choose a different one."

"It's *your* book," he said. He felt confused.

"Look," said Caterina, throwing up her hands in despair, "this conversation is going nowhere. Maybe we should try again, in a week or two. Or maybe you and I are just not very compatible, after all."

Petruchio grabbed another, and put his finger on a random page, near the end. "How about: 'he softly brushed her camel-toe with the tip of his throbbing manroot'"?

"That one's pretty tired," said Kate. "A 'throbbing man-root' is worn out. But you're getting warmer."

"Definitely," said Petruchio. Encouraged, he browsed further. "Here's something," he said, sounding intrigued. "She nibbled with her lips at the shiny end of his turgid manhood. She tasted his skin with her tongue and caressed his engorged staff with her fingers...' I think this thing is growing on me," said Petruchio.

"Or," said Kate helpfully, "how about: he filled her loins with the warm tumult of his lubricated sex-tool."

"Yes," said Petruchio, "yes, that's brilliant."

"Or how about: he wriggled his tumescent tube of fire into her hot sleeve of love?"

"Better still."

"Or: Standing tall, the bald avenger dived into her dark pit, head-first."

"Awesome."

"Or: The throbbing between her thighs exploded into a paroxysm of damp, hot pleasure as he laved her mossy cave with the spurts of his creamy man-love?"

"God, yes! I'm starting to understand romance, I think. It's making sense, I'm getting it."

Kate shook her head in disappointment. "No power of discretion," she said, as if talking to herself, or to a tree-stump. "It takes more than purple prose to make a romance."

"Look, I'm willing to learn," said Petruchio. "Teach me. What then shall we call my — my turgid manhood?"

"The most discreet writers simply call it *his sex*, without the bombast."

"What do they call your, um, the lady's, private part?"

"*Her* sex. Same idea."

"He thrust his sex into her sex, and they had sex?"

"Yes, but not at the same time."

"What, they take turns?"

"If it's a union of true hearts, he and she will always come together, sooner or later. But you cannot use 'his sex' and 'her sex' in the same sentence, that's all. 'He slipped the tip of his staff into the petals of her sex.' Or: 'between his legs his sex

was aching, straining for a satisfaction only she could give him.'
Try that."

"I'm ready."

"I mean, try saying it."

"No adjectives?"

"If you like. *Warm, moist, swollen, needy, eager,* whatever
fits."

"I'm still partial to *throbbing,*" said Petruchio. "Seems
pretty accurate."

"I guess."

"Trust me. It's throbbing."

"Okay, I guess we're ready, then."

"I feel we are, yes, definitely. I'm ready if you are."

"Rehearsal, I mean. No touching, yet. We need to exercise our imaginations together, explore our fantasies, allow our
souls to intertwine before our bodies come together. Start with
the praise. What am I like? Compare me."

"To what? to other women? a garden? a horse? a summer's day?"

"A summer's day — try that."

"You are more lovely, Kat, than a summer's day. Also,
less hot, but that's my fault, I'm working on it. Rough winds
do shake the darling buds of May, just as my hands will shake
your darling nipples into aching buds of desire."

"That's the idea. Now undress me — with your eyes and
words."

"Where do I start?"

"Unpin my hair and let it down."

"Done. Other end. Now I'm untying your left shoe and
slipping it from your delicate foot. I'm removing your right
shoe."

"Not so fast!"

"What did I forget?"

"A foot massage, for example."

"I rub your toes, the ball, the arch, the heel, the ankle."

"Yes, that's very nice."

"Gently, I pick you up in my arms and set you down on the
bed."

"First, remove my skirt, please."

"Good point. I undo the points and remove your skirt. Gently, I lift you..."

"I'm wearing a hooped underskirt also, and a petticoat."

"I undo the points that hold your underskirt on. I'm not sure how that works, Kat."

"Don't worry, you'll figure it out."

"Gently, I lift you onto the bed. I lie down beside you, and — which side of the bed is mine?

"Are you left handed?"

"No."

"Then you will lie to my right."

"Gotcha. So I lie down beside you. I lean on my elbow so that I can gaze into your stormy grey eyes and whisper sweet-talk in your ear. As I nibble on your earlobe, I toy with the lacing on your tight bodice. How am I doing?"

"You're doing well. Continue."

"I untie your poufy oversleeves, where they are attached with ribbons at the shoulder. Next, I unlace your bodice, from your bosom down to your skirt, and let it fall open."

"That's not quite how it works; first — "

"So I take out my pocketknife and I just zip right through the lacing, taking care not to scratch your tender skin. The bodice falls open. I can now feel the warm soft flesh of your tender breasts, just beneath your camica. I can see little bumps where your nipples are, which feels pretty exciting, and I want to see them, and touch them, and lick them. I untie your high-necked lace partlet. You lift your head as I gently slide the gauzy cloth from your upper breast and shoulders. You now lie beside me in just your camica, and your stockings."

"My oversleeves. Pull off my oversleeves. You only untied them, at the shoulder."

"I remove your oversleeves of slashed silk, and your white undersleeves. My God, you've got a lot of clothing to take off!"

"Keep going, please."

"Now it's just your camica and stockings, right?"

"And my jewelry. And my drawers."

"And by now it's all getting pretty scary, so I just lie there beside you, for a few minutes, and I hold you close, and maybe just hug you in my arms, for a while."

"That's okay. That's nice. Lovely, really."

"How do we take off the camica?"

"You don't need to take it off right away, you can explore, first."

"So maybe I fondle your breasts through the fabric of the camica, and then I slip my hand inside, to touch your breasts, and we're kissing of course, and, but — let's just take the thing off, can we?"

"It is not a *horse* race, Pet. But this is just practice, so, yes, okay. I sit up, and you help me slip the camica over my head, and we throw it from the bed. You see my breasts for the first time."

"Yes, yes, and they are the most perfect things I have ever seen. You are lying there now, beside me, naked from the waist up, and I know I am the luckiest man in the world to have married you. So I loosen the string on your drawers, or whatever you ladies call 'em, and I slip them down to your knees."

"Off, Pet. Remove my knickers. They'll only get in our way, later."

"So as you lift your knees one leg at a time to slip off your bloomers, I stare in wonder and amazement at your soft warm place."

"My kneecaps?"

"No, I meant: higher up."

"And I meant: my stockings have not come off yet."

"So I slide the first stocking down your leg, one inch— "

"Garters?"

"I undo your garters, then slide down your stocking, one inch at a time, whispering in your ear how much I need you, I want you, I love you. You're now wearing nothing at all except some jewelry and one stocking, and I can't stand it so I just leave the other stocking on your leg, and I rip my own clothes off as fast as I can get out of them, and I jump into bed beside you and we crawl under the covers and — do think we can try this thing now, Kat? I'm totally ready, I feel. Yes, I'm ready, definitely. I am so, so, so ready. This trial run has been very helpful."

A muffled conversation in the next room to which Petruchio and Caterina had paid no attention now became suddenly boisterous, deflating the romantic mood at the worst possible moment: "No! Stop! That's nasty! I can't! I won't!"

"What the — ?" exclaimed Petruchio.

"That would be my sister," said Kate, rolling her eyes.

Bianca cried, "Ouch! No! Ouch! Ouch! Oh! Oh! Ouch!"

"Sounds like he's beating her," said Petruchio, with furled brow. "Should we knock? See if she's okay?"

"No," said Kate, "but in the morning, you can watch for a bit of eggshell sticking to her tail. I didn't think she would really do it."

"Do it? Have sex?"

"Maybe that, too," said Kate. "Just wait. When the sobbing starts, it may go on for some time."

In about a minute, they heard the sound of a woman sobbing.

Petruchio looked ashen. "Sounds pretty upset," he said.

"She *must*," said Caterina. "Lucentio is your typical man of privilege, obsessed with being first. If he should discover his bride is not a virgin, he would doubtless sue Papa, shame the bride, annul the marriage, and go off in search of someone new. So what you do on your wedding night, is you conceal on your person an eggshell that has been emptied and refilled with chicken blood, and sealed with wax. At bedtime, when the groom grows amorous, you curl up into a ball. You cross your legs. You holler, 'I won't do that nasty thing!' When he touches you down there, you kick him. When he tries to come inside, you don't just lie there like a fish, you yell so loudly that even the servants run to their windows, to eaves-drop. When he's done, you bawl and sob. In the meantime, you reach for the eggshell, and smash it in your fist, beneath your buttocks. And by now, your father and siblings and the servants, and all the neighbors within earshot, are saying, '*It's done! And such a sweet, good girl!*' In the morning, the whole parish is celebrating your virtue, and holding you up as an example to other teenaged girls of the parish."

"So why are you telling me her secret?"

"It's no *secret,*" said Kate. "If a man is fooled, it's his own fault, for not knowing the literature."

"I may be in over my depth here," said Petruchio.

"Come," said Kate. "Lie down next to me. This is going to be *such* fun!"

Petruchio obediently lay on the bed beside Kat and gazed into her eyes. "You are *so* beautiful," he said. He touched her cheek — but he had lost his erection, now. And he feared he could not coax it back to life, that night — not with the sound of Bianca, sobbing in the next room. A minute later, he dozed off, from nervous exhaustion. Caterina decided to let him sleep. They could try again tomorrow, pick up where they left off. Petruchio was not yet fully groomed for romance. But true love waits.

• • •

VI. *Romanzo Fiume*

WHEN PETRUCHIO awoke in the morning, Kate was gone. Her wedding gown and other garments lay on the bed, along with a bath towel that was still damp. He kicked himself for having overslept. Kate poked her head into the bedroom. She was dressed for tennis.

"Ah. You're awake. Put on something comfortable. We're going to have quite the big adventure today, you and me."

"Such as?"

"We shall go punting."

For his sixty-fifth birthday, Signore Baptista had purchased a flat-bottomed, square-prowed punt — Caterina called it a "tender" — for fishing excursions. He never put it in the water. Five years later, the punt remained upside down, on blocks, out back. The punting-pole (the "quant"), plus paddles and oars, remained in the boathouse, unused, along with the fishing gear, which was used only by servants. Kate's idea was to put the boat into service as Queen Cleopatra's river barge, with Petruchio as her muscular and graceful gondolier.

Kate directed two of her father's servants to give the vessel a trial run on the Marsango Canal, which they did. No leaks. Meanwhile, she packed some extra clothes; a picnic hamper with cold baked meats, wedding cake, some fruit, and a bottle of wine; plus several small rugs and cushions, to make the journey more comfortable; plus a blanket — "because when wild nature calls" (as she explained to Petruchio, hours later), "a girl does not want to feel prickly weeds and harsh grasses beneath her soft white buttocks, or have bugs crawling under her back, or snakes." Petruchio agreed.

The morning was partly taken up with a late breakfast and the opening of wedding gifts. But as soon as Lucentio and Bianca were up and about, Kate took Pet's hand and led him out the back door and down to the water's edge. They followed a path along a stone wall, through a gate, and down to an ancient dock, half rotted away, which had escaped the recent renovations. Caterina's punt was now furnished and ready to launch.

The excursion began with a quarrel. Petruchio rummaged through his satchel.

"What are you looking for?" asked Kate.

"My gun."

"Your *gun?*

"My pistol. It's in here, somewhere."

"No, it's not. I removed it."

"Why would you take a gun?"

"Why would you bring it?"

"Protection, of course."

"No guns."

"I'm taking my gun."

"If you need to protect me, use your fists."

"Outlaws have guns."

"Guns are for men with small penises."

"Some grown men buy entire arsenals. Cannons, even."

"Yes, as compensation. Because their cocks are only two inches long."

"As in *rooster?* or *manroot?*"

"Their sex. Two inches long, fully loaded. No bigger than my pinky finger."

"How would you know?"

"Because I know the literature: the bigger his gun, the smaller his sex. If you're afraid to go out in the boat without your gun, fine, we'll stay here, and have lunch with my sister and brother-in-law; either one of whom may, in fact, need to be shot before the day is out."

"Fine. No gun."

Petruchio took his place in the stern, with the punting-pole. Kate sat up front, facing him, paddle in hand, to help keep their tiny craft — "Cleopatra's tender," as she called it — in the middle of the channel, so that they didn't get hung up in the rushes. They pushed off from the dock.

Although the canal was only a few meters wide, being out on the water on a sunny June day seemed a pleasure, at first. Coming to a stone bridge, they laughed, they ducked. Petruchio found his rhythm. Getting sweaty, he took off his shirt.

"Sing me a few old chanteys you learned in school," said Kate.

"Don't know any," said Petruchio.

Shortly before the canal emptied into the River Brenta, Kate announced that she was Cleopatra, queen of Egypt, preparing to sail down the Nile from the legendary Valley of the Kings. While Pet wore himself out thrusting the quant against the muddy bottom, pushing the boat forward little by little, Kate supplied a running third-person commentary on the action: "*Illumined by the setting sun, the barge in which Cleopatra sat glowed on the water like a burnished throne. The deck was gold, purple the sails, and so perfumed that the very wind was love-sick with the fragrance. Antonio's pole, thrusting to the tune of flutes, made the water to follow faster, made amorous by his strokes. Antonio with thirsty eyes gazed on Cleopatra and swallowed as if he'd just crawled in from the desert.*"

"I seem to remember something like that in *The L**** *Word*," said Petruchio."

"All true romance is crafted from the same essential ingredients," explained Caterina.

Every other boat, every landmark, every change of scenery, suggested to Kate's imagination some new adventure.

"*...in flight from the enemy, Antonio and Cleopatra passed through a steep and rocky gorge, between high bluffs from which Octavius and his Roman soldiers, in their heavy chariots, could not follow. The lovers left their enemies behind, lost somewhere on the trackless mesa, high above the mighty Nile....*"

As they moved beyond the mouth of the Marsango into the River Brenta, Kate and Pet changed places. He put down the quant, sat on the middle bench, and rowed. She sat in the stern, facing him.

"*The soldier's pole is fallen!*" said Kate. "*But why does the world report the hero's limp? O slanderous world! My hero, like the hazel-tree, is straight and tender, and his nuts are sweeter than the kernels of mighty Caesar.*"

"Where did you get all this goodly speech?" asked Petruchio.

"From my own mother wit," she said.

The boat went faster now. Kate waved to the men on a fishing vessel and called out: "*You cannot frighten us, Pompey, with your sails. On land, you know how much we outnumber you, but what of that? We'll fight with you at sea. Why? Because you have dared us to it! And because with Cleopatra by his side, Antonio is invincible.*"

"That's not how I remember the story, exactly," said Petruchio.

Impatient with her husband's pedantic footnote on battles that went poorly for Marc Antony, Kate abruptly skipped ahead sixteen centuries. An elderly fisherman in a rowboat, casting a fly, was "a lawless band of Turkish corsairs," said Kate; his rowboat was an Ottoman galleon firing cannonshot at their passing and defenseless Christian vessel, a Spanish carrack. She spotted a whale (an overturned boat, half-sunk along the bank), and a number of exotic sea-monsters. A tempest arose. Giant billows began to crash against the sides of their boat, shaking its frail timbers. As Cap'n Petruchio struggled with the storm (a fresh June breeze), Bos'un Kate climbed the topmast, watching for land ahoy.

"Keep to starboard, Cap'n," said the bos'un. "We're approaching the mouth of the Amazon." Petruchio guided the punt to the west bank and into the headwater of the Brentella. (This eight-mile stretch of canal — a shortcut from the Brenta to the Bacchiglione — was to be the longest leg of their fifteen-mile boat-trip to Padua.) Having reached the New World, Kate's Spanish carrack became a birch-bark canoe. Fallen logs on the riverbank were not dolphins but hungry crocodiles; one of whom, observed Kate, had recently eaten a cannibal chief, leaving no scrap of him behind but a few scattered feathers. A peasant's hut on the port side was the cottage of the chief's orphaned daughter, a cannibal princess named Bradamante, who ate Spanish missionaries until the right boy came along. A straight and tedious stretch of canal, in Kate's running commentary, became a hellish white-water rapids, death swirling around every rock as savages lining the banks shot poison-tipped arrows at the two intrepid adventurers.

For Petruchio, a little punting on the canal, a little rowing on the river, and a return to Villa Marsango for lunch, would have been just about right; whereas a boat trip from the Marsango canal, to the Brenta, to the Brentella canal, to the Bacchiglione, to the Tronco Maestro and downtown Padua — with a new and breathless adventure every few minutes, from one tortuous romance or another — felt like way too much of an okay thing. The Venetian gondoliers made poling look easy. It wasn't easy. While Kate told stories, napped, sang popular lovesongs, and gushed over the beauty of the landscape, Petruchio fought the mud, the reeds, the bugs, the overhanging vegetation. As the evening wore on, the pushing became tiresome, perfunctory, custodial. No Marc Antony, he felt like a workingman, a servant, wearing himself out just to give Caterina a pleasant ride.

At sunset, they had not yet reached the Bacchiglione. Petruchio felt exhausted, even a bit irritable. The channel of the narrow Brentella was now dark and they still had a long way to go.

Caterina throughout the journey remained fresh and cool as a summer flower, her laughter competing with the chatter of the unseen songbirds that thronged the trees along both sides of the canal. "Massive cataract, ahead, Cap'n! Just ahead! Oh, no! Hold on, we're going over the edge!"

"I like the swans," said Petruchio, wearily. "So serene. I like the way they sit glowing in the moonlight, so still, so quiet."

"Those are no swans, Cap'n!" said Caterina. "Those are giant South American albino hippopotamuses, who threaten to crush our tiny canoe between their massive teeth!" Kate kept watch with a paddle resting across her lap. "You just steer," she whispered. "If they attack, I'll shoot them with my Amazon hippo-gun."

As the punt rounded a bend, one noisy and unhappy swan, with a flurry of wings, took flight to get out of the way. Kate gave a sudden little shriek and clutched at her heart.

"You okay, Kat?"

"Sí, sí," she said at last. "Flying hippo. Scared the *shit* outta me."

A mist hovered over the water, disappearing here and there as the punt passed through a tunnel of over-arching trees, blocking out the moonlight. In need of rest, Petruchio set down his punting-pole, fluffed up a cushion in the stern, and collapsed. He had been on his feet for hours now, taking breaks only to sit and row. Caterina gingerly moved from stem to stern, to sit beside him and snuggle. Petruchio put his arm around her. She leaned her head on his shoulder. It felt nice. For the next hour or two, their punt drifted lazily downstream, with only an occasional paddle to keep them out of the rushes. It was a clear night, the purple sky glittering with stars. An enormous moon illuminated their way.

"See how the treetops shudder softly," said Petruchio, "when kissed by the gentle wind." It was a line he had picked up from one of Caterina's romances. He thought she would like it. She did.

"Ah, Petruchio, it was on such a night as this that Ginevra la Strega smiled at grief, pining away for Peloso Vasaio. The shy maiden never told her love for the boy wizard, but let her secret, like a worm in the bud, feed on her damask cheek." Caterina smiled and waited, then elbowed her husband in the ribs. "Your turn."

"Oh. On such a night," said Petruchio, thinking fast, "on such a night ... did big Bruce Bandiera sit high on a desert plateau, and sigh his soul toward the army tents, where Elisabetta Rosso lay that night, with the very man who had sought to destroy him; and he also accidentally killed a bunny rabbit he had taken to be his friend." [1]

"On such a night," said Kate, "did Heloise, great with child, steal from her wicked uncle's house, there to dwell with Abelard's sister, so that her love would not be known."

"On such a night," said Petruchio, "was Barbara Pipistrella shot in the back, and paralyzed from the waist down, but Ricardo was still nice to her, after that."

"On such a night," said Kate, "did Perseus rescue naked Andromeda from the cruel chains of Cetus."

"On such a night," said Petruchio," "was Gwendolena Stacio wafted to her love, from a bridge, as Pietro Parker stood with webline in his hand, above the wild river banks."

"On such a night," said Kate, "Medea gathered the enchanted herbs that did renew old Aeson."

"Can we be a little less hoity-toity?" said Petruchio. "It annoys me a little, when you reference stories that no one knows. I never heard of 'Cetus' or 'old Aeson.' In fact, no one has."

---

[1] Petruchio here references *The Marvelous Tragedy of Bandiera,* a Renaissance tale that inspired *Hulk: Gray,* Book Three: "C is For Cry" (Marvel Comics: January 2004).

"Just two of the great ancient romances of the Western world," said Kate. "Like anyone has heard of Pietro Parker or Bruce Bandiera?"

"Just two of the great heroes of the graphic novella world, is all. Anyway, you win. Next game. Something different."

"It was not supposed to be a contest," said Kate.

"Whatever," said Petruchio.

A few minutes later, out of the blue, Kate said: "Poor Bianca. You have to feel sorry for her."

"Now you feel *sorry* for her?"

"I had a chat this morning with Fiametta. Bianca married Lucentio for the wrong reason."

"For his money."

"Well, that too, of course, but mostly, it was for his footman. When he first came to Padua, Lucentio swapped clothes and identities with Tranio, his drop-dead gorgeous valet."

"Why?"

"Just men being men, David-and-Jonathan thing, who knows? I suppose it was so that Lucentio could go gambling and drinking and wenching without being detected. At the awards ceremony, when Bianca set eyes on Tranio, handsome, stylishly dressed, she took him for a wealthy man. Lucentio, twice her age and dressed in a servant's livery, she mistook for the valet. Bianca fell in love — a first, for her — with Tranio; and Tranio, with her. Meanwhile, the real Lucentio fixed his eye on Bianca as the ideal trophy wife. He approached Papa to negotiate the prenuptials. So now it was like something out of a stage-comedy. Bianca could reject Lucentio's offer, and never see Tranio again. Or she could run away with Tranio, and never see Papa again, because he'd disown her, and Tranio would of course lose his job with Lucentio. Bianca's solution was to marry Lucentio, to be with Tranio. The footman gets the girl. The girl gets the money, plus her truelove, plus a well-groomed if somewhat superfluous husband. And the husband gets cuckolded. Bianca ought to have chosen romantic poverty, with Tranio. But oh, well."

Caterina yawned, adjusted the cushions, and curled up against her man, for a snooze. Petruchio longed to get up and start poling again, or row, but he could do neither with his wife napping on his shoulder. He thought he might go to sleep, but only his arm did. It tingled. When he moved it, Kate awoke. "Petruchio," she said, with sudden enthusiasm, "We have lost Villa Patria. It was burned by the Turks."

"Huh? You're dreaming."

"This is a romance that I'm writing in my head, tell me how you like it. All of the help have been slain, or captured and carried away as slaves to the Ottoman. Petruchio, you are a mail carrier, named Carlo."

"Or maybe Carlo is a soldier, a war hero returning to Italy after years at the front, fighting the Turks. But before he sees his girlfriend again, he'd like to visit the old fishing hole one last time. He grabs his pole and tackle box, he catches a few grasshoppers for bait, he — "

"Carlo is a mail carrier, come from Venice, to deliver a letter."

"Is there a good reason why he cannot be a war hero?"

"Yes, because I'm the one writing the story. So Carlo comes to the villa, on his horse, to deliver a letter, but he finds only a smoking ruins where the Villa Patria once stood. Searching for life among the rubble, he finds a girl hiding in the hollow cleft of an ancient oak tree. Her name is Rosa. Carlo and Rosa don't seem to be one another's type, but Rosa chooses to stay with him anyway, because there's just something about Carlo that seems, I don't know, sweet and innocent."

Petruchio interrupted. "But Rosa is *not* so very sweet and innocent, so when Carlo comes a-courting, she stabs him in the groin with a letter-opener, then she mothers him."

"Hush. Rosa's beautiful sister, named Angelica, has married a rich Russian lord and moved to Moscow, or some place like that. In her letter, Angelica apologizes for all the horrible things she always used to do to Rosa, who forgives her, of course, but Rosa now has bigger fish to fry, such as saving Italy from a secret invasion by the barbarian hordes. She must go to Padua by river, sound the alarm, warn the Italian people. Carlo does not want to do that. Carlo just wants to ride his horse around and deliver mail, because that's his job. Carlo says if he has to go anywhere, he will take the main roads; and when he gets home, he'll have a beer. He is reluctant to explore the river, which he fears may be unnavigable. But Rosa insists. So I stock the boat with supplies."

"Where'd you get the supplies? I thought the Turks killed everyone, and burned down your house."

"Vegetable garden. I gather food from the vegetable garden, also some strawberries, and I stock the boat, a ramshackle supply-launch called the Paduan Queen. The journey begins, but all is not well. Rosa is a free spirit. Carlo is a good Catholic who worries too much about respectable behavior, and his job; and also about such questions as: 'Where did the veggies come from?' At first, they cannot find much to talk about, so Rosa curls up with a good book. When Carlo discovers that she is reading a steamy romance, he gets jealous and throws the book into the river. They have a big fight. But they both feel just terrible, because they are falling in love. They each learn to appreciate the other's incredible uniqueness.

"The river starts getting pretty wild. White water rapids ahead! The current sweeps them suddenly downstream with breathtaking violence. It's a thrilling ride, it's scary, they nearly capsize! But when they reach the bottom, it's like, wow, that was right on the money! Rosa wants to keep going. But Carlo can't, he's tuckered, so they take a rest.

"They discover now that their boat has been damaged by the rocks. It leaks. They have lost their food and supplies in the raging turbulence. And Carlo's punting-pole has been splintered."

"Saw that one coming."

"...But they are still together, and still alive, which is all that matters to her, now. Rosa makes a splint for the quant while Carlo rests. We start out again. But as we move on, the river seems to be petering out. It's just like, I don't know — it becomes more like a *swamp,* or something. After a while,

Carlo loses his sense of direction. They get lost in the dense reeds. The tender gets stuck. So they strip to their underwear and jump into the water and sink in muck up to their knees. Their pale legs get attacked by creepy blood-sucking leeches, and Rosa has to pull them off herself because Carlo is too busy dealing with his own. They cannot get the boat moving again. They get cross with one another. They start arguing, even about little things. Carlo says: 'It's no use. We shall end up like all of the others who tried to come this way: we are doomed. Plus, I told you so.' But it's not possible to go back upstream. Besides, they have come too far. Rosa offers up a little prayer to Aphrodite — "

"Aphrodite?"

"Venus, the goddess of love. So Rosa prays, but nothing happens. The sun goes down. Lost and hopeless, they climb back into the stranded boat. They fall asleep, and wait for death.

"During the night, somewhere upstream, there is a huge rainstorm, which floods the river. When Carlo and Rosa awake, they find themselves floating right through downtown Padua, on the Tronco Maestro! So they think, 'Phew, we made it!' But then they see the heads of the enemy popping up all over the place, along the banks of the river, from windows, from rooftops, from church steeples. Though dressed like ordinary Italians, the barbarians have already taken over the city." Kate stopped speaking.

"And?" said Petruchio, after a pause. "That's *it?*"

"No. That is not *it*. I don't know what you mean, by *it*. But what do you think?"

"How does it end?"

"I thought you might have some ideas."

"I like it. But we haven't gotten very far. It's your story. Write chapter two, or pray to Aphrodite. Time to punt." Petruchio resumed his perch on the stern. Progress was difficult. The canal in this stretch was narrow and shallow and curtained with drooping branches. They came to a fallen tree limb. To get past it, Petruchio actually had to sit, and put down his pole, and fight his way through the branches and foliage.

His passenger, meanwhile, dozed off. He was okay with that. It was not Kate's slumber, but the rest of the honeymoon-travel package, that was driving him crazy. Not infrequently, his quant got stuck in the oozy bottom. On those occasions, he had to jerk the pole free from the mud, very quickly, or he'd have been dumped in the water as the boat, and his wife, continued downstream without him. Once he ducked too late or too little to avoid bumping his head on the arch of a stone bridge. That added a headache to his other miseries. The earth grew quiet but for the lapping of water against the prow, and the drip of his punt-pole. Each minute passed more slowly than the one before. Feeling blue and miserable, Petruchio at last sat down and got himself comfortable. A mosquito buzzed in his ear. He killed it, and fell asleep.

When he awoke, the punt was hung up in shrubbery off to the starboard side. Pet's right arm, and his hair, were tangled in Urtica nettles. The bugs were eating him up. Curiously, they seemed not to bother Caterina. "Some honeymoon," he muttered. "Ludicrous."

Worse than ludicrous. He felt a growing fear that he had lost his way. The Padua region since the twelfth century has developed a web of canals and irrigation ditches, with new ones being built all the time. Around Verona, it was just the Adige. Here in the Padova region, you could easily lose your bearings; especially late at night when the local fishers and pig-farmers were in bed and you had no one to ask for directions.

What kept him going was the knowledge that he had a special passenger on board, one whom he was sworn to protect. Which bugged him. If it were not for that, he'd have dragged the boat ashore and hired a ride back to Padua, by oxcart if necessary. Or, better yet, to Verona.

"I need to pee."

Kate's voice startled him. Petruchio had thought she was asleep. "Pull over," she said, "by that hawthorn grove."

"Here, in the middle of nowhere, in the middle of the night?"

"Yes, unless you want me to pee in the punt."

Petruchio guided the boat to a stretch of solid ground and helped his wife up the steep embankment.

"If I'm not back in five minutes," she said, "come get me."

Kate hurried into the grove.

Two minutes passed. Five. Six. Petruchio moored the punt to one of the many pseudacacias that lined the bank, and went to look for her. He half expected to find her gathering wildflowers or conversing with a frog; but Caterina was nowhere to be seen.

As he approached the hawthorn grove, Petruchio hesitated. From the woods came the sound of a man's voice, surly and gruff. That could not be good. He now cursed himself for having left his gun at the villa. Foraging, he found two fist-sized throwing-rocks and ventured into the wood, one stone in each hand, to investigate.

Then, there she was, standing in a brake beside the glowing embers of a dying campfire. With her were two men — very scary-looking outlaws. They appeared to be Barbary corsairs — feared Muslim pirates, sworn enemies of the Venetian state. Petruchio was astonished to see them so far inland. Both men wore baggy pantaloons, cinched at the ankles, and loose shirts bound with a colorful sash. The taller man, who was speaking, wore a white, ball-shaped turban, pinned in the front with a large jewel of some sort. The shorter man wore a fez. Both men had full beards.

Petruchio saw now that the taller fellow, in the white turban, held a gun; while the shorter one held a Turkish scimitar, a razor-sharp weapon known to be effective for turning Christian men into thin-sliced sandwich meats.

"Come, you beetch, say your prayers," said the turbaned fellow. He spoke Italian with a foreign accent that Petruchio could not place.

"Just tell me what you want," said Kate. "If it's money you need, I can get it.

"We don't care about the money, so much," said the Pasha. "We rape and murder. Eet's what we do."

"Not always in the same order," said the other. "Sometimes, we murder, then rape. Right, Pasha?"

"Shut up, Barbuto," said the Pasha. "And save your breath to cool your chai. Zees one ees mine. I found her first."

"Why would you murder me?" pleaded Caterina. "I have done you no harm. I have hurt no one, in all my life. I oppose cruelty to any living creature. Believe me, good sirs, I would not kill a mouse, or hurt a fly. I *did* step on a small snake once, against my will, and smooshed it, but I wept for it, afterward. I'm a good person. I have lived a good life. What use is my dead body?"

"Camping pillow," said Barbuto.

"Food for worms," said the Pasha, "My Tunisian brother-in-law runs a baitshop."

"Please let me live. You'll never see me again, I promise."

"We'll never see you again, either way."

Caterina was stalling — doubtless waiting for her knight to appear in shining armor. Her bravery, in debating with these heartless villains, quite astonished Petruchio. He felt proud of her. And he knew he would rescue her, or die trying.

Petruchio now stood within throwing range. He hurled the first rock into the woods off to the left, where it hit a tree and bounced noisily to the earth. Both scoundrels jumped. Petruchio then tossed the second rock off to his right. The unexpected disturbance startled the villains, putting them on edge. They jabbered at one another in their strange tongue.

Cupping a hand over his mouth, Petruchio bellowed, "Polizia! Drop your weapons, and put up your hands! You're surrounded!"

To Petruchio's amazement, the villains dropped their weapons and put up their hands. He barked a command to Kate. "Milady, return at once to the *soldiers* on the *barge*, and GO!

Kate turned and fled from the grove in the general direction of the canal. As she ran away, she shouted, "I love you!"

"Was she talking to us?" asked Barbuto. He shouted after her: "Love you, too! *Would* have!"

Now or never. Petruchio like a raging bull charged straight for the Pasha, who saw him coming and made a lunge for his gun, but Petruchio tackled the villain before he could get off a shot.

Their struggle lasted only a few moments. The Pasha's partner, Barbuto, grabbed both the gun and the sword. "Freeze," he said.

"Don't shoot," said Petruchio. "I surrender." But he knew they would certainly kill him. His only hope was that Kate had been able to make a safe getaway. He hoped that, someday, she would remarry; and tell her new husband, and her children, and grandchildren, the story of his heroic death. And he hoped the villains would kill him painlessly before they chopped or shot off any body parts.

"I had somesing going here weeth a pretty lady," said the turbaned Pasha, dusting himself off from the scuffle. "I don't appreciate Chreestian interference." The Pasha gently pinched Petruchio's cheek. "But you're cute enough," he said.

"He's got a real pretty mouth, don't he?"

"That's the truth," said the Pasha. "Compared to you."

"Just for the record," said Petruchio, "I am a man, and not a maiden, as you say."

"Aha! Barbuto, this is no budding girl. This here is a budding bardache, fair and fresh and sweet. Tell me, Barbuto, have you seen a fresher virgin? Such contest of roses, red and white, in his pretty face? His lips, as red as coral! his eyes, like stars, his cheeks, like peaches."

"Whatever works," said Barbuto, with a shrug. "But hurry up, because I got a itch to keel him."

Barbuto wandered about the grove, swooshing his scimitar through the air, as if for homicide practice. "I'm gonna chop hees fooking head off."

"Not yet."

"One leg?"

"Later," said the Pasha.

"Just his left hand, for starters?"

"Not yet." The Pasha scrambled to his feet. "On your knees, culo," he barked. Petruchio kneeled in the dirt. "Hands behind your head!" Petruchio folded his hands behind his head.

Petruchio said, "Can we talk this thing through, my friends?" (trying to be sociable).

"We ain't your friends," said Barbuto, still swooshing his sword, left and right.

"What are you doing here?" asked the Pasha.

"Headed down river," said Petruchio. "Little boat trip. Hope to reach Padua by daylight."

"Padua?" said the Pasha. "You better pray good, or you won't see Padua. It's daylight already, and I don't see Padua. Look how brightly shines the sun."

"The sun?" said Petruchio. "The moon shines still, it's not daylight yet."

"You call me a liar? Do it, Barbuto! Keel the son of a whore!"

"No, wait," cried Petruchio. "That *is* the sun that shines so bright!"

"What did he just say?" asked the Pasha. "Did zees fooking idiot say the moon is the sun?"

"That's what he said, Boss," said Barbuto. "Makes me want to keel him."

"Not yet," said the Pasha. He turned to Petruchio. "I say it is neither the sun nor the moon, but a large cue ball."

"I agree with you, sir," said Petruchio.

"Nay, then, you lie. It ees a round brie cheese."

"Then it is cheese," said Petruchio. "I don't care. It's none of my business."

"That's right, culo," said the Pasha. "My radical Muslim cheese is none of your Chreestian Italian business."

"This dialogue is boring," said Barbuto. "Let's cut to the part where we keel him."

"Not yet." The Pasha was not done humiliating his captive. "Hey, culo, you see that cloud, that's almost in the shape of a camel?"

"Yes, sir," said Petruchio.

"Well, I think it looks more like a weasel," said the Pasha.

"Very weasel-like," said Petruchio.

"Barbuto, does that cloud look like a weasel?"

"Don't look *nothing* like a weasel," said Barbuto. "That's a whale. Culo here is lying to us."

"Sir," said Petruchio, "whatever you think that cloud looks like — a dragon, a bear, a lion, a towered citadel, a pendant rock, a forked mountain, a blue promontory with trees upon it, or a pig's ass — that's what I think, too. I acknowledge your power over me. And now, sir, I should like your permission to depart, if it please you. I am sorry to have intruded, I regret having given offense, and I beg your pardon for my mistake."

"See, zeess here woods is *our* woods," said the Pasha. "That moonshine is *our* moonshine. And this canal is *our* canal. It don't go to Padua."

"And you said this one goes where, again?" asked Petruchio.

"Barbuto, did I say this fooking canal goes somewhere?"

"No, Pasha, you never said nothin' like that. No man's reputation is safe with him. He dies."

"Not yet," said the Pasha.

"Can we talk?" asked Petruchio.

"No. Zeess canal stays right here," said the Pasha. "Find your own goddam canal."

"I didn't take it anywhere," said Petruchio. "I'm just a little lost."

"Looks like you may be *way* the hell lost," said Barbuto.

"Well, I have quite a long journey ahead of us, gentlemen, I guess I'll just push on. We're not looking for trouble. Take my money," said Petruchio, "but spare my life."

"How much money you got?" asked the Pasha.

"What I have on me is yours," said Petruchio. "I have but little. Take that, plus these poor garments, and you behold all my wealth."

"Give us what you've got," said the Pasha, "and we'll love you like a gentleman."

"Deal," Petruchio, with a sigh of relief. He untied his money pouch from his belt and handed it to the Pasha.

"Now drop your breeches," said the Pasha.

"Drop? What?"

"Gonna take your money, and your poor garments, like you promised, and zen we gonna love you like a gentleman. Deal's a deal."

"I call halfies," said Barbuto.

"Which half do you want? Top or bottom?"

"You take the back," said Barbuto. "I'll take the front. But if he bites me, I swear I'll keel him."

"Yes, if he bites you," said the Pasha, "keel him."

"I think," said Petruchio, "we may have had a slight cultural misunderstanding — "

"Shrink not, but down with 'em," said the Pasha.

"But — why?"

"First, we love you. Then, we castrate you. It's what we do. We're famous for it. Infamous, rather. I'm surprised you didn't know."

"Surely, you jest! What can you do with a man's testicles?" inquired Petruchio.

"Eat them."

"You wouldn't!"

"We would," said the Pasha, "and do. We cook them first, of course. They're quite tasty, in a zesty béchamel sauce, you'd be surprised. Drop your breeches."

"You'll have to kill me first."

"Death before dismemberment?"

"Exactly."

"Relax, mate," said the Pasha. "No one's gonna castrate you. I said that to test your valor."

"He was toying with you," explained Barbuto. "It was a *joke*."

"That's right. But I had you worried, there, didn't I, pretty boy?" said the Pasha. "Muslim terrorists gonna cut off your testicles. Muslim terrorists gonna eat 'em, like meatballs. Ha ha ha! We were just messing with your cultural stereotypes, dude."

The two villains had a good laugh together, at Petruchio's expense. Petruchio laughed, too, partly from relief, and partly to help facilitate a sense of camaraderie. "Heh. Well, I'd best be moving on, now."

"Not yet," said the Pasha. "You still haven't dropped your breeches."

"What, now?"

"Will you stop *worrying*, for chrissake?" said Barbuto, irritably. "What, do we have to draw you a picture? We *ain't* gonna cut off your friggin' balls. How many times does the Pasha have to tell you that eet was a *joke*? We're just gonna have us some buzerones, then you're free to go."

"Oh, no thanks. I'm not really into that."

"You won't be."

"I refuse," said Petruchio.

"Death before dishonor?"

"Exactly."

"He chooses *death* before *dishonor*, Barbuto."

"Alphabetically speaking?"

"Good point, Barbuto. Death to the infidel! But first, some buzerones."

"No," said Petruchio. "Absolutely not."

"Is your gun ready, Barbuto?"

"Ay, ay, sir. Loaded and cocked."

"Look, culo," said the Pasha, angry now, "you get naked before I count to ten, or Barbuto will have to shoot you, and zen he'll chop you as small as meat to the pot. He toss you into the canal, in bite-sized choonks. If you ever reach Padua, eet will be on a dinnerplate, as a fillet of catfish."

The Pasha counted slowly: "One...two....three.... Change your mind yet, you dumb dago?"

Petruchio looked the devil straight in the eye, slapped his left palm inside his right elbow, and jerked his fist upward, in blistering defiance. "Mille cazzi nel tuo culo," he said. "Ma vai a cagare."

"....Seven....eight....nine... Have you any last words, by which you wish to be remembered?"

"Yes," said Petruchio boldly. "Omnia vincit amor! I love you, Kate."

"Ten!"

BAM! At the sound of the blast, Petruchio's first surprise was that he felt no pain. His second surprise was to see Barbuto drop the gun to the ground and stagger about, clutching his stomach. He was bleeding. After some frenzied six or seven steps, whirling about, he fell.

The Pasha quickly snatched Barbuto's gun, and the scimitar, and ran off with both weapons into the woods, shouting some gibberish, Algerian cursewords, perhaps.

BAM! a second shot was fired, somewhere in the dark. Diving for cover, Petruchio hid in the underbrush, and waited.

The ensuing silence could not have lasted more than a few minutes, though Pet said later that it seemed an eternity.

Hearing footsteps, Petruchio peeked through the branches — and beheld what he took at first for an apparition. Stepping calmly into the hawthorn brake, all aglow in the moonlight like an angel from Heaven, was his bride, Caterina Miniola Ramusio di Baptista, in her white tennis dress, holding a pistol and blowing smoke off the end of the barrel.

"Kate?"

"Sì, Signore."

Rising to greet her, Petruchio stood before her, speechless.

"Thank God, you're safe," she said.

"It wasn't just God," said Pet, dusting himself off. "The Lord had ground support. Where'd you learn to handle a gun like that?"

"Nothing special about the gun," said Kate. "Seen one, seen 'em all."

"No, I mean, where'd you learn to shoot like that?"

"Not to brag, but I've been in girls' shooting competitions since I was six years old. My second bullet hit that turbaned Turk right between the eyes. Dead as a ducat. How's his pal doing?"

"Not well. Still breathing, I think."

Kate strolled over to Barbuto, and kicked him. "Nope. Dead. I guess he messed with the wrong lovers." She bent over and picked up the man's fez, which lay in the dirt, and dusted it off, for a souvenir.

"You saved my life, Kat."

"You saved mine first. You tackled the danger, unarmed, while I just hid myself in the woods, with the gun."

"I thought I was a goner." He was struck now by another thought entirely. "Not to complain," he said, "but if you're a crack shot, why did you wait so long before shooting?"

"First, I prayed to see deliverance."

"Well, that explains a lot," said Petruchio, somewhat grumpily.

"Plus, I had to load."

"But where'd the gun come from?"

"It's yours, honey! I knew you wouldn't need it, so before we left the house I strapped it to my leg, beneath my camica. Just in case, you know. But then, we *did* need the gun and I couldn't get to it, not until you with your dauntless courage gave me the opportunity to run away."

The horror of one man's bloody corpse, and another one off in the woods somewhere, left Petruchio feeling a bit jumpy. Unsteady on his legs, he sat down upon a log. Kate sat beside him. "I've got the munchies," she said, somewhat too cheerfully. "Would you mind running back to the tender, to grab our picnic hamper?"

Petruchio looked as white as a canal swan. "How can you think about that, right now?"

"Um, because I'm *hungry?*"

"Jeeze, Kat. You are one tough woman."

"And you are one tough man." She handed him the pistol. "Here. Thanks."

"I thought you don't believe in guns."

"I said a real *man* doesn't need one. And now, I don't need one, either, because I have a real man. How many husbands would rescue their wife, single-handed, unarmed, if she were to be kidnapped by pirates? That was the most incredibly romantic thing that ever happened to me. Now I can I die happy."

"What are you talking about?"

"Padua's courts never show mercy to female homicides. I expect to be tried and hanged, for having shot those evil bastards."

"No, you won't. I shall say that I am the one who killed them. Let them hang me instead."

"Petruchio?"

"Yes?"

"I love you, Petruchio."

"I love you, too."

Petruchio's expression was grim. Caterina seemed more chipper. "Anyway, help is not far off," she said, cheerfully.

"How's that?"

"As the crow flies, we're just three miles from home. Around the next bend of the canal is the Bacchiglione, with a straight shot to Padua. Besides which, my Papa owns this land, these woods. His players rehearse at the Fattoria di Sotto, hard by. I very recently saw two of them perform, in this very grove. Guillaume, Bertramo! Stand forth, and take a bow!"

As Petruchio watched in open-jawed wonder, the Pasha stepped forth from the woods, his stage-beard in hand and no bullet-hole in his forehead. Barbuto then leapt to his feet. Standing side-by-side, the two men took a bow. Caterina jumped up from her seat on the log and applauded their performance. Petruchio jumped up from his seat and shouted "Freeze." He held the two actors at gunpoint. His arm was shaking.

"Relax, honey," said Caterina. "The gun is not loaded. It never was. Neither was theirs. Just powder, no bullets."

"But ... the blood!" said Petruchio.

"Oh, that's just your usual theater-mix of arrowroot and red tempera powder," explained Caterina, cheerfully. "The gun fires, the sword stabs, the victim clutches his stomach and squishes the eggshell. Looks like real blood, but it washes right out, with warm soapy water. Stage trick. They do it all the time. Guillaume, Bertramo: Terrific! Very scary show! I'm thrilled!"

"We are your humble servants, milady," said the Pasha, bowing like a courtier. "It was your script that deserves praise. We merely improvised."

"Really, you liked it? Because I had *so* little time to cobble something together. I just kind of threw it together, from scraps I've picked up here and there."

Petruchio was not smiling, which Caterina mistook for puzzlement. Bubbling with enthusiasm, she explained: "These two very talented actors, Pet, belong to my father's company. I knew you would want to meet them, and see them in action. Allow me to introduce you. This is Guillaume Ragnatela, who played the Pasha; and Bertramo Mostardino, who played Barbuto. Guillaume, Bertramo, please meet my love, my hero, my white knight, my Petruchio — the bravest man in Italy."

"You're beautiful, man," said Guillaume.

"And as wise as he is beautiful!" added Kate.

"Culo carino!" said jealous Bertramo.

"Great job, fellas," said Caterina. "I hope that Pet and I didn't keep you waiting here too terribly long," she said. "It was a long paddle, from the Marsango."

"Not at all. We arrived a bit early, built a nice campfire, and rehearsed."

"Swing by my father's house tomorrow, in Padua," said Kate, "and I'll see that you get your check." They bowed, and thanked her. "Oh, and I still want to do the Antony and Cleopatra sketch for Petruchio," she said. "It will have to wait for a day or two. Maybe Wednesday evening. Say, seven-ish?"

The actors nodded. "Sounds good."

Caterina never felt happier. She was proud of her husband, for his heroism. She was proud of her "reality play" (as she called it), which had gone splendidly. And she was proud of her own convincing performance as the damsel in distress. She turned to Petruchio, to take his hand, and give it a squeeze — only to discover that he was sulking.

"Are you crazy?" Petruchio said. His tone was more irritable than Kate could have predicted. "I see your knavery," he said. "This was to make an ass of me."

"No! a hero!"

"Lady, you are out of your mind."

What really devastated Caterina was the way that he said, "Lady, you are out of your mind." So cold, so icy. So insensitive!

My readers will pardon me for omitting the next quarter-hour of dialogue, a screaming match. Both Caterina and Petruchio said bitter things that they would later regret.

[* * * * *]

WHAT eventually turned Petruchio's wrath and Kate's wounded feelings into mutual adoration was Caterina's sincere and contagious belief that her man's heroism in the hawthorn brake was as good as the real thing; *better*, even. From Kate's point of view, Petruchio had proved himself to be the quintessence of true love and masculine honor. Her unstinting praise and adoration began to have a salutary effect on his self-confidence.

"Don't you see it, Pet? Outnumbered, outgunned, you dared to rescue me, taking no thought for your own safety. Incredibly, recklessly, courageous! Plus, who these days would choose death before dishonor? You would! So idealistic! And even after the seeming villains were slain, you chose to be hanged for my crime — to suffer dishonor *and* death so that my honor, my life, might be spared. So incredibly romantic. Pet," she cooed, "You are absolutely, positively, the most *amazingly* scrumptious man. You are my rock."

As the lovers' quarrel subsided into tenderness, Caterina noticed that Petruchio was favoring his right leg. "Honey," she said, "are you okay? Were you hurt, in the scuffle?"

"Little scraped up. Little bruise, maybe."

"Oh, my," said Kate, alarmed. "The way you collided with that pirate, and his terrible scimitar! They should not have brought a real sword. Pray God your leg is not half cut off."

"Seriously, it's— "

Kate cut off his speech, unwilling to hear him modestly understate his heroic self-sacrifice. Before Pet himself could say "it's nothing," or "just a scratch," she stopped his speech with a kiss.

It was a good kiss; their best, so far. Passionate. So full of desire, so full of infinite need to be together, to be one flesh. This was the kiss that Ulysses, returning from the horrors of Troy, received from Penelope. This was the kiss Marc Antony received from Cleopatra, after the Battle of Actium. This was the kiss Tristan received from Iseult after being wounded by the poisoned lance of jealous King Mark. And this was a kiss that caused Pet to turn blue before Kate released him for a breath of air.

Petruchio suddenly jerked himself away. His eyes grew wide. "Phew." He was panting.

"You okay?"

"Oh, yeah. Just needed some air, is all. If that's what they call 'delicious torment,' I want more of it."

"The field is won," said Kate. "Take me!"

Bertram, the shorter actor, cleared his throat as a gentle reminder that spectators were present. Caterina scolded them.

"Guillaume! Bertramo! Why have you not gone home? May I not plant one passionate kiss on the sensuous lips of this high-spirited innocent, without an audience? We would like some privacy, please."

"Yes, milady. You had not yet dismissed us."

"You're dismissed!"

The two actors hurried off, taking the canal tow-path toward nearby Fattoria di Sotto.

Caterina called after them. "See you in Padua! And don't forget Wednesday evening!" She turned again to Petruchio. "Darling," she said, "Your leg-wound may be dressed when we get home. But I won't."

"Won't what?"

"Be dressed. Come, let's get out of here.. True love waits, they say, but if it waits much longer, I swear to God I'll have to settle for losing my undies and virginity in the back seat of my father's boat before we get home tonight

• • •

VII. *Punto Culminante*

AROUND THE VERY NEXT BEND, the canal merged into the Bacchiglione, as Kate had predicted. Here, the water became suddenly deeper; the current, more swift; and Petruchio's rowing, more vigorous. Caterina sat in the stern, with her knees drawn to her chin, thrilled to watch his powerful body at work. Keeping a steady pace, Petruchio hoisted the dripping oars like angel wings; lunged toward her, his strong hands clenched on the grips; then arched backward into the pull. Again. Again. Again. Each time he thrust the oars into the water, the boat surged forward. Such rhythm, such grace, such strength.

Such cold water.

"Sorry, love." Missing a beat, Petruchio arched into the pull prematurely. The oars slapped at the water, showering Kate from both sides.

"It's okay," she said. "I needed that." She curled up in the cushions, and pulled the blanket over her to stay warm, and fell asleep. When she awoke, they had reached downtown Padua. It was nearly midnight. Kate felt refreshed. Petruchio did not.

Signore Baptista's palace at the west end of Via Patriarcato had its own docking platform on the Tronco Maestro, with stone steps leading up from the water's edge. It took a few minutes to get their things unloaded, and to hoist the punt up onto the embankment.

Weary but triumphant, Petruchio planted his feet on the landing, one fist upon each hip, and stood tall. Their ordeal was over, at last. Now that his bride was brought safely home, a part of him just felt incredibly strong, and vibrant, and manly. And that part of him was throbbing again.

Feeling the chill night air on his sweaty torso, Petruchio threw on his shirt. It was wrinkled and damp. He left the shirttails untucked.

Kate, still a little sleepy, rummaged in the satchel and pulled out his cloak.

"I won't be needing that," said Petruchio.

"Oh, good," said Kate, and tossed his gun into the water.

"I meant the cloak."

"Oh. But you might need the cloak, up top. Our property, along the dike, tends to be a little dampish."

He donned the cape and hooked the clasp.

"You look gallant," said Caterina, sincerely. "What about all this other stuff?"

"Leave it. Or throw it in the river. I never want to see it again."

Kate left it. All of it. The cushions. The blanket. The quant and the oars. The picnic hamper. Even the satchel, which contained her make-up kit and some money. Perhaps the servants would come for it. Perhaps it would be stolen. She didn't care. All she needed was her man. Arm in arm, she and Petruchio climbed the stone steps to the garden behind her father's palace.

Up top, at the Palazzo del Ramusio, a party was winding down. Baptista's rear portico remained bright with colored lanterns. Bottles of wine stood open, mostly empty now. Servants came in and out, clearing away dishes and glasses. No guests remained except the few who were staying over.

"Buongiorno!" Hortensio Lando was the first to spot Petruchio and Kate coming up the walk. Beside him was a stately dame, in her early fifties, elegantly dressed.

"What's the occasion?" inquired Caterina.

"What's not to celebrate?" explained Hortensio. "Your father's retirement. Your sister's birthday. Lucentio's wedding. Your wedding. Soon, the birthday of St. Anthony. A full moon. Whatever. Cheers." The woman beside him pinched his buttocks. He very nearly spilled his wine. "Oh, yes, it's also my wedding party. Come meet Isabella, my bride. Some few hours ago, she and I were committed to one another. In fact, we still are. A scurvy priest, by the authority of the Venetian state, has committed us to the bonds of holy matrimony, without chance of parole."

Joining Hortensio and his bride at the banister now, to greet the newly arrived pilgrims, were Signore Baptista;

Fiametta, his housekeeper; Bianca and Lucentio; Tranio, a footservant; and Tabatha, the cook.

The low ground nearest the dike's edge remained soggy. "Come around to the front," called Baptista. "Damn mess, this time of year."

"No problem," said Petruchio. Unclasping his cloak, he gave it a quick shake as a toreador might do, and spread it on the ground. He bowed low. "For your convenience and pleasure, m'lady," he said.

"Thanks, hon." Taking Petruchio's arm, Signora Caterina Miniola Ramusio di Baptista walked dry-shod over the velvet cloak and continued on toward the house, without looking back.

"Did he just do that?" said Lucentio.

"I would not have believed it by report," said Hortensio.

"Sweet Jesus," said Isabella, clutching her silk hanky with both hands against her bosom.

"Dear Lord," said Lucentio, "if ever I am brought to such a silly pass as that, for a woman, may my cazzo fall off."

"Luche, dear," said Bianca, "If you fail to do as much and more, for your wife, at the first opportunity, may your cazzo fall off."

The cloak remained on the wet ground like a forsaken beach blanket. No one seemed to think of retrieving it but Hortensio, an itinerant scholar who earned less in a year than the cost of a velvet cloak; nor had he ever owned one. Glancing down at the yard below, Hortensio had the look of a tender-hearted child who has just beheld the tragedy of a baby fawn torn by wolves.

The two weary pilgrims, meanwhile, joined the party as if nothing extraordinary had occurred. Petruchio collapsed in a chair and would have fallen asleep but for Caterina, who launched into a rhapsody of their honeymoon journey from Villa Marsango. Gushing with enthusiasm, she spoke of fertile vineyards and bright gardens with sinuous rills, where butterflies flitted and birds sang; and of the mighty Brenta, enraged with the spring flood, its turgid waters sweeping their vessel along through an otherwise serene landscape of humble thatched-roof cottages and stately pleasure domes made more golden by the setting sun. She spoke of being swallowed into the open jaws of the snaky Brentella, of probing its dark entrails, far from home, past Limena, past the windswept ruins of Colmelloni castle. She spoke of getting caught past sunset in nearly impenetrable vegetation; and how a fierce swan appeared out of the darkness to attack them, to protect its young; but then the giant bird saw Petruchio standing tall and the thing flew away like a scared chicken, it was just so funny. How Pet, on the canals, with his powerful thrusts, zoomed past the other boats as if their punters had mere straws, or swizzle sticks, for a quant; and how, when he rowed, Pet drove the oars with such bullcalf force that the turbulent waters splashed skyward, and got her bottom all wet and she didn't even care but said, "Splash me again, good sailor, splash me again."

In the retelling, Caterina omitted unsavory details and added a few savory ones. The gist was that she adored her big, strong, intelligent, considerate, and heroic husband; that Pet was simply the most wonderful man on earth; and that, while life may yet offer some compensation for women who were not married to him, she did not really know what that could be.

Before Kate's story was over, Petruchio had revived and was sitting up again, with excellent posture.

Lucentio the while sipped his wine, checked his nails, and rolled his eyes, looking bored. He had seen Petruchio before, at the wedding; and he was less impressed with him for a brother-in-law than Caterina was with him, for a husband. The cost of a velvet cloak was nothing. But he would not have his wife's sister's husband raising the bar on spousal expectations with foolish displays of abject gallantry. Plus, he felt suspicious: it did not compute that a boy like Petruchio, who appeared to have no real earning power, would pull such a stunt as throw a silk cloak in the mud, unless to curry favor with Baptista. "What's next, Poochi?" said Lucentio, "For that's your name, I hear. Will you write love poetry to your wife, and submit yourself to be published?"

"I have the inspiration," said Petruchio, "but not the talent."

"What, to see yourself bound in leather, and sold in gilt sheets, for a lady's pleasure?"

"I should like to write poems of my soulmate every day of the year, every year of my life," said Petruchio (laying it on a bit thick), "but if my words are seen by her eyes only, and forgotten with my death, I am content."

"Most women would rather receive a blank check than blank verse, would be my guess," said Lucentio.

"And your guess would be wrong," said Isabella.

Lucentio would not let it go. "Shall a gentleman throw his wardrobe, or himself, upon the ground as a floormat? I think not."

Caterina, sotto voce so that her father did not hear, uttered a word of indelicate counsel ("*Fottiti!*") that does not translate well from Italian to English; in which she abruptly suggested that Lucentio, for all she cared, could go perform an act that is not anatomically possible.

"Don't get your drawers in a wedgie," snipped Bianca at her sister. "Oh, I forgot, Petruchio is wearing them. Petruchio, don't get my sister's drawers in a wedgie."

"Be nice to him, Bianca," said Lucentio. "The sweet Pooch is composing a sonnet in his head. Hurry, Petruchio, it seems you may be just minutes away from having your first period."

"He is all the man I'll ever need," said Kate. "What have you ever done, to defend your love, Lucentio?"

"Don't have to defend it," said Lucentio. "We're married, it's legal."

"I mean, to defend Bianca."

"Oh, her. Why, I defend my wife all the time. Just this morning, someone said, 'Hey Lucentio, I think your wife's getting fat,' and I defended her, I said she wasn't. Ha ha ha. Get me a beer, will you Bianca? This one's almost gone."

Bianca made no reply — which amazed Caterina. Obediently, Bianca walked inside to fetch her husband a beer. Moments later, she poked her head back out the door and barked an order to young Tranio, Lucentio's gorgeous valet: "You! boy! Come assist us. We're having some trouble in here, with the cork." Tranio got up and hurried inside. He did not come back outside, for a while. Neither did Bianca.

When the young Mrs. Lucentio finally returned with the beer and sat down, Kate announced a contest: "We ladies love to be praised," she said, "but not all husbands have the wit or courage to do it. I should therefore like to hear each of these men speak well of his wife, in twenty-five words or less. We women shall judge which husband is most fit. If each man receives one vote, we shall have a second round. Who will begin?"

"Good night, children," said Baptista. "I need to retire." He shuffled off to bed.

"Come," said Kate, "who will begin?"

"That will I," said Lucentio. Without turning toward Bianca, he chugged the last swig of beer, smacked his lips, set down the bottle, and announced: "My wife has wavy hair, sexy eyes, rosy cheeks, coy smile, slender neck, nice rack, good curve, small hands, long legs, and....Is that it?"

"...a tight unit," added Tranio. He chuckled. The jest was not fully appreciated, even by Bianca. "Just kidding, boss," said Tranio. "What would I know? I'm a footman."

"Anyway, I think she's great," said Lucentio. He sipped his drink, cool, nonchalant, contented that he had spoken eloquently enough of Bianca's essential virtues to receive at least one vote, if not all three.

"I should hope I can do better than that, when praising my Isabella," said Hortensio.

"Come, husband," said Isabella, "ram your eulogy in my ears."

"Isabella," said Hortensio, "you are a woman of the highest intellect, the most formidable memory, a great repository of wise sayings, and your fruit tarts are delicious."

"Thank you husband. Keep talking like that, and you may have a special treat tonight, in bed."

"Oh, goodie," said Hortensio. "I love hot tarts."

"And maybe some hot love, too," said Isabella, as a tease.

"Never mind that," said Hortensio. "Once a week is enough, for that. I can't be doing it constantly, at my age. But a blueberry turnover would be exquisite."

"Vai a cagare, darling," said Isabella, and kissed him. Hortensio was not offended.

"O, you are novices!" said Petruchio, to Hortensio and Lucentio. "To his wife, a man should bare his heart."

Lucentio, inspecting his nails again, said, "Say, Pooch, what's that you're wearing on your sleeve? Oh, never mind, I see it's just your little heart on there, for your wife, of all people."

Ignoring Lucentio, Petruchio pushed back his chair, took Kate's hand, and dropped to one knee: "Caterina, my love, my angel, you are perfection. Language itself is not rich enough, nor life long enough, to say how much I love you."

"Well, I guess *that* contest is over," said Isabella.

"Not so fast," said Kate. "I shall not cast my vote for Pet until I know what he would say if we had never met."

"My darling," said Petruchio (still on one knee, gazing into her face), "if we had never met, I would sail unto the farthest corners of the earth. I would explore the deepest jungle. I would ascend the highest peak. I would mount unto the roof of heaven itself, to find you, Kat. Truly, I think it would be an easy leap to rescue pretty Caterina from the pale-faced moon, or to dive into the deep where fathom-line could never touch the ground and to pluck up Caterina by the locks, if, by reaching you, I might win your love and respect."

"That was a helluva lot more than twenty-five words," said Lucentio.

"And if I scorned your lovesuit?" said Caterina.

"Then I would pitch a tent below your bedroom window, and there keep watch for my lost soul until you came to the window. I'd write pop tunes of unrequited love and sing them loud even in the dead of night." Petruchio stood, and stretched his arms wide. "I would call out your name to the echoing hills and teach the howling wind itself to sigh, 'Ohhhh, Caterina!' You would not rest on sea or land, until you pitied me."

"Phew," said Isabella. "Works, for me."

"Stalker behavior," said Lucentio. "Sick."

Petruchio said, "Kiss me, Kate."

Caterina did not just kiss. She met Petruchio in mid-air, an attacking octopus, wrapping her arms about his neck and her legs around his waist. He teetered, off-balance, falling back against the wall for support. When he opened his mouth to speak, she opened hers to meet it; and she silenced him with a lingering, open-mouthed kiss in which you just knew there was some tongue-action going on. At last they parted, with a clamorous smack.

"You've been a bad boy," said Caterina. "Go to my room! Time out — for a little time, in! Oh, *god*, I love this man."

"And now, if you will excuse us, ladies and gentlemen," said Petruchio, "my wife and I have some things we need to do, upstairs. Come, Kat, let's to bed."

• • •

DROPPING from her lover's arms, Caterina hit the floor running. "I'll race you!" she said, giggling. In a flash, she was inside the house and taking the back staircase two steps at a time, with Petruchio at her heels in ardent pursuit. Kate was first through the bedroom door. Petruchio closed the shut behind them.

"Where are you?"

"Here."

"Too dark."

Groping about, Petruchio missed Kate but found the doorknob; whereupon he opened it, and fetched a lantern from the corridor.

The intermission lasted a few minutes as the lovers lighted the bedroom candles. Then, they recreated the moment, beginning from the top of the staircase. Kate ran into the room, laughing. Petruchio pursued her, and closed the door behind them. Kate locked it.

"Ah, that's much better," said Petruchio.

"Come, Pet." Taking his hand, Kate led him to the foot of the bed. She pulled back the curtains, and commanded: "Let us dive and bellyflop, on the count of three: *One ... two ... three!*"

The young lovers launched themselves onto the mattress, landing together with a crash. The headboard slammed into the wall. The bedframe held. Their bodies became hotly, breathlessly, intertwined — a greedy embrace that might have looked to an outside observer like the desperate flailing of two swimmers in trouble and about to go down.

Kate stopped to pull something from her hair. "What's this?"

A sheet of stationary paper, folded in thirds, had been left on her pillow. It was marked: "IMPORTANT." Kate tossed it aside.

"Shouldn't we open it?" asked Petruchio.

"No, probably just a love-letter from one of my old boy-friends," she said, with a grin.

Petruchio snatched the letter but Kate wrested it from him, tearing the paper almost in half. She flattened it and began to read aloud: "*Beloved daughter Caterina...* Crap. It's from my father. *Pardon the brevity of this letter....* That'll be the day. If my father's *life* depended on his ability to say 'pass the salt' in twenty-five words or less, he'd choke. Kate resumed reading:

...At age 70, one hasn't the privilege to go on for as long one may wish. You're a grown woman now, Kate. I'm proud of you. I recognize that you and I have had — still do have — some issues. I know I was not a great father. When your mother died, I was not strong enough to bear the loss. My daughters — a motherless toddler and a newborn baby — were placed in the care of others, and were thereby made fatherless as well. I wish I had it to do over. Since that is not possible, I wish only to be forgiven.

"I can't read this," said Kate, suddenly irritable. "You read it. I'm sick and tired of his bloody excuses. And he *always, always, always,* chooses the worst possible moment to get in the way. This being a case in point." Petruchio continued:

In my retirement, at the villa, I intend to take strolls, plant a vegetable garden, establish a vineyard, go fishing, continue my study of geography. Perhaps I shall do some painting. I

*should like also to visit my two daughters, if they will have me;
and I hope I shall live to see my grandchildren. Your father in
his old age shall not be a vexation to you...*

" —My father has never *not* been a vexation," said Kate.
"The man was *born* to vex me. That's what he *does:* vex.
He's worse than a Barbary pirate. Almost. Anyway. Put it
down. I'll read it later."

Petruchio flipped the paper over once, glanced at the word
"IMPORTANT," and resumed reading:

*...Your father in his old age shall not be a vexation to you.
Fiametta will live with me at the villa. If I should dote, or
become feeble, she will care for me. Ours is not an intimate
relationship, but we love each other. And even though Bianca
treats her poorly, Fiametta has always loved you girls as if you
were her own daughters.*

*Which brings me to the point: I am aware, Kate, that you
dislike everything about our home in Padua — my design, my
furniture, my geography books, my art collection, even the
street address. So you will perhaps reject the gift I offer: if
you and Petruchio can content yourselves to remain in Padua,
you shall have the house rent-free for as long as I live; and I
shall bequeath the property to you when I die. Who knows?
perhaps some of your distaste for the house, and for Via
Patriarcato, will dissipate when the patriarch is gone ....*

"You don't like this house?" asked Petruchio, amazed. "I
love this house. What's not to love? This house is a palace.
He's *giving* it to us!"

"It's starting to grow on me," said Kate.

*...The street address, I cannot change; but I have renamed the
property after your mother: henceforth it shall be called the
Palazzo del Miniola. Nor shall I be offended if you redecorate
the interior.*

*I am leaving professional life with my affairs in good order.
My investments and rents can be capably managed without my
residence in the city. And yet, the future management, per-*

haps the very survival, of my theater troupe, remains up in the air. Signore Baptista's Men — and woman — had a banner year, thanks in part to your sister. Bianca has now made her exit. But other young female stars wait in the wings, and the company will doubtless prosper, even as Italy's national theater grows. As principal shareholder, I have been offered a substantial sum — one hundred thousand crowns — for my stake in the company. The thought occurs to me, however, that you may wish to have some say in that.

Petruchio has expressed interest in the theater. And I am aware that you, Kate, have been writing plays (albeit without my encouragement), for some time. If it please you, I will assign to Petruchio, as a wedding gift, my controlling share in Signore Baptista's Men, Ltd.; on this condition only, that he must do a better job than I have done in supporting your goals both personal and artistic. Perhaps I will live to see a romantic comedy written by my daughter and produced by my son-in-law. I would like that, very much.

Your sister, as you know, leaves tomorrow for Pisa, or as soon as her things are fully packed. After which, I expect never to see her again, in this life. I do wish you girls were more fond of one another. You say I never treated you the same way. That may be true. I know you think I always loved Bianca best. That is not true. Bianca has always had a fierce drive to succeed. She got that from me. You inhabit an ethereal world of romance. You got that from your mother.

Bianca is my star. But you, Caterina, are my angel.

As you know, it is Bianca's birthday. It was seventeen years ago today that your mother died. But she did not altogether perish. As you stand before me, Kate, in your gown of red silk and white polkadots, with that happy smile on your face and a bow in your hair, the father who failed you beholds, in you, a beloved image of the mother who left us, too soon.

Your beauty, Kate, your imagination, your wit, your goodness. These are gifts that you inherited from Topa Miniola — your dear mama, my sweet Minnie.

Such gifts as your father is able to give, he wishes you may receive as well: with my love.

Papa

P.S. Please inform me, as soon as you can, of your decision.

The prospect of a career in the entertainment industry, with dependable income; the thought of commanding his own dramatic company, a team that included some of Italy's most celebrated actors and writers; the idea of dwelling in one of Padua's finest mansions, with his mother and aunt conveniently situated a hundred kilometers away in the old homestead; these thoughts convinced Petruchio, down to his very toes, that his future with Caterina was a bright one. "Cool," he said. But when he looked up, he saw that Kat's jaw was trembling. "You okay?"

"Yes," she said. She chewed on her lip.

Petruchio gazed at her, without speaking.

"What? I'm fine, it's good." A crystalline tear now spilled over onto her cheek. She sniffled. "I just feel so..."

—and then, suddenly, his wife was bawling like a monsoon in the tropics.

"I am just so...so *happy*! Oh, Papa!" Snatching the letter from Petruchio's hands, Kate barely managed to say, in a cracked voice: "Wait here. I'll be right back."

She fled from the room, weeping.

Petruchio listened as Kate's footsteps receded from him, through the hall and downstairs. His bride had evidently been overpowered by an irresistible need to reconcile with her father; not just by and by, but at that exact minute.

Petruchio sighed. For one passionate moment — just before the Papa Baptista letter intervened — there had been such explosive energy, such desire, such promise of imminent consummation. Petruchio was not ungrateful for his father-in-laws's generosity; nor was he jealous of Kat's newfound affection for the old man; but as he lay on the bed alone, Pet could not help but feel as if a very special moment had been lost, together with his erection.

Nothing for it but to wait for Kate's return.

Five minutes later, he was still waiting. Ten minutes. Fifteen minutes.

Petruchio felt he could not go back downstairs; not when his wife and father-in-law were busily compressing eighteen years of parent-child fireworks into a quarter-hour of impromptu reconciliation and quality parenting time.

"Just for something to do" (that's what he told himself), Petruchio's thoughts turned to romance. So many books! Caterina's library collection here looked five times larger than at the villa.

Rising from the bed to choose a book, Petruchio noted a stack of paperback quartos on the chiffarobe, together with a sales receipt. At some point in the brief interlude between their first meeting and marriage, Kate had visited Padua's book market, returning home with an armful of new and used paperbacks. (She had said nothing to him, of this.) Judging from her selections, Petruchio inferred that his fiancé upon their sudden engagement must have had made a beeline to the romance section, there to conduct research on heroes who bore his name or nickname. Her new acquisitions included a half dozen romances with steamy woodcuts on the front cover: *The Hunter's Pet, The Boss's Pet, My Pet Petruccio, For the Love of Pooch, Smooch Your Pooch, Pamper Your Pooch*, plus one sad story of a girl's disappointment in love (*La Piccola Pooch*); a hard-core novella in the style of Aretino (*Screwed Pooch*); and one title that Kate had evidently purchased in haste, by mistake (a dog-training manual called *Don't Pet a Pooch While He's Pooping*). She had also bought a well-worn copy of Munthio's *Memories and Vagaries*, a volume of short stories featuring "The Tragic Tale of Petruccio di Salvatore." This was the book that Petruchio opened first. Flipping through its chapter headings, his eyes became riveted on page 66: "Petruccio grew worse and worse. His mother no longer left his side. And it was scarcely a month after, that Salvatore's accident happened: he fell from a scaffolding and broke his leg...."

"I'll none of that," thought Petruchio. He replaced *Memories and Vagaries* to the stack, on the bottom, hoping that Kate would not get to it any time soon. He turned instead to her vast library. Scanning the shelves, he pulled one from the shelf called *The Accidental Bride*, which he thought might contain practical strategies for the night ahead (what was left of it), such as how to keep your wife focused. With that one under his arm, he opened another, called *When Strangers Marry,* and began reading somewhere near the climactic chapter: "She pressed the tips of her breasts to his chest. The shaft beneath her hands was full and thick now, and she plucked at the carved onyx buttons of his breeches to free it. With the help of the straining pressure beneath the thick cloth, the buttons popped easily from their holes...."

• • •

Kate returned to the bedroom on tiptoe, supposing that Petruchio might have fallen asleep. She was of course pleased to find him still awake, reading at her desk, by candlelight. "What ya' got there, Pet?" she said.

" *When Strangers Marry.*"

"Oh, I love that one," she said. "Spoiler alert: True love finds a way."

Caterina still held in her hand the (ripped, and now tear-stained) letter from her father. She was full of sighs, smiles, and complicated expectations. "Excuse me for having tarried so long," she said. "I just needed to talk with Papa about where things stand, with us."

"The thing was standing with us, right here, when you left," said Petruchio, somewhat sulkily. "I was abandoned."

"Shamefully abandoned! But that's what makes a rake so irresistible. A woman's heart knows no stronger drive, nor instinct more basic, than the impulse to make a bad man, good, or a good man, even better."

"Your very absence is why the rake has made no progress."

"Thirty minutes."

"The separation seemed fifteen years or more, to me," said Petruchio.

"So are you still up for it?"

"I wasn't. But now I am. These stories are really perking me up. Listen to this one, *The Accidental Bride*. "The salty taste of him entranced her...."

"I think you mean, 'en-*tranced* her.' Not '*en*-tranced her.'"

"Sorry. '...The salty taste of him en-*tranced* her. Taking him fully within her mouth now, she drew her lips up the length of the stem as her hands continued to stroke and knead between his thighs.'"

"Okay, maybe you were right the first time. But we shall not start with me taking you in my mouth and drawing my lips up the stem. I want us to be perfect partners."

"I'm with you. Love between equals. No arguments."

"No, I mean I want us to try a famous scene from *Perfect Partners.*"

"I don't know that one."

"I'll teach you. Off the chair." Petruchio stood. "Drop your pants. Hurry." Petruchio untied his points, and dropped his pants.

"My underbreeches, too?"

"Not yet." Kate removed her white tennis dress but not her camica. She hooked her index finger in the waistband of Pet's drawers, and walked him across the room until she had backed herself into to the corner. "Put one hand against the wall. This is just for starters."

He placed one palm against the wall. "What are we doing?"

"Little warm-up exercise. You're Giolo, I'm Leticia. I'm going to ride you."

"Ride me?"

"It's not what you think. Put your arm around me." Petruchio his arms around her. "No, just one arm. Keep your other hand against the wall."

"Why's that?"

"For support. Okay, lean into me a little." Caterina spread her feet apart. "I'm ready. I want you to slide one knee between my legs. Okay, move it up. *Slowly.*"

"Don't worry," said Petruchio. "I had no thought of getting even." He brought his knee up slowly, tentatively, as far as it could go.

"Keep going. Let me sit on you. I want you to lift me off the floor."

Leticia's ride. Kate knew what to expect. A sense of lost control. Fiery intimacy that could possibly leave her feeling dazed, disoriented. A feeling of incredible warmth scorching the softness between her thighs, as if she were already naked. Heat.

Leaning into the wall, Petruchio hoisted Kate on his thigh, and braced his knee against the wall. As he thrust his leg upward, Kate's feet lifted off the floor. She gave a little shriek of delight. She felt wobbly all over. She crossed her ankles and squeezed her legs together, to keep from losing her balance and falling off. She slid forward a little. Back, a little. Petruchio put his free hand beneath her buttocks to steady her, and bounced her gently up and down, which she seemed to enjoy, quite a bit. With one hand gripping Pet's shoulder, she waved her right hand in a little circle, and shouted loudly, "Ride 'em, cowgirl!" (forgetting people were downstairs).

Getting tired, Petruchio hoisted his knee higher against the wall, to support his rider. Kate slid down his thigh into a tight embrace and melted into a long, wet kiss.

"Oh, my God! Oh! Oh, Pet, put me down."

Petruchio, breathless himself, lowered her back to the floor.

"Thank you, honey. Leticia was right. The warmth is *astonishing*. It was glorious. Heavenly. But now my undies are wet."

Kate reached under her dress and untied the drawstring of her bloomers. They dropped to her ankles. She stepped out of them and kicked them off to the side, then looked up into his eyes. "Nuts. We forgot something."

"What?"

"While I was riding, you were supposed to move your thumb along my jaw, tracing the shape of me as if you intended to sculpt my face. I forgot to tell you about that part."

"Shall we do it again? I can give you another ride, if you like."

"Not right now. Your turn," she said.

"My turn?"

"To choose a model romance."

Petruchio went to the desk and returned on the instant with a paperback called *Rock My World.*

"Terremoto Mio Mondiale? Oh, yum! Which scene? No! Surprise me. There are so *many,* in that one."

Petruchio hooked his left hand under Kate's armpit and pulled her close with the inside of his elbow — not because it was in the book for him to assume that position, but only so that he could hold the book open just above Kate's shoulder to read it, and yet keep his right hand free for following the step-by-step. "*...She could feel his heat through the flannel of the pajama pants. Had he been like that all day, wanting her as much as she wanted him? His chest was bare.*" Petruchio stopped reading and handed Kate the book. "Keep your finger in the spot for me, will you?"

"You mean, in the book?"

"Um, yeah." Pet hastily pulled off his shirt, and took up the book again. "Thanks." He resumed reading. "*Before she could speak, he pulled her close to him and kissed her. It was an urgent, heated kiss, his lips pressed to hers, his tongue sweeping between her parted lips, stealing breath and sense and speech.*" So they did that. Petruchio found that he liked kissing his wife, very much. The way she opened her mouth, and it fit so perfectly to his. The way she tasted. The way she moved her tongue around. The way she knew how to keep right on kissing him until he was breathless and senseless and speechless.

"'*What next, my love?' he said. 'I'm sure you —* '"

"*I'm sure you will think of something nice,*" said Kate, full of anticipation.

"You know this by heart, or something?"

"Not really. But I remember the best lines. Keep reading. He does think of something nice. And you read so very nicely. So dramatic!"

"*...'I'm sure you'll think of something nice,' she said. He slipped his hand between her thighs, his pinky resting against the folds of her sex.*"

"Your pinky meets my pinky! How fun! Let's try it!"

"Now?"

"Now!"

Petruchio obediently slipped his hand beneath Kate's camica and ran his palm up the inside of her incredibly smooth thigh, stopping halfway. "Seems twisted," he said.

"Perfectly normal."

"No, I mean, my hand doesn't want to *go* that way. Either it's a misprint; or the author has made a digital error; or Adam, the guy in this book, has his hands on backward. It will be the index finger that ends up resting against the folds of her sex."

"I doubt that it matters, which finger."

"Which do you like best?"

"Most romance authors seem to prefer the middle one. Or else, the middle two, at the same time. Experiment, a little."

"*He pressed his finger between her folds, feeling the growing wetness there. She widened her stance.*'"

Kate spread her feet a bit farther apart. Petruchio seemed to be reading ahead, in silence.

"Well? Christmas is coming. Don't just stand there. The suspense is killing me."

Reaching again under Kate's camica, Pet guided his palm along the inside of her left thigh until it reached what seemed like a natural stopping point. It felt very hot. "Here?"

"A little farther. Ooh."

"What?"

"Again."

"Which?"

"That. Oh, yes. Oh, honey!"

It was just his anxiety, but Petruchio had the distinct sensation of his fingers being scorched off.

"No, don't stop. O, Pet that is, that is just ... mmmm... sensational!"

Petruchio stopped for a second, to rest his hand.

"Funny," said Kate, "it just dawned on me for the first time what's meant by the phrase, *tickled pink.* It's very nice. God, this is romantic!"

"More?"

"Absolutely. Stroke it! Yes, there, ... oh, my ... just keep ... doing that ... until somebody says, *When*."

Pet moved his fingers up and down, and back and forth, and around, a bit clumsily at first, but he found his rhythm, assisted once or twice by Kate's guiding hand on his wrist as she slumped against the wall, moaning softly with each breath. Her lips parted. Her eyes rolled back in her head. Petruchio found he was suddenly having to bear her entire weight on the crook of his arm; and that made it hard for him to keep *Rock My World* open to the right page. But he kept stroking the while, gently now, and quite earnestly.

"When!"

Petruchio stopped.

"Phew! Wow! Had to catch my breath there. O god, I never felt anything like *that* before...."

"O god, me neither," said Petruchio.

"...Nor shall any man but you ever tickle my fancy. I love you, Pet, and not just for your beautiful hands."

Kate's praise developed in Petruchio a growing sense of confidence, of accomplishment. He felt proud and he felt swollen, although not with pride. He resumed reading aloud. "'*Adam cupped her breast in his palm, running his thumb along the satiny underside, then up over her nipple.*'" Petruchio put his hand on Caterina's breast. He could feel the nipple beneath the cloth of the silky camica. He swept his thumb over the nub, back and forth and around. He moved to her left breast, same thing.

"I'd like a little more of that, if you don't mind," said Kate.

"Wait. What comes next is, '*He swirled his tongue around the sensitive peak, then took as much of her as he could into his mouth.*'"

"So maybe I should take off my camica?"

"I was thinking, maybe, yeah."

Petruchio stepped back. His heart was racing. This was easily the most thrilling moment of his twenty years on the planet.

Kate criss-crossed her arms, and with one graceful motion slipped the camica over her head and let it drop to the floor. She stood before him, naked. The book fell from his hand.

Kate saw the flash of panic in his eyes. "Leave it," she said. "I can guide you. Take my two peaches into your greedy hands."

Pet took one plump peach into each of his greedy hands.

"Take me into your mouth. Swirl your tongue around the sensitive peaks."

Petruchio swirled the sensitive peaks, first the right, then the left, then the right one again. Kate felt his stiff sex pressing against her abdomen. Which interested her.

Kate pulled back a little. Reaching for Pet's under-breeches, she touched the wet spot. Suddenly grabbing the shaft in her hand, she opened and closed her hand around it, two or three times, though it was still wrapped in his damp and baggy drawers. "Oh my goodness!" she said. "A manroot, when throbbing, becomes somewhat larger than I expected. What I've got in my hand feels more like the entire throbbing tree trunk." She let go and untied the drawstring of his under-breeches, to have a peek. But his drawers did not immediately fall to the floor. They become suspended, as if from a clothes-hook.

Petruchio lowered his eyes, in modesty; or perhaps just to check himself out. "Thank you for saying so," he said. "But I think it's actually fairly ordinary."

"Ordinary, you call it?" said Kate. "My god, Pet, it's like you've got a *cucumber.*" With a flick of her wrist, she caused his undies to fall to the floor. "My, just look at you!"

Petruchio felt shy. "I mean, really? You think it's a big one? Because I have been worried, ever since I was maybe thirteen, that mine could be on the slightly below average size. I wish it was a little longer. Not a lot. But maybe an inch, or so.

"Longer? Any longer, and we would have to trim it!"

Petruchio winced.

"Joke."

"Heh," said Petruchio, trying to be a good sport. But Caterina's jest acted on him like a bucket of ice-water.

"Timberrrr...." she said, with a giggle.

"Kate, can we hold off on the jokes? That was not helpful."

She pulled him close and hugged him to her bosom. "Oh, but here comes a furry little squirrel! She scurries up the tree!

Down the tree! Up the tree! Down the tree. Such a big, tall tree! and so slippery! (How's that feel?)"

"Like the tree is loaded with dynamite, and about to explode."

"So big! and slippery! and explosive! But look, our soft, fearless squirrel scoots right up to the tippy-top branch, to seek a little drop of moisture to relieve this parching heat!"

"Kate, stop! oh, no! I can't hold it! Damm, it's gonna blow!"

Readers who have come with Caterina and Petruchio thus far will be happy to read that the young lovers formed a blessed union, just in the nick of time. Kate jumped into Pet's arms, wrapped herself around him, and slid down his torso. A moment of unpleasant stinging gave way to a rapture of warm shivers. Petruchio collapsed backward onto the bed, with Kate on top. They laughed, they moaned, they said "Oooooh!" and "Oh, yeah!" and "Ohmygod-ohmygod-ohmygod."

As the climactic moment subsided into a rosy glow, the two lovers just lay there intertwined, facing one another, feeling spent, with a smile on their lips and a sparkle in their eye. They recovered just enough to say such things as "Wow," and "Phew," and "Mmmmm." But before he fell asleep, Petruchio opened up his heart, to make a confession: "My Love," he said, "when you first introduced me to romance, I had my doubts. But now, I believe."

• • •

PETRUCHIO and Caterina slept soundly, in a close tangle of arms, legs, and bedding.

Kate awoke first, at dawn, to the song of the lark. Not wishing to disturb Pet's slumber, she lay there quietly, contented just to watch the window curtains lift and fall, coyly flirting with the breeze.

Petruchio awoke to a gentle kiss on the cheek. Blinking open his long-lashed eyes in the morning light, he looked dreamy, as if unsure for a moment whether this room, this bed, this girl, this love, could be really real.

Moments later, as in *Blessing,* or *Fever Dreams,* or *Nobody Does it Better,* the entire household awoke to the drumbeat of a headboard slam-slam-slamming against the wall with incredible, almost frightening vigor. Aphrodite, Kate's beloved ragdoll cat who had been asleep under the bed, took off like a shot, jumped upon the library table, and then up onto the bookcase; where she remained for the duration. The storm subsided at last amidst howls of feminine ecstasy and a savagely masculine groan. No one went back to sleep that day except the two young people who created the disturbance.

As the sun rose, and as the house downstairs stirred to life, Kate cuddled into Petruchio and napped with him like two spoons in a drawer, or like Nikki Martinelli and her beau in *Just Another Pretty Face.*

Caterina was the first to awake. Feeling amorous, she roused Pet back to life with a scene she called Tooty Flutey, from *Lovers' Reveille.* But the tired boy just lay there on his back, grinning like a happy idiot. So Kate swung a knee over the top and took him on what she called a Backwards Pony Ride, as in *A Dangerous Return.*

("How was it?" asked Isabella Lando, over tea and scones, at Thursday's brunch meeting of the Ladies Book Club. "Yummy," was Kate's reply; "so far, I have found nothing more delicious than a Backwards Pony Ride." "How about the other?" asked Isabella. "Yummy is not the word," said Kate, "but Petruchio liked it.")

For a breather, the young lovers took turns reading to one another, in bed; which Petruchio, an aspiring actor, found perfectly satisfying as a post-coital entertainment. But a scene he was reading from *Head over Heels* infused Kate with a fresh spirit of adventure. "Put down the book," she said. "You read so beautifully, Pet! Let's try Yin Yang. Would you rather be Yin? or Yang?"

Petruchio said his leg injury was bothering him a bit, and maybe they should have some breakfast first. Excusing himself, he put on a robe and slippers and ventured downstairs in search of Tabatha, the cook. Caterina remained in bed with a stack of novels beside her, and browsed. So many romances, so many lovely scenes of passion! Subtle seductions, sudden ravishings, mutual temptations, cat-and-mouse, hot burn, slow boil, easy-does-it; even the impetuous, but often satisfying, quickie. And in so many interesting arrangements! Villain-and-Virgin, Sitting-Savages, Happy Missionaries, Frisky Puppies, Wheelbarrow, Topsy-Turvy, almost too many positions to name.

Downstairs in the kitchen, with some coaching from Tabatha, Petruchio made breakfast. (This was a first. Back home in Verona, Pet's mother and aunt did all the cooking.) He squeezed fresh orange juice, then fried up some bacon and a batch of buttered hotcakes; which he brought upstairs upon a food tray, with forks and napkins, and served to Kate in bed.

While the newlyweds ate breakfast, Tabatha heated kettles of water and filled the tub. Which was a good thing, because breakfast in bed proved to be a bad idea, with so many other things going on. ("Damn syrup got into everything," explained Kate.)

Bathed and dressed, feeling much refreshed by the morning's labor, Petruchio and Caterina emerged from their love suite just as a minor drama was unfolding outside the palace: Lucentio had been to Padua's horse-and-carriage market, and returned with a new rig. Parked out front was a luxurious Hungarian coach. It was drawn by four white horses, a team of muscular Holsteins. The servants crowded around the parlor windows, full of oohs and ahs. Baptista hobbled outside to have a look. He received from his son-in-law the full sales pitch. It was a gilded carriage in the new style, with an arched roof and every possible amenity, including hand-carved wood, a wine bar, and interior lighting; reclining seats (to accommodate sleep on a long journey, and amorous play, when parked); plus the latest design in leather-strap suspension for a smoother ride. The old man liked the coach so well, he said he intended to get one just like it.

Bianca was upstairs still deciding what she and Tranio, or rather, she and Lucentio, would need for their life together in faraway Pisa. Her academy award, her knick-knacks and stuffed animals, her jewelry, all of that was a given. But choosing which shoes, which clothes, to take — that was tough. Most of her dresses she had already worn once or twice; but fashiongazers in Pisa would have no way of knowing that. In the end, she decided it was best for the servants to just pack up everything. That way, she could decide at the other end what to wear and what to toss.

Coming indoors, Lucentio called upstairs to Bianca, excitedly announcing he had a surprise for her. When she appeared some minutes later — her hair was still in curlers — she inspected the new rig from the doorway, without going out. She said that it looked quite adequate.

Kate and Petruchio assured Tabatha they would return in time for dinner and slipped out the back way. They hurried off on foot, holding hands. The young lovers had no time, right now, to inspect Bianca's new set of wheels. Their sad farewells — to Lucentio and Bianca, to Baptista and Fiametta — could wait. It would be a day or two before Bianca shipped for Italy's west coast, and probably a week or more before Baptista transported his books and artwork and personal effects to Villa Marsango. Caterina would have to take Petruchio shopping for new furniture, new artwork, new kitchenware; but that, too, could wait. What could not wait was an urgent appointment: Petruchio had to be at Signore Caroso's studio, by two p.m., for his first lesson in Beginner's Dance.

finis

Why Shakespeare?
By Alf Dotson

> *Who is it that can tell me who I am?*
> — William Shakespeare

THE "SHAKESPEARE INDUSTRY" — by which is meant, not the makers of such popular novelties as the William Shakespeare bobblehead doll, but rather a global cartel whose membership includes scholars, university professors, actors, directors, and book editors — has been accused of intellectual thuggery. It is said that the academic establishment in particular can be counted on for a knee-jerk dismissal of any Shakespeare news that did not first appear in a refereed journal or university press. Nowhere is that resistance more fierce than when it comes to evidence that Shakespeare may not have been "Shakespeare" — a theory that is today defended or refuted on nearly 143 thousand Websites (and rising). To hear some experts tell it, the human race has produced more fringe theories about William Shakespeare than about the assassination of JFK or the discovery of undocumented aliens in Area 51. But that kind of academic snootiness received an unexpected reality check last winter when Robert Shakespeare of Eureka, MT, broke open the dusty footlocker of his father, the late Clark H. Shakespeare. Robert, a disabled Iraq War vet, discovered among family papers a trove of manuscripts that has put the reputation of the great Bard up for grabs, and perhaps his very identity.

In light of the recent headlines, reporters have been asking me how a trucker's son from Zap, North Dakota, became mixed up with William Shakespeare of Stratford-upon-Avon. Where I grew up, the name "Shakespeare" meant just one thing: fishing gear. The Shakespeare Company, founded in

1897 by an American angler named William Shakespeare, Jr., is North Dakota's most trusted name in tackle. It was at age ten, with my Shakespeare Ugly Stik® and my Shakespeare Synergy® reel, that I pulled from Lake Sakakawea the greatest catch of my life, a 46-inch northern pike. That's just two inches short of the all-time Dakota record set by Melvin Slind in 1968 — a year before my father (wherever you may be) and mother (may she rest in peace) were even *born*. A loyalist, I would not have traded my lucky Shakespeare combo-kit for a snowmobile or a dirt bike. Indeed, I shall always remember my initial disappointment, in my ninth grade class at Beulah High School, when I was assigned to read a "Shakespeare" play (i.e., *Romeo and Juliet*), only to discover that its author had no real interest catching fish.

A second demerit against Shakespeare, to my young mind, came when the teacher asked us to watch a "wonderful" version of *Romeo and Juliet* directed by Franco Zeffirelli, filmed in 1968. My grandmother, Dolly ("Nanna") Ford, a New Age hippie with expertise in astrology, had brought me up to believe that nothing of interest happened before 1969. That was the year of the dawning of the Age of Aquarius (she believed), as formally announced by a pop band called The 5th Dimension, in a tune released on May 10 of that year. May 10, 1969, was also the exact date on which my mother, Sunshine Dotson, was conceived. (Her life was an unforeseen consequence of Nanna's one-night-stand at the "Zip-to-Zap," a festival that put my hometown on national TV and is still recalled with horror by the mostly church-going, mostly gun-toting, mostly beef-eating Baby Boomers of my home state and county.) Nanna often reminded me as I was growing up that three of her Sixties heroes took bullets in 1968 — Martin Luther King, and Bobby Kennedy, and Andy Warhol — only one of whom survived and it was not her top choice. That was also the year of the Tet Offensive, the Mi Lai Massacre, and of Richard Nixon's election to the White House. According to my grandmother, what the world saw in 1968 was nothing less than the death throes of the Age of Pisces.

Nanna warned me that the New Age could yet suffer a few aftershocks. When I caught my 34-pound, 46-inch, northern pike, Nanna was the first to recall that 1968 was the year in which "that Roseglen man" caught his 38-pound, 48-inch trophy — due to a June 21 alignment of stars that made the more fortunate Mr. Slind a lifetime member of the Top Whopper Club (North Dakota Fish and Game Department), while forever excluding her grandson's name and fish and hometown and lucky Shakespeare stick from the record books. I would not want Nanna's New Age star-gazing to be blamed for my own immature Bardophobia: but let's just say that when I sat down as a high school freshman to watch *Romeo and Juliet* for the first time, I had low expectations: here was one more thing from 1968, a year that I already knew had produced nothing but tragedy.

But that Shakespeare movie, and Olivia Hussey in particular, gave my heartstrings an unexpected tug. The final scene in the Capulet tomb, when Romeo thought his true love was dead ("Ah, dear Juliet, / Why art thou yet so fair?"), made me cry — which was embarrassing — but I just felt strangely moved by it; first by the film, then by reading the playwright's original script. Watching, and reading, and re-reading, *Romeo and Juliet* at age fourteen, it felt to me as if William Shakespeare (like no one else in this world, including Nanna) understood the deep, secret longings of my heart. For one thing, the story painfully exhumed the buried anguish of my own first romance, in the sixth grade, with my Sioux princess, Winona Littlebird; whose mother had a history of looking for love in all the wrong places; and who decided on a whim that another good place to look would be somewhere in California. One chilly October day, at the height of my innocent prepubescent romance, Jesse Littlebird stopped by the Middle School; removed Winnie from Mrs. Bauer's classroom; hustled her out to the car (an old boyfriend's rusty Chevy wagon with Utah plates); and drove away. That was it. No goodbye, no explanation. The line just snapped, and she was gone. They stopped in Dodge, fourteen miles west of Zap, where Winnie's mom posted an angry message on the Main Street bulletin board; then continued west with no forwarding address. In the ninth grade, as I watched Franco Zeffirelli's *Romeo and Juliet,* it all came back — her angelic goodness, and long black hair, and dewy eyes, and soft smile. Juliet as played by Olivia Hussey reminded me exactly of my lost angel, Winona Littlebird.

So I started reading Shakespeare. I was the only boy in the ninth grade who liked *Romeo and Juliet.* Juliet, especially. (If the playwright had wanted to have fans in *my* state and high school, he'd have written a play about cowboys in prison and called it "Rodeo in Joliet.") Nor did I get much encouragement at home: Nanna picked up the Signet paperback edition I brought home from school and said: "What has this got to do with anything? Why do they still force you kids to *read* this shit?")

In tenth grade we studied *Julius Caesar.* Next year, *Hamlet.* And *Macbeth,* in our senior year. By that time Shakespeare had me hooked. I loved his wit, his word-play, his uncanny ability to see a problem from every angle. I loved his wildly improbable plots. I loved how the verse sounded, especially when my English teacher, Mrs. Heller, read it aloud. Shakespeare transported me to another world. His stories helped me to envision myself having a life somewhere beyond Zap (who knows, maybe even in California — Winona's mother could have died by now, I know mine sure did). As a freshman in high school, living alone in that tin can with my grandmother and with "Zepp" (short for Led Zeppelin, Nanna's dog), I had no realistic future besides a 9-to-5 job at the coal gasification plant, with fish and beer on weekends, the same place Nanna worked (and my Mom, too, before she couldn't take it any more). Padua, Verona, Venice, even Elsinore and Dunsinane: these dramatic settings existed in my imagination as a golden world where people more eloquent than myself still loved and lost, but at least had more interesting conflicts than over why a boy cannot remember to turn off the lights, and to put down the toilet seat, and to return the television remote to the cupholder in Nanna's La-Z-Boy recliner.

Taking my inspiration from Shakespeare, the world-class genius who appeared out of nowhere, I took up writing. I contributed to *Miner Incidents,* our student newspaper, published six times a year. I composed sonnets. I penned two plays (one of which was performed by the BHS Drama Club), and a novel. My teachers at Beulah High, seeing in my written work a spark of talent, fanned the flames. Most important, they made a reader of me. As a more-or-less accidental result, when it came time for me to apply to college, my SAT scores got me into Harvard — that, plus the fact that the Harvard Admissions Office tries always to bag at least one freshman from each of the fifty states, and I may have been the only North Dakotan, that year, to apply. A generous financial-aid package did the rest.

At eighteen I had no car and could not afford the airfare. Camping in the Badlands was the farthest I'd ever been from home. But I wanted to go. So I went. Weird thing is, once I went off to college, home itself just kind of disappeared on me. Two months after I graduated with honors from Beulah High School, I said goodbye to my grandmother and our dog. With a pack on my back and suitcase in hand, I hitchhiked 1,895 miles to Cambridge, Massachusetts, to begin four years at Harvard, most expenses paid. By the time I reached my destination ten days later, Zepp was dead — from grief, my grandmother said (but he was a very old dog). Then Nanna herself died a year later, of lung cancer treated, though unsuccessfully, with aloe vera, broccoli, and homeopathic teas. I don't even know what happened to her stuff. I've been pretty much on my own since then. Doing okay, though. Double major in History and English. When someone blasts a hole in your heart, I'm not saying that reading Shakespeare can fix it. But for me, it always seems to shed a kind of light.

Anyway, in answer to your question, how did I get mixed up in Shakespeare: I was already pretty mixed up, when we met.

• • •

Discovery of the Jamestown Shakespeare Manuscripts

> *Why, how now, gentlemen!*
> *What see you in those* papers, *that you lose*
> *So much complexion?*
> — William Shakespeare

THE SHAKESPEARE INSTITUTE in Church Street, Stratford-upon-Avon, received a letter last year from Robert Shakespeare of Eureka, Montana, forwarded to the Institute from the Shakespeare Birthplace Trust on Henley Street. Mr. "Shakespeare" — no one believed that was his real name — wrote to request assistance with some "chicken-scratchy" handwriting — papers that the self-identified Bob Shakespeare represented as "hunderds of pages of really old stuff from hunderds of years ago" — documents he alleged to have inherited from his "daddy, Clark Shakespeare." The Institute's faculty — Dr. Dobson, Dr. Fernie, Dr. Jowett, and the rest — are brilliant scholars who know more about Shakespeare than William Shakespeare knew about Shakespeare. I was then in Stratford for my Harvard semester abroad, taking the Institute's curriculum-modules in "Shakespeare's Theatre" and "Research Skills." In the four months I studied there, I never asked a single question to which those amazing scholars did not already know the answer — except one: "Who is Robert Shakespeare?" Expert opinion in Stratford was divided, three ways: Bob Shakespeare was either a prankster, a lunatic, or a blinking idiot. (There are many of all three types of people out there, thousands of whom are indefatigable letter-writers, and professors get more than their share.)

I knew of this overture from Mr. Shakespeare not because it was part of my curriculum but because someone posted a copy on the bulletin board outside the Shakespeare Centre Library Reading Room, for a laugh. (The letter had already bounced around for a week or two before I saw it.) But Mr. Shakespeare's inquiry, with its claimed possession of old manuscripts, piqued my curiosity. So when no one at the Shakespeare Institute, or at the Shakespeare Birthplace Trust, or at the Shakespeare Centre Library, showed any sincere interest in "Bob" Shakespeare, I thought, *What's to lose?* I poked around online for a week or two, looking for him. Facebook and a dozen online people-finders turned up 26 Shakespeares in the State of Montana. I found one "Roberta A. Shakespeare," mid-60s, in Browning, MT (population: 1,016) but no Robert, and no Shakespeares at all in the town of Eureka. My tutor advised me to give it over: "At best," she said, "this bloke is an amateur genealogist looking for help with his family tree — which cannot possibly lead to the playwright because Shakespeare has no living descendants with his surname." At worst, I thought, the author could be another angry Montana hermit with an axe to grind, or a pipe-bomb to mail, not unlike, say, Ted Kaczynski, seeking revenge perhaps for having failed a college Shakespeare class. But even the merest chance of working with historical documents, texts never seen by professional scholars, fired my imagination. The way I looked at it, if the papers were of no importance, they could be returned without comment. I wanted to have a look at what this Montana fellow had discovered, even if his Shakespeareana proved of no greater interest, to scholars, than rod-and-reel ads torn from back issues of *Field and Stream*, or *Crappie World*. So I wrote to Shakespeare, from Stratford:

Dear Mr. Shakespeare,

At the instant of receiving your letter I am quite incapacitated with an ague: but I have with me at present a visiting Harvard scholar, named Alfred Dotson, who's just the man to examine your manuscripts. I beseech you, let his lack of years be no impediment; for I never knew so young a body with so old a head. I have acquainted Master Dotson with your inquiry. He is furnished with my opinion, bettered with his own learning pursuant to our Research Skills Module at the Shakespeare Institute (the greatness whereof I cannot enough commend). If you dispatch your parcel by USPS ground, Master Dotson will be back home by the time your documents arrive. I leave him to your gracious acceptance.

Best wishes,

Dr. J. P. Collier, professor emeritus

Okay, so I lied: "J.P. Collier" is no Institute lecturer, but a documents-forger, an infamous scoundrel long dead. I cribbed my text from *The Merchant of Venice.* I'm not a professor. And for my "office" address, I gave Bob Shakespeare my dorm room on the 5th floor of Mather House. That way, if he proved a madman or prankster, the last laugh was mine, not his. But I had a hunch. Now in my third year at Harvard, I was mulling over a topic for my Senior Thesis. And it seemed a remote possibility that Mr. Shakespeare might here have offered one on a silver platter that no one else in academia was willing to touch.

Bob's parcel, which had once served as a shipping-carton for twelve one-liter bottles of Southern Comfort, arrived at Harvard only two days after my home-return. I had to go pick it up from Receiving. Upon lugging it back to my dorm room I did not, as you might expect, tear it open but slit the wrapping tape with a utility knife, half-persuaded that I'd be resealing and returning the package, with time to spare before the next pickup. But when I saw the actual content — bundles of old paper tied with string, and three rolled parchments tied with ribbon — my heart leapt into my throat. The manuscripts certainly *looked* authentic. This looked to be my best catch since Lake Sakakawea.

One problem: every document in the box except Bob's cover letter was penned in the sixteenth century, in a half dozen individual scrawls, much of which I found hard to make out even though we had covered calligraphy in my Research Skills module. The spelling was irregular, often atrocious. A few were in Latin. Much of the paper was dusty, smelly, and damaged by moisture. Over the next several months, as I transcribed texts to my computer, I had to become a junior expert in Elizabethan handwriting. (Toward that end, I received much helpful assistance from the archivists at Harvard's Houghton Library, for which I am grateful. Any remaining errors in the stories themselves or in my notes are of course my own.)

Now that word of his discovery has been leaked, Mr. Shakespeare is being wooed by librarians from Edinburgh, Scotland, to San Marino, California, with pleas to donate his manuscript collection to their archives. Even the Shakespeare Institute would like a piece of the action. I have asked Bob's permission to publish photofacsimiles, along with my transcriptions, online. That may not happen any time soon. Bob is thinking more along the lines of Sotheby's or Christy's auction house, and a new Dodge Ram pickup truck. In the meantime, his documents are securely stored in a climate-controled safe deposit box at the East Cambridge Savings Bank.

Here are the essential facts: The Jamestown manuscripts once belonged to a William Shakespeare ("Wilm Shaksper," b. Nov. 1602, not the poet) who came to Virginia in his teens as an English colonist.[1] He died in 1626. Some of his belongings were then passed down from generation to generation, as historical curios without any special importance attached to them by his descendants. The bulk of the manuscripts are comprised of ordinary household accounts for the years 1618-1628, and will be of no special interest except to American historians of the colonial period. But among those yellowed parchments and papers are a number of manuscripts pertaining to the life and works of William Shakespeare the famous playwright, and relating also to various of his contemporaries, people whom William Shakespeare of Jamestown, Virginia, cannot have known. Many of these narratives are quite extraordinary and unlike anything previously discovered about Shakespeare from the early modern period.

True Shakespeare represents the first publication of four documents in the Jamestown collection, issued here in a modern-spelling text:

> *Othello l'Amour; or, the Tragedy of the Handkerchief,* by Christopher Marlowe.

> *The True Mystery of Hamlet, Prince of Denmark,* by [Thomas] Watson.

---

[1] "Willm. Shakespeare" (not the actor) was baptized in Coventry on 5 December 1602 (as the illegitimate issue of one "Allice Forde of Rowington," county Warwickshire).

The Taming of the Pooch: An Actually True Romance, by Isabella Sforza, lady Porcigliano; trans. Anne Cook-Bacon.

Romeo — plus Juliet: True Confessions of a Ghoastly Father, by Friar Lorenzo Frier; trans. Richard Barnfield.

Readers may be surprised to learn that several popular plays "by William Shakespeare," for which the poet has received so much posthumous acclaim, began as true stories that the Stratford fellow cribbed from earlier writers: Lady Porcigliano wrote her true, girls-on-top romance of Kate and Petruchio thirty-some years before Shakespeare reduced her actually true romance to a sexist farce. Richard Barnfield completed his translation of Friar Lorenzo's shocking *Confessioni* in 1589, three years before the so-called Bard of Avon reworked it as a play about star-crossed puppy-love. Christopher Marlowe wrote his hard-boiled *Othello,* and Thomas Watson, his true-crime *Hamlet* in 1588, more than a decade before William Shakespeare of Stratford took a professional interest in detective fiction. Isabella Sforza, Friar Frier, Christopher "Kit" Marlowe — these are the literary giants from whom Shakespeare learned how to write. (Not slavishly so: Shakespeare was not someone who wrestled with his demons, such as inflated diction, and verbosity, and a disdain for accuracy; if anything, one could wish the playwright had studied these original tales more thoroughly, as modern scholars shall do, thereby to perfect his slapdash narrative structure and his often obscure style.)

Every story, every statement of fact, every personal letter in the Jamestown Shakespeare Manuscripts invites the kind of microscopic scrutiny that has been lent to the Dead Sea Scrolls, and the Book of Exeter, and the poetry of the bard Ossian. In the rough-and-tumble, often cutthroat world of professional Shakespeare studies, reputations will be made or destroyed in scholarly discussion of these incredibly important documents. Shakespeare's own reputation may take some bruises with the publication of earlier stories, more original, more witty, than his own, from which the world-famous playwright borrowed so much of his famously clever material.

Anti-Stratfordians — crazies who believe that "William Shake-speare" was just a pen name for Francis Bacon, or Edward de Vere, or Christopher Marlowe — may find in these pages much to crow about, citing fresh evidence of the playwright's secret identity. More traditional academics, such as doctors Dobson, Fernie, and Jowett (in Stratford), or professors Marjorie Garber and Stephen Greenblatt (here at Harvard), may find themselves in a state of mild apoplexy. I would not go so far as to say that the genius of "the Stratford man" has been laid to rest. There are *problems* — I would put it as simply as that. Perhaps the most puzzling one is this: When confronted with "The Taming of the Pooch," and "The True Mystery of Hamlet," "Othello l'Amour," or "Romeo" — quite possibly, the four greatest stories ever told — why did William Shakespeare not leave well enough alone? The Bard of Avon wrote well, and much. But the Baroness Porcigliano, and Master Watson, and Christopher Marlowe, and Friar Lorenzo Frier — does one dare say it? — wrote even better.

With the Complete Works: food for thought

Make the meat *be beloved, more than the man that gives it.*
— William Shakespeare

PROFESSIONAL ACADEMICS tell a story — which means it may not be very accurate — about a clairvoyant named Madame Bukuroshe, who lived in Birmingham, England. This was in the 1920s, when the worship of Shakespeare was still at its height. Someone asked her, "Madame Bukuroshe, which of the many possible Shakespeares is the *true* one?" (Francis Bacon? Edward de Vere? Queen Elizabeth? William Stanley? Simon Wastell? Christopher Marlowe? John Ford?) According to the story, the old woman looked into her crystal ball, a cheap-looking thing that she might have bought at any Woolworth's store. She muttered some skimble-skamble stuff that sounded like Albanian. In fact, it probably *was* Albanian, she was from Albania. She then sat quietly for a moment with her fingertips on the glass ball — seeking necromantic answers from the dead, concerning the true identity of William Shakespeare.

At last, Madame Bukuroshe spoke (very slowly and with an accent that I cannot perfectly reproduce): "The plays and poems of William Shakespeare were written," she said, "not by William Shakespeare, but by another man with the same name."

Well, that's an old chestnut. But the anecdote contains this kernel of truth: canonical Shakespeare is not finally a question of who dunnit. Who is Shakespeare? John and Mary Shakespeare (his parents), are Shakespeare. The poet's Stratford schoolteachers, are Shakespeare. Anne Hathaway is Shakespeare. Sir Francis Bacon, and the seventeenth earl of Oxford, and the sixth earl of Derby, plus Thomas Watson, Christopher Marlowe, Queen Elizabeth, and Joseph Fiennes — these people are Shakespeare. Each one of them contributed a spark, a candle's glow, to the heavenly sun of our greatest poet. The heroes of the Old Testament, and of Greek tragedy, these are Shakespeare. Chaucer is Shakespeare. Henry Potter. Golding's *Ovid.* Spenser's *Faerie Queene.* Richard

Barnfield's *Affectionate Shepherd...* but never mind that. The Anglican Church is Shakespeare. England is Shakespeare. Winston Churchill. Princess Diana. JK Rowling. In one sense, all humanity is Shakespeare: the highest and best thoughts, the hardiest ideals, the deepest aspirations: these are Shakespeare.

It's not all good, of course. With the advantage of scholarly hindsight, everyone now is able to see that the British patriarchy was Shakespeare. English imperialism was Shakespeare. So, too, was the Oedipal crisis. Plagiarism. Paternalism, colonialism, militarism, capitalism, elitism, classism, gynophobia, white racism, ethnocentrism, anti-Semitism, escapism, esotericism, lookism: each one of these illiberal discourses is regrettably Shakespeare, Shakespeare, Shakespeare, up one side and down the other. Some 16,000 academic books and 37,000 scholarly articles published about hegemonic Shakespeare in the past quarter-century will back me up on that.

The one ineffaceable difference that remains, between William Shakespeare and the Shakespeare Establishment, is that most literary scholars cannot write very well, and Shakespeare could; so while the publications of liberal Shakespeare professors never seem to influence anything except their own case for tenure and promotion, William Shakespeare, with his conservative thought on almost every earthly subject from aardvarks to zygotes, has had a profound impact on the shape of Western culture.

By providing us with the original and early narrative sources for four of Shakespeare's greatest works, *True Shakespeare* does not undermine the playwright's achievement. Far from it. These volumes simply help us to understand how all kinds of writing, by different writers throughout history, male and female, rich and poor, right and left, tend to get mixed together in the wonderful machinery of our literary tradition, and yet are made fresh daily by the seasoning of tradition and the transformative power of art. However it came to be, Shakespeare – our *Shakespeare* – is surely the biggest literary sausage ever made.

A. D.

160

Works Referenced in *Taming of the Pooch*

Aretino, Pietro. *Ragionamento.* Venice, 1534.

Axon, William E.A. "Ortensio Lando, a Humorist of the Renaissance." *Transactions of the Royal Society of Literature.* Vol. 20 (London, 1899): 159-196.

Collins, Jackie. *Hollywood Divorces.* New York: Pocket Books, 2004.

Cook-Bacon, Lady Anne, trans. *An Apologie or Answere in Defence of the Churche of Englande.* London, 1564.

— , trans. *Fourteen Sermons of Barnardine Ochyne of Siena.* London, 1548.

— , trans. "The Taminge of the Pooche, by ye Ladye Anne Cooke Bacon." [Trans. A. C. Bacon from an Italian original, not extant.] With prefatory letter to her son, Sir Francis Bacon. Edited by A. Dotson (2010). The Jamestown Shakespeare Papers [1561-1603], MS JSP 14. Private collection of R. Shakespeare.

Forester, C.S. *The African Queen* (1935) and Bogart/Hepburn film (1951).

Grendler, Paul F. "Ortensio Lando." *Critics of the Italian World, 1530-1560.* Madison: Univ. of Wisconsin, 1969. 21-38.

Lando, Hortensio. *Sette libri di Cataloghi.* Venice, 1552. Trans. A. Dotson (2010).

Munday, Anthony, trans. "The Heaven of the Mynde, or the Myndes Heaven. A moste excellent, learned and religious Treatise, declaring the way and rediest manner how to Attayne the True Peace and Quiet of the Mynde. Written in the Italiane tongue by the right honourable Ladie, Madonna Isabella Sforza, sister to the Great Duke of Mylane; and translated into English by A[nthony] M[undy]" (Dec. 1602). Colchester: Kendall collection.

Sforza, Isabella, Lady Porcigliano. *Della vera Tranquillità dell'Animo.* Venice, 1544.

— . — . [English trans.] See Munday.

— . *l'Addomesticamento del Cucciolo.* Ital. original not extant. English trans., "The Taminge of the Pooche"]. See Bacon, Anne Cook.

Shakespeare, William. *The Taming of the Shrew.* In *Mr. William Shakespeares Comedies, Histories, and Tragedies.* [First Folio]. London, 1623.

Story of the Learned Pig. Anon. London: R. Jameson, 1786. Available online at http://www.sirbacon.org/learnedpigbook.htm.

Susann, Jacqueline. *Valley of the Dolls.* New York: Bantam, 1966.

Willis, George. "Isabella Sforza." *Willis's Current Notes.* London, 1857. 70.

Mentioned: Dwan Abrams, *Only True Love* Waits; Jonis Agee, *River Wife*; Megan Alexander, *His Lordship's Dilemma*; Caroline Anderson, *Saving Doctor Gregory*; Catherine Anderson, *Three Times a Bride*; Judith Arnold, *Father Found* and *Married to the Man*; Pietro Aretino, *Secret Life of Wives*; Kay Arthur, *For the Love of Pooch*; Elizabeth Ashtree, *An Officer and a Hero*; Kathleen Ball, *A Love So Deep*; Christian Black, *Restless Spirits*; Tracey Bateman, *Thirsty*; Larry Bates, *Sex for Christian Couples*; Lexi Blake, *Nobody Does it Better*; Judith Bowen, *His Brother's Bride*; Sandra Brown, *The Devil's Own*; Willa Cather, *My Antonia*; Marion Chesney, *Our Lady of Pain*; Jackie Christian, *Nasty Night (Spank Me Right)*; M. Christian, *Licks and Promises*; Kresley Cole, *A Hunger Like No Other*; Elaine Coffman, *Escape Not My Love*; Kathleen Creighton, *One Good Man*; Sam Crescent, *The Boss's Pet*; Jude Deveraux, *Ever After, Knight in Shining Armor, The Temptress*, and *Velvet Song*; Helen Dickson, *An Unpredictable Bride*; Karla Doyle, *Gift-Wrapped*; Judith Duncan, *Beyond All Reason*; Dawn Eden, *The Thrill of the Chaste*; Jane Feather, *Beloved Enemy, The Accidental Bride* and *The Diamond Slipper*; Barry Franklin, *Wired for Sex*; Christine Feehan, *Burning Wild*; Julie Garwood, *The Lion's Lady*; Hannah Grace, *Wildfire*; Heather Graham, *Conquer the Night* and *Rides a Hero*; Lois Greiman, *The Princess and her Pirate*; Gena Hale, *Paradise Island*; Cassie Hamilton, *Our Little Secret*; Beth Webb Hart, *The Wedding Machine*; Virginia Henley, *Desired*; Ryan Howes, *What Wives Wish their Husbands Knew about Sex*; Christian Ibegbu, *The Man I Love*; Rique Johnson, *A Dangerous Return*; Joan Johnston, *Colter's Wife*; Nicole Jordan, *Fever Dreams*; Brenda Joyce, *Dark Victory*; Jillian Karr, *Something Borrowed, Something Blue*; Brenda Kennedy, *Destined to Love*; Sherrilyn Kenyon, *Born of the Night*; Lisa Kleypas, *When Strangers Marry*; Diana Knightley, *Promises to Keep*; Kathleen Korbel, *Outlaws and Lovers* and *Perchance to Dream*; Laura Leone, *Fever Dreams*; Caroline Linden, *What a Rogue Desires*; Elizabeth Lowell, *Winter Fire*; Juliet Marillier, *Daughter of the Forest*; Lynn Mason, *The L*** Word*; Heather McCollum, *Highland Warrior*; Jenna McKnight, *A Greek God at the Ladies' Club*; Lois Menzel, *Celia*; Gwyn Merello, *La Piccola Pooch*; Cassie Miles, *Guarded Moments*; Jan Millsaps, *Screwed Pooch*; Karyn Monk, *Surrender to a Stranger*; Axel Munthe, *Munthio's Memories and Vagaries*; Janet Nissenson, *Splendor*; Pascal, *Rebel Heat*; Carly Phillips, *Perfect Partners*; May Jo Putney, *The Marriage Spell*; Jennifer Quasha, *Don't Pet a Pooch While He's Pooping*; Amanda Quick, *Deception* and *With This Ring*; E. G. Radcliffe, *The Last Prince*; Loki Renard, *The Hunter's Pet*; Nora Roberts, *Treasures*; KV Rose, *Ecstasy*; Taylor Ryan, *Birdie*; Sharon Sala, *Missing*; Candace Schuler, *Just Another Pretty Face*; William Shakespeare, *Romeo and Juliet*; Sharon Shinn, *Angel Seeker*; Teddy Slater, *Smooch Your Pooch*; Anna Small, *Tame the Wild Wind*; Lass Small, *An Obsolete Man*; Nicholas Sparks, *The Wedding;* Anne Stevenson, *Flash of Splendour*; Jennifer Stevenson, *Bearskin Rug*; Marla Taviano, *Is That All He Thinks About?;* Sylvia Thorpe, *Beloved Rebel*; Michelle Valentine, *Rock My World*; Heather Vivant, *The Erotic Lives of Christian Wives*; Teresa Warfield, *Make Believe*; Patricia Wentworth, *The Fire Within*; Rachel White, *The First Time*; Sarah Whitehead, *Pamper Your Pooch*; Diana Whitney, *Daddy of the House*; Karen Toller Whittenburg, *Million-Dollar Bride*; Susan Wiggs, *Miranda*; Eric Wilson, *The Jerusalem Undead Trilogy*; Sherryl Woods, *To Catch a Thief*; Kathleen E. Woodiwiss, *The Reluctant Suitor*; Christian Zanier, *The Honey Lickers Sororiety*; Christian Zillner, *Angel's Delight*.

Other hilarious Tales edited by Alf Dotson
from The Jamestown Shakespeare Manuscripts

Othello l'Amour, by Christopher Marlowe, edited for 21ˢᵗ Century gumshoes by Alf Dotson:

From the Jamestown Shakespeare Manuscripts comes the first hard-boiled detective story ever written; possibly, the most thrilling. In 1588, in Venice, the daughter of a white senator eloped with the commander of the armed forces, an African, and fled to the island of Crete. Her father, Signore Brabantio, hired Christopher Marlowe (1564-1593) — poet, university wit, playwright, atheist, homosexual, and government agent — to find the doll and bring her home. Here is a tough-guy case that has it all — scandal, gold, pearls, a magic totem, a doting patriarch, a husband war-hero, a cross-dressed lover, a rosy-cheeked boy, a femme fatale, a stupid constable, ethical ambiguities, and five violent deaths in one night — all five murders being solved before breakfast.

The True Mystery of Hamlet, by [Thomas] Watson, edited for 21st century detectives by Alf Dotson:

From the newly discovered Jamestown Shakespeare Manuscripts comes a 100% solution to the greatest mystery ever conceived by the mind of man: *Hamlet, Prince of Denmark.* The historical Sherlock Homes (1525-1589) investigated the deaths of Prince Hamlet's father and uncle, the queen mother, Hamlet's school chums, his girlfriend, his girlfriend's father and brother, and of the sulky prince himself. Homes plucked the heart from Hamlet's mystery three hundred years before Sir Arthur Conan Doyle (in 1887) cribbed a similar name for his fictional detective, and before Sigmund Freud (in 1900) traced the young hero's strange fixation to an unresolved Oedipal Complex.

Romeo; plus Juliet: True Confessions of a Ghoastly Father, by Friar Lorenzo Frier; unexpurgated text edited for 21st Century readers by Alf Dotson.

From the Jamestown Shakespeare Manuscripts comes an autobiography begun in 1550 by Friar Lorenzo Frier (1503-1555), written to justifiy his tragic infatuation, as a Catholic priest in his late forties, with a teenager of Verona named Romeo Montague. "Part One: Adonis" is full of sunshine and youthful *joie de vivre.* The story is chiefly comprised of a laugh-out-loud erotic narrative, in verse, of Friar Lorenzo's first great romantic fling. At age eighteen, before he was ordained, Frier fell in love with "Adonis" (not his real name), the son of Russian nobility who visited Umbertide in the year 1521. And yet, readers with no patience for cheerful boyish poetry may simply scoot ahead to Part Two, by which time the tormented clergyman, years later, surrounded now by decadent aristocrats and a corrupt Church, has morphed into a spiritual monster.

Also from Wicked Good Books

Women's Works, volumes 1-4

Edited by Donald W. Foster

In high school and college, the curriculum in history and literature virtually ignores one half of the human race. You can now remedy that oversight on your own. Twenty-five years in production, *Women's Works* gathers together the best of the early women's tradition, from the ancient Celts to Colonial America. All early women's texts in this amazing collection have been edited in modern spelling from the original manuscripts and printed books. Works originally in Welsh, Norman French, Old or Middle English, or in Latin are provided with a parallel English translation. Historical and biographical context is supplied for all selections. Here, at last, is the education in women's culture that you never got in school — poetry, drama, autobiography, satire, women's medicine, birthing manuals, life inside medieval nunneries, witch confessions, Elizabethan cookery; legal history of rape, domestic violence, and reproductive rights; early feminists, English queens, lesbians, prostitutes, celebrities, saints — it's all here. History and literature are not just by and for *men*.

"[*Women's Works*] is a gem. It provides witty, lively introductions to a large gathering of women's writing across a range of subjects [...] the most complete and compelling collection of its kind, combining meticulous scholarship and engaging presentation with fully teachable texts. The anthology we have needed for so long has finally arrived."
   — Valerie Wayne, Prof. Emerita of English, Univ. of Hawai'i

"A remarkable contribution to scholarship that is also a pedagogical treasure, *Women's Works* ... should be in every university and college library and open on the desks of everyone teaching courses on or including seventeenth-century English literature."
   — Prof. Margaret Ferguson, Distinguished Professor of English, University of California at Davis, and 2014-15 President of the Modern Language Association

"This collection is a revelation, even to those of us who have long been interested in women's writing. From now on, it will be an indispensable resource."
— Phyllis Rackin, Professor of English emerita and past president of the Shakespeare Association

"Women's Works captures...the vast range of early modern English women's literary contributions, providing students with the historical and cultural context necessary to understand women's poems, plays, and prose writings. It will teach scholars a thing or two as well. No other anthology on the market offers a comparable sample of women's printed and manuscript texts from the period..."
--Prof. Jennifer Higginbotham, Ohio State University

"As the reader for countless journals and university presses in the field, I can place Foster in a rather wide range, a rather huge number, of Renaissance scholars. And he is surely one of the best: learned, bright, witty, winning — compelling in his argumentation and attractive in his style and presentation.... *Women's Works* is simply breathtaking. Not in its concept — we have long needed, and said we have needed, a thorough anthology of the best writing of Medieval and Renaissance English women ... — but in its execution. ... And he has prepared, for the first time, a work that is authoritative and comprehensive, complete and final. It will not, because it cannot, be superseded."
— Arthur F. Kinney, Thomas W. Copeland Professor of Literary History and Director of the Center for Renaissance Studies at the University of Massachusetts

Women's Works, vol. 1 (900-1550). 444 pp. illus. $39.95.
Women's Works, vol. 2 (1550-1603). 444 pp. illus. $39.95.

Women's Works, vol. 3 (1603-1625). 444 pp. illus. $39.95.
Women's Works, vol. 4 (1600-1650). 424 pp. illus. $39.95.

Also from Wicked Good Books, Inc.

How to Write:

Not Your Usual User's Guide to the English Language

Angie English

EVER WONDER why you get *B*s (or worse) on your classroom writing? why you get poor reviews (or none) for your blog and your published books? why your letters to the editor go unpublished? your job-applications go unrewarded? your love-letters go unrequited? Here's why: you may know how to write, but you don't know *How to Write.* At long last, from Wicked Good Books, comes a writer's guide worth reading, a book for those who need to write well compiled by those who already do. Most writing manuals are tedious and often wrong. *How to Write* compresses the wisdom and expertise of best-selling authors and educators into a single witty and indispensable volume, a book that should never be far from your nightstand or writing desk.

How to Write comes in four sections, beginning with part one, "The Ten Commandments." Memorize them. Then just follow the easy steps (also supplied) for writing original works of incredible genius.

Part two, "How do they *do* that?" unfolds the wisdom of the ages concerning the kinds of writing you are most often asked to do for others, whether in the classroom or at work or in the book industry.

Part three, "Write or Wrong," is a guide to words, thereby to prevent you from emulating the many scholars, athletes, and presidents before you who have made fritters of the English language.

Part four, "Index and Ready Reference" directs you, in a jiff, where to go, within *How to Write,* for the help you need.

ISBN-10: 0-9882820-1-1
ISBN-13: 978-0-9882820-1-8
235 pp.

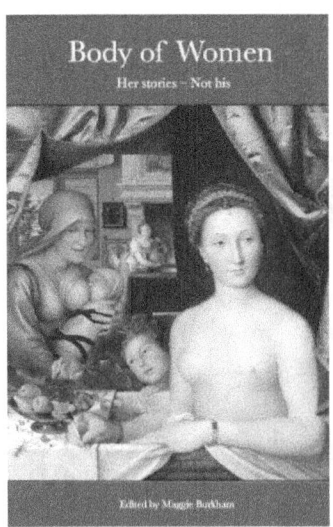

Body of Women: Her Stories (2025).

Few English-speaking women know much about their own cultural past, and very few men know the first thing about history from women's point of view. *Body of Women* addresses that gap in social knowledge. Beginning with the 10th Century CE, this volume traces the concerns of women in the bedroom and birthing-chamber, in markets and prisons—housewives, midwives, mothers, and physicians; paupers, servants, merchants, and countesses—as they struggled for autonomy, prosperity, happiness, and (not least) for safety from poverty, disease, beatings, and sexual assault—much of which is recorded here in their own words. Included are texts written by and for women, from the magical charms of Anglo-Saxon *hæġtessan* ("cunning women"), to the Church's about-face in the 19th Century with respect to abortion and "ensoulment" of the human fetus; also, early instruction manuals concerning fertility, sexual intercourse, midwifery, birth control, miscarriages, childbirth, and breast-feeding; self-care, hygiene, diet, and cosmetics; homeopathic medicine; historical records of rape and domestic violence; as well as church doctrine and secular law with respect to women's bodies and women's rights.

—Edited, with introductions, by Maggie Burkham

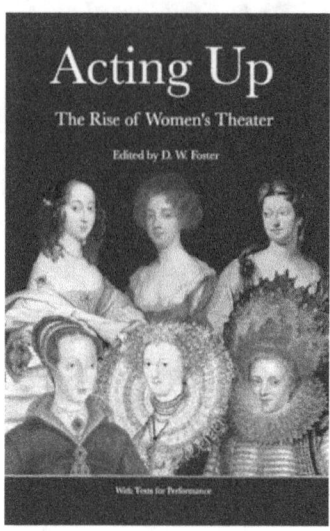

Acting Up: The Rise of Women's Theater (2025) traces women's performative texts from Anglo-Saxon and Celtic verse for women's voice, through medieval liturgical drama, to dialogues and closet drama penned by women of the 16th-17th Centuries, to Jane Cavendish (the most misunderstood poet of the Civil War); to the great flowering of women's stage drama, represented here by Aphra Behn and Susanna Centlivre; together with fresh revelations concerning Cavendish, Behn, and Centlivre drawn from the National Archives, genealogical records, and their own letters. Here as well, for the very first time anywhere, are accurate, stage-ready scripts for performance. A must-read for students and thespians.

—Ed. D. W. Foster